Of the Earth

Of the Earth

Book 1 of the
Clashing Kingdoms Series

Kim Cousins

RESOURCE *Publications* · Eugene, Oregon

OF THE EARTH

Resource Publications
An Imprint of Wipf and Stock Publishers
199 W. 8th Ave., Suite 3
Eugene, OR 97401

www.wipfandstock.com

PAPERBACK ISBN: 978-1-6667-0241-5
HARDCOVER ISBN: 978-1-6667-0242-2
EBOOK ISBN: 978-1-6667-0243-9

02/23/23

For Norah and Caleb, Dejana and Aviana,
the Lord bless you and keep you.

Preface

I REALIZE SOME READERS look for "Easter eggs," clues buried within books. These clues lead readers to a bigger competition at the end of a mystery; maybe even leading intrepid readers online to find prize money. As an author, I'm not that clever or that wealthy, but sometimes, I am subtle. So, with respect to my readers, I want to identify a few of my subtleties.

Animals talk in this story. To differentiate conversations between animals and humans, the dialog of animals is written in italics. This is such a small detail that most readers wouldn't notice the variation except in instances when animals and people talk simultaneously.

The other subtlety involves footnotes. Much of the drama in this book mirror actual events documented in the Holy Bible. In those instances, I inserted footnotes so curious readers can refer to the Bible for clarification, or revelation. I encourage readers to investigate, to dig deeper, to challenge perceptions.

So, dear readers, I invite you to explore. You can read this little book for its story, or you can read it to hunt for answers. Either way, you might find something more precious than Easter eggs. Maybe you'll discover Easter.

Acknowledgments

I can't relate to the child-raising correlation, but I can attest that it takes a village to publish a book. And I belong to a wonderful village! A village filled with church members, professional experts, dedicated friends, and loved ones.

From serious discussions on futuristic scenarios, military weapons, and marketing strategies to lighthearted observations on format—Hey, your book needs page numbers!—I deeply appreciate the contributions of my family, friends, and publisher. I specifically want to recognize my son, Sam Cousins, for his thorough editing; my friends, Deb and Reese Matoy, for their unwavering support; and Michael Gillespie of Brite Ideas for his illustrations. For patient and prompt guidance throughout the publishing process, I thank the fantastic professionals at Wipf and Stock Publishing, especially George Callahan. For my wonderful husband, Woodie, who grew accustomed to waking up at weird hours in the night to find me upstairs typing, rather than downstairs sleeping. For everyone involved with this book: your hard work, your dedication, your prayers, and your encouragement, I thank you for blessing me so richly.

List of Characters

1. Boss Jedidiah "BoJed," gang leader
2. Elizabeth, sixteen-year-old former prisoner
3. Garcia family
   a. Emanuel
   b. Rosa
4. Jeremiah "Miah," seventeen-year-old teenager
   a. Papaw, grandfather
   b. Bill, dad
   c. Nora, sister
5. Jim Wilkins, Army veteran
   a. Mattie, Australian Shepherd
   b. Carl, orange tabby
6. Juan Peña, Army veteran
   a. Happy, Newfoundland
7. Marcus Washington family
   a. Constance "Connie," wife
   b. TJ, sixteen-year-old son
   c. Talia, thirteen-year-old daughter
8. Sara, former prisoner
9. Nellie, valley resident
   a. Brant

    b.   Toynell

10. Ryan McGuire family

    a.   Shirley, wife
    b.   Jason, fifteen-year-old son
    c.   Destiny, fourteen-year-old daughter

11. Sara, former prisoner

12. Sean McFadden "Mac" family

    a.   Patricia, wife
    b.   William, five-year-old son
    c.   James, two-year-old son

13. Neighbors

    a.   Alicia
    b.   Monica
    c.   Pastor Greg
    d.   Patsy and Ralphie

Autumn

1

"Peacekeeping, open up!" a man thundered as he pounded on the flimsy wooden door. "Mr. Ehrmann, we have a warrant for your arrest!"

Inside the home, an old man, startled, looked up from a tattered book which constituted one of his most prized possessions. Anticipating this unwanted visit, Mr. Ehrmann deliberately stood in silent resolve. The front door splintered, hanging pitifully by broken hinges as a team of PeaceKeepers rushed into his living room.

Clad in TAC[1] gear and carrying M4s, the men violently secured the small apartment before scrutinizing their newest quarry.

"Mr. Ehrmann, the Security Council has reported your failure to comply with regulation NWL Section 25.807 by the prescribed time. As a citizen of the New World, it was your duty to receive the mark of allegiance. You have failed to act in accordance with the laws laid out by our great leader for our benefit. What do you have to say for yourself?"

"I've been busy," he mumbled.

Looking around the empty room, seeing nothing but a book, the team leader replied, "Busy! Busy with what? Reading . . ." looking at the book's title, "a Bible? Do you really think that answer will fly with the Security Council?"

Smiling, Mr. Ehrmann stared at the team leader, replying, "Well . . . not just reading; sometimes I pray too."

Furious at the man's blatant disregard for his authority, the team leader hit the old man in the face with the stock of his M4. The sound of bone cracking filled the room as Ehrmann slumped to the floor. Laughing erupted from the corner of the room as another PeaceKeeper walked over to look down at the body, "That sounded like it hurt."

---

1. Tactical.

"Good! Hopefully this Holy Roller stays out for a while. I'm tired of listening to them whine for mercy, or worse still, hearing them cry out to an imaginary god. I have better things to do than babysit a bunch of half-crazed fanatics!" His words met with resounding approval from the others.

As blood oozed from the wound on Mr. Ehrmann's face, another PeaceKeeper reached down to check the old man's neck. "Sir, there's no pulse. What should we do with him now?"

Disgusted, the commander replied, "Leave him! Call in an EKIA to HQ.[2] Let 'em know that another Bible-thumper resisted and was killed during his arrest. We got a bunch more to round up today. Don't bother going through his stuff; it doesn't look like he has anything of value."

With that final directive, the men exited, leaving the old man lying motionless on the floor and a small puppy, which none of the men noticed, quivering under a fuzzy, blue blanket.

As the seconds turned into hours, the sun began to set. Eventually the puppy slowly ventured out of her hiding place. She licked the old man's aged face and settled quietly beside him. As the room darkened, the puppy nudged her owner's hand, whimpering softly to wake him. With no response from the kindly man and overwhelmed with sadness, the puppy began to cry. Trying to stay quiet, the puppy's muffled sobs streamed out of her as a low mournful howl from the bottom of her heart.

Distracted, the puppy didn't hear a visitor who walked carefully, quietly, through the splintered doorway. Once secure with the surroundings, the mysterious visitor stood behind her and said sternly, *"What's wrong with you?"*

Caught by surprise, the puppy yelped and swirled around to face this newest intruder. Before her stood the biggest cat she ever saw. The cat, pumpkin orange fur with piercing green eyes, focused directly on the puppy's face, watching her dispassionately.

"Who are you? Wha . . . what do you want?" the puppy asked, her voice trembling.

"My name is Carl," the cat said. An awkward silence filled the room while the cat glanced down at the lifeless man on the floor. Looking back at the puppy, he said, *"I'm sorry about your human; he must've been kind to you. But I gotta warn you, all your blubbering is going to attract*

---

2. Enemy killed in action to headquarters.

attention—the wrong kind of attention—and in these days of starvation, dogs make a perfect dinner for hungry people."

"What?! Are you kidding?"

"I wouldn't kid you about a thing like that, precious." A moment later Carl asked, "By the way, what's your name?"

"I . . . I don't have a name." She looked at the body on the floor, "My person brought me home a few days ago. He said he'd name me as soon as he got to know me better."

"Ah, it's just as well. Maybe someone will give you a name," he studied her closely, "but if you live with two or three different people, they'll all give you a different name. It gets really confusing." The big cat sauntered over to the puppy, rubbed his shoulder over her eyes. "Let's dry those tears and get outta here. I'm guessing that you haven't been outside much at night, but let me tell you, this is the scariest time of day for animals, or people."

Carl walked cautiously to the door, looked down the hallway, and said softly, "Follow me and do as I say. I know a safe place in the alley where we can sleep tonight. We might find some food in the trash cans, if we're lucky."

The puppy fell in step with Carl. Although she was only twelve weeks old, she was both beautiful and smart. As a tricolored Australian Shepherd, her black, white, and brown coat blended well with most surroundings and her acute intuition told her to trust Carl. She licked the old man's face again, looked around the apartment one last time, and slipped out the door into the inky blackness of the city night.

ഏറ്റ

The two wanderers crept down three flights of stairs, slipping out of a hole in the wall on the bottom floor. Carl advised the puppy, "Stay close to the building, if we get separated, find a dark corner to hide. With walls to your back, no one can sneak up behind you. I will look for you at daybreak."

"I don't think you'll have to worry about us getting separated; I'm staying right on your tail."

Carl chuckled and edged quietly down an alley. The passage was dark. With no electricity in the city, every alley was a terrifying corridor of darkness. At the end of the passageway sat a dilapidated dumpster with garbage overflowing on all sides. "Ah, here it is! Dinner at the Ritz," joked the fat cat. The puppy grimaced at the foul odor of the trashcan, but said nothing.

Carl coached, *"I'll see if I can find some food in the dumpster and throw it down to you. Hunt for a quiet place to hide the scraps, then come back to get more. I'll jump down when it looks like we have enough to eat, or if I can't stand the smell any longer."*

Carl's unselfishness earned the puppy's devotion. Despite the many dangers of having an extra mouth to feed, this cat was willing to share his food and keep her safe. *"I will do whatever you need, Carl,"* she said gravely.

Carl looked at her with surprise. *Whoever heard of a serious puppy?* he thought. Carl smiled to himself and began rummaging through the trash. While there was little real food, he found many wrappers or containers with bits of food here and there. He kicked out several wrappers, a few pieces of moldy bread, and gooey pastries stuck inside a plastic bag. When he thought he had found enough food, Carl jumped out of the dumpster, licking his paws, *"Hey, princess, where are you?"*

"Over here," she answered. Carl padded over to a corner—behind a rusty metal barrel—where the puppy hid the food.

Carl stopped to look at her with amazement. *"You're pretty smart. What kind of dog are you?"*

"A very hungry, scared dog," she replied.

"Well, let's see what treasures we have to satisfy that hunger," laughed Carl as he walked over to the pile, selecting a small parcel.

After their initial taste of the food, the two friends began to eagerly tear into bags, eating the assorted treats. Suddenly, the puppy yelped. *"Ouch, something stabbed my leg!"* she cried.

"Nobody stabbed you," an oily voice growled behind her, *"I bit you."* The puppy spun around and looked into the beady eyes of a rat. As she backed up, she saw several sets of unblinking eyes gleaming in the moonlight. *"This is our alley, so this is our food. If you back away now, we won't hurt you, if you decide to be a hero . . . well, you'll find out how sharp our teeth really are!"*

With his back arched and his tail frizzed, Carl walked straight over to the head rat, slapping it with his claws. *"Back off, coward! Find your own meal,"* hissed Carl. Suddenly four rats jumped on Carl, making the big cat squall as he clawed his attackers ferociously.

That's all the prompting the puppy needed to see. She jumped into the fray, snarling ferociously, biting rats, throwing the wretched beasts against brick walls. Within seconds the battle was over. Carl relaxed his stance as the rats hastily retreated to their hiding places. He saw the puppy standing her ground, panting, anxiously searching for other rats to fight.

"*Whoa, gorgeous, the battle's over. Are you okay?*"

"*I'm fine. A . . . a . . . a little shaky, but I'm fine. Are you hurt?*"

"*Nope, not a scratch on me. Let's take a look at you.*" Carl led the puppy to a gap between buildings to study her in the moonlight. "*Well, you took a beating, that's for sure. I'll clean the bleeding cuts tonight and look you over better in the morning.*"

Exhausted, the puppy laid down to let Carl cleanse and untangle the knots in her fur. His gentle purring was a comforting sound. As Carl bathed her wounds and brushed her fur with his sticky tongue, the puppy fell into a restless sleep.

The next morning presented a whole new level of agony for the little dog. Not only were her gashes and cuts swollen and red, but every joint seared with pain. When Carl asked how she was feeling, she opened her eyes slightly, groaning, "*Carl, I feel terrible. I'm so cold, I can't stop shivering.*"

The orange cat sat next to her to scan her injuries. Trying to hide his concern, Carl said, "*Let's move out of this dark backstreet, find a safe, sunny place, catch a few rays.*" Carl twitched his ears to listen, then walked cautiously to the front of a building. Once he found a secure spot behind some boxes, he stretched out and said, "*Come sit beside me. We can watch the street for a while.*"

As the puppy ventured out of her hiding place, she froze in place, shocked by the stark misery of city life. She saw buildings torn apart, ripped curtains blowing out of broken windows, cars abandoned, charred furniture on sidewalks, streets strewn with garbage. In the distance, she heard faint screaming, people cursing, and dogs barking, yet she didn't see anyone. If it wasn't for the skirmish the night before and the terrible sounds she was now hearing, she would've thought they were the last living creatures on earth.

"*What's happening? Where is everyone?*" she cried.

"*Huh? Haven't you seen the city yet?*"

"*No!*" she exclaimed. "*I lived on a farm until a few days ago. That nice man brought me to his room in the city; he said I was going to be his protection. I had a mother, and brothers, and sisters; we played together all day in the fields! I swam in a pond, barked at birds, and chased rabbits for fun! Where are we?"*

"Um, we live in a very bad place with very bad people. I lost my human family a few weeks ago; now I wander the streets trying to stay alive. You say there really are places with grass and water?"

"Yes," she wailed, "and if I could, I would take you back to the farm to live with my family!"

"Hmm, well it sounds like we need to find a way out of this city and get back to those green pastures," Carl murmured. "I always thought stories about the country were just lies told by old cats with wild imaginations. Try to relax; I'll think of a way to get us outta here; get you back to a life we'll both enjoy."

Although Carl doubted he could deliver his promise, he wanted to say something to reassure the injured, frightened puppy. The puppy limped over to a sunny spot, lay down, and closed her eyes. As she slept, Carl watched the street, trying to devise an escape plan.

Late in the afternoon, an opportunity arose. Carl woke to the banging of a truck door. He watched a powerfully built man, wearing a beat-up cowboy hat over his dark, curly hair, walk around the back of a truck and study its flat tire. "Perfect," Jim Wilkins said dismally, "could anything else happen today?"

Frustrated, Jim looked at abandoned cars and trucks on the street for a suitable replacement. Luckily, in the distance he saw another Ford Ranger just like the truck he drove. Carl watched as Jim found a tire iron and a small bottle jack before walking down the street toward the other vehicle.

As Jim drew near the Ranger, he saw the discarded truck was in rough shape. Dirt and grime covered its cracked windshield and leaves piled around the wheels. "I don't suppose anybody would miss a tire from this ol' girl," he muttered. Looking over the tires, Jim noticed some dry rot, but he chose the best tire out of the four; afterward, he began the process of jacking up the truck and removing lug nuts.

When he pulled the wheel off the dilapidated truck, Jim strolled back to his vehicle, rolling the wheel beside him. Once he changed his flat tire, Jim put a box under the cannibalized truck to retrieve his jack. As Jim stood up and stretched, Carl walked over to him.

The orange tabby rubbed his head against the man's faded jeans. "Hey, who are you?" laughed Jim. "Are you here to make friends or are you just looking for a scrap of food, you big beggar?" Carl continued to rub himself against the man's legs, purring loudly. "Well, I have to say, Gigantor, that you are bold and certainly not starving."

In response to the man's friendliness, Carl immediately ran over to the puppy to rouse her. *"Wake up, sleepyhead; I think I found our ticket out of this dump."*

The pup rose and limped obediently behind Carl. When Jim looked down at the huge cat and the battle-weary puppy, he was overcome with pity. "Whoa, what happened to you?" he asked the puppy. "Let me get a good look at you." He stroked the pup's fur carefully, "Don't worry; I'm not going to hurt you."

The puppy sat wearily on the sidewalk while Jim examined her wounds. "Some of these cuts need stitches; they're definitely infected." Jim continued to inspect the puppy, "Lucky for you, I know a little bit about treatin' wounds." Smiling, Jim mused, *I'd just never worked on a dog before.*

Jim reached for a toolbox in the back of his truck filled with simple medical supplies. "If you'll bear with me, I'll get you all fixed up, little lady."

The man threw a blanket on the truck's open tailgate, then gently placed the puppy upon the makeshift examining table. Jim pulled out a bottle of antiseptic and a bag of sterile cloths from the box. Using scissors, he trimmed some fur around her wounds. He wiped her abrasions, talking softly to her, stroking her coat. After cleaning her cuts and applying surgical adhesive, Jim gave the pup an oral antibiotic, which she swallowed grudgingly.

"There you go; you're all set. After all that fuss, I guess I should take care of you while you're healing. We better get out of here though . . . it's gonna get dark soon." Carrying her to the cab of his truck, Jim patted the bench seat, "You can lie down here, if you want." The puppy graciously accepted his invitation, promptly sitting against the backrest.

Feeling something on his leg, Jim looked down to see the orange cat rubbing against him. The man bent down to pet the cat, "You wanna come too, big guy?"

Carl, while not a fan of car rides—no cats are—still wanted to follow the puppy to see if green pastures really existed. Having made up his mind, Carl leaped into the cab of the truck, joining the puppy on the cloth seat.

Paying more attention to the animals and excited about having companions, Jim missed the approach of three men walking menacingly toward them. Suddenly aware of the danger, Jim nonchalantly assessed his surroundings while putting the medical box into the cab of his truck. Before closing the door, Jim slipped a revolver into his pocket before greeting the men, "Evenin' fellas, how's it goin'?"

"What's up, guy," snarled the first man sarcastically, "is we ain't doin' so good."

"Really? What's wrong?"

"You're what's wrong!" shouted a scrawny man with stringy, blonde hair. "You don't belong here!"

"You're right; I was just fixin' to leave when you boys stopped by to send me off," Jim answered amiably. "So if you don't mind, I think I'll just load my gear and be on my way."

"Think again, pal; you owe us for the wheel you stole."

"That truck doesn't belong to any of you," Jim countered, "so I don't owe you a thing."

Agitated, the man clenched his teeth, "You better watch your mouth," he threatened as he stepped closer to Jim, swinging a pipe wrench by his side.

"Fine. You want money for the tire? So be it," Jim said tightly. He slipped his hand into his pants pocket to retrieve a silver coin, "Here's payment for the wheel." When he flipped the coin with his thumb and index finger; a third man caught the silver in midair.

All three of the men gathered in a circle to look at the coin. "Lemme see that," gasped the scrawny man. "Looks like a legit Morgan silver dollar! Ya know what that means don't 'cha?"

"Yeah, I know what it means," growled the first man, "it means this guy's got silver lining those pockets."

"Yeah, not only that, he don't got no tattoo on his hand neither!" taunted the third man.

"No mark on his hand or forehead, silver in his pockets, animals in his truck . . . why boys, we got us a gold mine!" laughed the leader. "Well, buddy, since you ain't from around here, let me fill you in on a few things." Holding up one finger, he sneered, "First, everyone has to have the mark or you're wanted by the government, so we might get a reward for hurtin' you. B," holding up a second finger, "silver and gold are also illegal but very valuable for trading," he laughed maliciously. "And last," holding up a third finger, "dogs and cats make wonderful dinners so it looks like you're not going anywhere; neither are Fido or Fluffy."

"Now let me tell you what *I* think," Jim said in a low, threatening tone, "I paid you for the tire so we're square. Now I'm goin' to get into my truck and be on my way." The boldness in his voice threw the men off guard, they stood momentarily in silence. Taking the opportunity to leave, Jim turned, walked to the driver's side of his truck, and slid behind the steering wheel, slamming the truck door.

Regaining their senses, the men ran toward the truck. The leader reached his arm through the driver's window, grabbing Jim by the collar, "Give me one reason why I should let you go."

Pulling the revolver from its hiding place, Jim cocked a snub-nose .357 Magnum and jammed it into the man's mouth. "I'll give you one reason why you're going to let me go. As for your friends . . . they can have the other five if they're interested." The leader backed up, revealing a broken tooth with blood running from the side of his mouth. The bloody man backed away, rage flaring in his eyes.

Without wasting time, Jim started the truck, dumped the clutch, and raced away. Picking up speed, Jim headed for a turn to get out of sight of his attackers. Taking a right turn as fast as the old tires could manage, Jim was suddenly overwhelmed with fur, and paws, and claws scratching his leg!

Dazed with excitement, the puppy lost her balance and tumbled into Carl. The two rolled end over end, landing right into Jim. With a quick laugh, Jim warned, "Not the time, guys!"

Using one arm, Jim pushed them back to their side of the truck. Stunned by his lack of balance, Carl dug his claws into the seat with the resolve that he would not fall over again. Following Carl's lead, the puppy squatted down, trying her best not to slide into Jim as he raced the truck through empty streets.

Not sure if he was being chased, Jim slowed his vehicle and turned off the headlights. Although the sun had set, there was still enough light for Jim to take several more turns as he evaded any would-be pursuers. Looking down at his furry companions, Jim said, "We need to get off the road, guys; they'll be lookin' for us."

As they slowly drove down a once-beautiful suburban neighborhood, Jim saw an abandoned house with a semi-collapsed garage. *Perfect*, Jim thought. Backing the truck in, Jim quickly got out to cover the hood and windshield with a canvas tarp and discarded wood he found in the crumbling structure. Content with the crude camouflage, Jim got back into the truck and reclined his seat to get a better view of the road through a hole in the tarp.

"Well, pals, we're going to need to hunker down for a little while," Jim whispered. "They'll be looking for us and we don't have much gas left. If those idiots find us stranded down the road, we'll never see daylight again." Jim stroked the animals' coats, reassuring them, while he watched the street, bracing himself for an attack.

Before long, several ratty cars filled with raucous, hollering men raced past the garage. Jim knew they'd be safe as long as they didn't draw attention. Most of these neighborhoods looked so bad that the truck was nearly indistinguishable from the rest of the junk. Doing the only thing they could, Jim and the animals sat quietly in the darkness, waiting for the trouble to pass. After several hours, and what felt like an eternity in the silent darkness, Jim saw the cars driving back to their original destination.

"Looks like they gave up searching for us," he said. They waited in the truck for another half hour before moving again.

Confident they were off the hook, Jim opened the driver's door. He stepped into the garage, inviting his two furry companions out to stretch their legs and relieve themselves. Although his eyes were not as sharp as Carl's, Jim decided to look around the dark garage for anything useful. While not seeing much, he did find a few rusty sockets and a spanner; he wiped rust off the tools and added them to his collection.

On his last pass through the garage, the man quietly gasped, "Will you look at that!"

There, hidden on a back shelf, he found two large gas cans. Pulling the cans out of their hiding spot, Jim noticed they were heavy and filled with liquid. Excited with the prospect of fuel and a way out of town, he opened a can's cap to smell the contents.

Sniffing the first can, he detected a sweet scent, with a hint of oil. Deflated, "I think this is bad gas, guys." Grabbing the second can without much hope, he took another whiff. To his surprise, this fluid smelled like good, clean gasoline!

"That's what I'm talkin' about. Someone must have put stabilizer in this one."

Encouraged from finding gas, Jim quickly poured the good fuel into his truck's gas tank. He dumped the bad gas out of the other container and secured both empty cans into his truck bed. "It's time to go," Jim said in a calm voice, but the two animals just looked at him. In response, Jim patted the seat of the truck.

The puppy crept into the cab, still unsure about this new man, or sliding around on a bench seat. Carl followed behind her. As the Aussie glanced at Carl, she noticed the cat suck a mouse's tail into his mouth. *"Yeech, what are you doing, Carl?"* she grimaced.

"Just having a little celebration dinner, sweetie; a guy can't maintain this physique without proper nourishment."

2

JUST BEFORE HE STARTED the ignition, a clap of thunder shook the garage. Almost instantly, a torrent of rain drenched the streets. Jim said exuberantly, "You two must be my good luck charms. With this storm, no one will hear our engine turn over. Besides, no one will want to get out in this weather to look for us." Admiring the downpour, "This is great!"

As thunder crashed outside, Jim started his truck inside the garage, then rolled inconspicuously into the street. He left the headlights off as he moved down boulevards using the glow from window lamps to avoid obstacles on the road. After ten minutes of white-knuckle driving, he switched on the parking lights, increasing his speed. Within half an hour, the trio merged onto a highway, driving faster.

The thunderstorm raged intensely but after facing PeaceKeepers, rats, and neighborhood thugs, the weather seemed like a minor inconvenience. While the windshield wipers quickly swept away the hammering rain, the three weary travelers kept their eyes focused on the road. Relaxing a bit, Jim started to talk with his companions.

"Since we're going to be traveling together, I need to have some names for you. Neither of you have collars with tags, so I'm going to come up with my own names." He looked at the puppy's bright, inquisitive face, "Let's see, what's a good Australian name for a beauty like you? How about Matilda? I could call you Mattie for short." The puppy wagged her stumpy tail at the sound of the man's voice. Jim grinned, "Alright, I'll take that as a yes. Mattie it is.

"And what about you, Mr. Orange? What would be a good name?"

Carl stared intently at Jim trying to send him a telepathic message, *"My name is Carl. My name is Carl."*

"Hmm, how about Fatty?" Carl closed his eyes, flattening his ears. Mattie wagged her tail and gazed at the man.

"My name is Carl. Carl means majestic; at least, that's what my family used to say."

"Let's see, Ralph . . . Chester . . . hmm, how about the name we heard this evening, Fluffy?" By this time, Jim was chuckling and the big cat acted like he was asleep.

"Arright, let me think of a more serious name for a serious cat," pondered Jim. "I once knew a man with hair about the same color as yours, orange not red. He was a good man. Strong, upright, a distinguished soldier. I'm guessin' that you're a solid friend because you wouldn't leave Mattie when she was sick. His name was Carl. How does Carl sound?"

Carl perked up his ears, opening his eyes. The big cat pressed next to Jim's lap as he started to purr. "Okay, now I have names for my two friends: Mattie and Carl."

"Mr. Majestic," corrected Mattie as she snuggled next to Carl. Within minutes, she fell fast asleep as she listened to his soothing purr.

☙◌◐◑◍◌❧

To stay alert while he drove, Jim scanned radio stations in search of music or news. Most radio stations had closed two years ago when the United States lost its international dominance but he found a New World–sponsored channel that would sporadically report news.

> [Static crackling] "PeaceKeepers continue in the effort to round up any persons refusing to obey the laws of rededication and marking." [garbled words] ". . . pockets of insurgents are discovered . . ." [hiss] "Keepers detain . . ." [trailing words] "prisoners to processing facilities. These facilities seek . . ." [static] "to process and educate through cutting-edge training programs . . ." [garbled language] "great success. The few who reject the New World philosophy or refuse to show this allegi . . ." [static crackling] "by refusing to take any of our sacred marks . . ." [silence] "stand before a tribunal court to be tried for sedition."

The newscasters began to laugh. The male anchor said, "I sure wouldn't want to face the tribunal."

The female newscaster scoffed. "Me neither, but who cares? In my opinion, if you have to meet with the tribunal, you're a despicable person anyway."

With his brow furrowed, Jim remembered his friends who rebelled against the New World Order's PeaceKeeping forces. *Where are my friends now? What decisions did they make today? Are they even alive?*

Then he reflected sadly, *I'm no better off than my buddies. We're all AWOL; renegade soldiers considered armed and dangerous by the world government.*

Jim hit the steering wheel with the palm of his hand, cursing his life. "I vowed to uphold the Constitution," he said miserably, "to defend our nation against enemies, both foreign and domestic. What can I do now that the U.S. is paralyzed? How can I fight such insidious enemies?"

When he thought about the past few years, Jim struggled to make sense of the world. Wars, famine, plagues—catastrophic occurrences, certainly—but not uncommon events in the course of human history. As a Special Operations medic, Jim was trained not only to identify but to overcome problems; he could live with human and weather disasters.

But later, really bizarre things began to happen. A worldwide pandemic erupted. Asteroids fell to earth. Huge volcanos erupted which triggered massive earthquakes, killing millions of people. Yet when seas turned to blood, Jim knew he needed to find more secure surroundings. This was not global warming or climate change; this was otherworldly!

Jim did not delay. He heard about preppers living in the Appalachian and Rocky Mountains. In fact, after refusing to serve in the New World Armed Forces, a few of his Army buddies planned to set up an outpost somewhere in the Smoky Mountains. Since Jim lived in Virginia, he decided to travel to Tennessee in search of his friends. Obtaining topographical maps of Virginia and Tennessee, Jim felt that even if he didn't find his buddies, he would look for a safer place to stand his ground.

To accomplish this goal, Jim needed a vehicle to flee the city, so he traded his M4 rifle and ammo in exchange for an aged Ford Ranger and a tankful of fresh gas. Without a mark on his hand or forehead, Jim couldn't buy anything in a government-sanctioned business; moreover, owning weapons and ammunition was against the law so Jim did all his transactions through the black market. Fortunately, Jim developed a network of likeminded people to acquire his basic necessities. He used this network to barter for a truck and get out of town.

As he drove south, Jim mentally listed the strengths and weaknesses of his truck. Trucks were great for hauling and driving on long, rutted roads with some measure of speed, but all vehicles needed gas. Fuel was a major problem.

He thought of the gasoline warning light blinking at him before he stopped to rest; now acquiring more fuel was his primary concern again. Typically, when he drove through cities, he siphoned enough good gas from older cars or punched holes in the gas tanks of newer vehicles to drain fuel into a pan. Out in the country, with fewer people and less discarded vehicles, finding useable gasoline was going to be a much bigger problem.

After being on the road all night, Jim exited the freeway to drive down a single-lane dirt road. After they traveled a few miles, he saw a picnic table next to a stream, surrounded by stately elms. The colorful autumn leaves rustling in the trees and the babbling water provided a perfect reprieve from the last twenty-four hours. Jim parked his truck in a small grove of elms. Out of sight from the road, Jim turned off the engine and sighed.

He opened the door, stretched his long legs, and snapped his back. Mattie and Carl stepped out of the dented truck to stand in the deep grass. At first Carl looked haltingly at a tree, but once he realized what he saw, he immediately climbed up its trunk until he reached the first branch. He squalled at the top of his lungs, *"Look at me, Mattie, I'm free! Like a tiger prowling in a forest!"*

"See, I told you that there really are trees and grassy fields. Isn't it fantastic?" Mattie yipped.

"'Fantastic' isn't a big enough word. I feel like a lion; I could run and play all day! Hey, do you want to go hunting with me? I'm starving." Invigorated by the prospect of dinner, *"I'll bet I find something to eat in this great place,"* bragged Carl, flattening his ears and twitching his tail.

"You go ahead and explore, Carl," barked Mattie. Sore from her wounds, she walked rigidly through the deep grass. *"I want to keep an eye on Jim to make sure he's safe while he sleeps. But don't get too full of yourself; if I felt better, I would catch a fish for dinner before you could even get out of that dumb tree."*

Responding to her challenge, Carl climbed down the tree and stood on the stream bank. He dipped his paw into the brook a few times, frowned, then backed away from the water's edge. *"I don't need this,"* he scoffed, *"I hear my dinner bell squeaking in a field over there."* Excited with his newfound freedom, Carl pounced off into a hayfield to search for food.

Slightly feverish, Mattie ambled slowly toward an old, gnarled tree. She lay down carefully at the foot of the tree, putting her head between her paws. She looked up as Jim sat next to her.

"How're you feelin', Mattie?" he asked gently. Jim studied her wounds, pleased to see a decrease in the swelling and redness. "You'll feel better in a few days," he assured her as he leaned against the tree, tilting the brim of his hat over his eyes. As he listened to the pleasant sounds of water tumbling over rocks, and leaves tossing in the wind, Jim fell peacefully to sleep.

When Jim woke up a few hours later, he felt completely refreshed, almost optimistic. He was going to live another day in this cruel world, and that was a great accomplishment in itself. When he glanced down, he saw Mattie still sitting next to him, watching the river. "What do you say we try our hand at fishin'?"

Mattie stood up, a bit stiff-legged, and wagged her tail, pleased to hear his voice. Jim noticed, "Even when you're hurting, you want to help." He petted her head, "Take it easy, Mattie. Someday I might have some livestock for you to herd, but today you can keep an eye on Carl." Jim stood up to retrieve his tackle box from the back of the truck.

When he escaped the city, Jim packed his truck with everything he could find to survive. He collected fishing gear, dehydrated food, tools, weapons, a first aid kit, two newly acquired gas cans, plus a wide assortment of rope, wire, and hardware. Whenever he found something useful, he threw it into the bed of his truck.

Scanning the afternoon sky, "This is the perfect time of day to catch a fish," the slim man said, winking at Mattie. Taking his tackle to the river, Jim sat down to cast his line. *I'm alive. I'm fishin'. I'm looking at a field of wildflowers on the other side of the river. Things could be a lot worse.*

Wearily, he thought, *In this day and age, things couldn't get much worse.* Jim remembered the debt-ridden society, partisan politics, and lack of civil discourse that created an environment of anger and resentment. "And the straw that broke the camel's back ruined everything," he lamented. Jim shook his head, recalling the orchestration that led to the fall of the United States of America.

To suppress these dark memories, Jim turned his attention to fishing. Within an hour, he caught five fish. After cleaning and skewering the fish, Jim roasted the meat over a warm, orange glow of open flames. The aroma drew Carl out of the woods, and soon the three travelers anxiously waited to pull meat off the sticks. The meal tasted exquisite! After Jim shared his fish with Carl and Mattie, the three relaxed together under a shade tree near the river.

"Well, guys, as much as I'd like to sit under this tree all day, we still have a few hours of sunlight left. We need to find gas soon or we'll be walking to Tennessee." Stooping down at the river's edge, the cowboy cleaned his fillet knife, grabbed his fishing gear, and threw everything back into the truck bed. "Let's get rolling." Mattie and Carl jumped onto the front seat, Jim started the engine, and the three companions drove down the dusty country road.

After riding together for almost a day, the animals settled into a traveling routine. Mattie preferred to sit next to the open passenger window; Carl liked to sit next to Jim. Carl hated wind in his face but Mattie loved to feel the wind rumple her hair, wiggle her ears, and flap her tongue. Sitting on the seat, she stuck her head out the window so she could laugh into the wind.

"Dogs are really dumb; you know that, don't you?" complained Carl.

"You just don't know how to have fun," commented Mattie. She stood up to bark at cows grazing placidly in the fields. The cows lifted their heads to watch the truck but continued to munch on grass sticking out of their mouths.

Staring at the cows, the wide-eyed tabby exclaimed, *"Whoa, never mind dogs; those are really dumb-looking animals!"*

"Those are cows. If you lived on a dairy farm like I did, you would love cows. Maybe someday you'll get a chance to drink fresh milk; it's wonderful!"

Carl grumbled under his breath. It wasn't that he didn't like to learn new things; he did. He just didn't like to learn new things from a puppy, a very smart puppy.

Both of the animals stopped talking because the truck came to a sudden stop. Jim slipped on his work gloves and pulled the tattered cowboy hat a little lower on his forehead. As he stepped out of the truck, Jim tipped his hat and said politely, "Howdy, ma'am."

A sixty-year-old woman stood next to a broken barbed wire fence. She wore a dingy, mid-length calico dress covered by a frilly lime green apron, men's work boots, and a ragged straw hat. The woman reached into her apron pocket and asked cautiously, "Whadda you want?"

"You can take your hand off that shooter because I'm not gonna hurt you," Jim said evenly. "I wanted to know if you'd like some help with your fence."

Eying him suspiciously, "Do you know how to string a barbed wire fence?"

"Yep."

"Well, before we get too friendly, take off your gloves. I wanna look at your hands."

Jim slowly removed the leather gloves and held out his hands. The woman studied his hands before adding, "Now off with your hat. Let me get a good look at your forehead."

Jim slipped the hat off his head. After studying his hands and forehead, she asked in a friendlier manner, "Are you a Christian?"

"I don't know if I'd call myself a Christian, ma'am," Jim replied. "I was raised in the church, but after leaving home, it didn't take long to lose my faith."

Narrowing her eyes, "You don't have the mark on your skin."

"I don't really like the idea of someone tellin' me I have to have a tattoo to buy or sell something. I don't like folks knowing my every move or even my financial history, for that matter." With an edge in his voice, "And to be honest, I don't much care for a stranger giving me the third degree when I offer to help fix her fence," Jim growled as he angrily put his hat back on his head.

"Now hold on, darlin', I didn't mean to upset you," she drawled, "but we have so many city folks coming out here to steal our animals that we're mighty distrustful of new faces."

"Who is 'we'?" asked Jim.

"Folks in this area," related the old woman, an edge of skepticism still lingering in her tone. "By the way, my name is Nellie, and you are—?"

"—Jim. Jim Wilkins." He nodded toward the truck, "And traveling with me are my dog, Matilda, and my cat, Carl."

Standing on her tiptoes to peer into the cab, Nellie remarked, "Any man that travels with his pets, dudn't have the mark, and offers to help mend an old woman's fence deserves to eat a home-cooked meal."

"That sounds great," Jim replied, "but let's get this fence fixed before dark. We'll make sure your animals are safely tucked away before we start talkin' dinner."

"It's a deal, Mr. Wilkins," smiled Nellie. They restrung and tightened the wire fence together before driving down a densely forested path to Nellie's house. The forest parted at the end of the gravel driveway to display a two-story farmhouse, various outbuildings, and fenced animal pens organized neatly on a lush green carpet of mountain grass.

Nellie's farm was quaint, homey. The farmhouse walls were built from large river rocks and the roof was covered with mossy wood shingles. A mass of flower blooms spilled over stone walkways, completely surrounding the house's foundation, filling the air with sweet fragrances. In the fading daylight, Jim saw an amber light flickering from within the house and a thin wisp of smoke escaping the chimney.

Nellie smiled, "It looks like Miah's home. Good. I'd like you to meet him; he's a great kid."

When Nellie, Jim, and his pets walked into the living room, a teenager turned around from his kitchen work, beaming brightly. "Miah," Nellie said, "I'd like to introduce you to my new friend, Jim, his dog, Matilda, and Carl, the cat." Miah swept a lock of blonde hair from his eyes with his forearm, smiled, and shook Jim's hand. Miah's gesture surprised Jim because most people nowadays feared touching new acquaintances. Disregarding social norms, Jim shook Miah's hand without a second thought.

"It's nice to meet you," Miah responded respectfully. "My name is really Jeremiah," grinning, "but most people call me Miah, for short." Getting on his knees, the young man stroked Carl's soft fur and ruffled Mattie's ribs with both hands. "A puppy! I haven't seen a puppy in years."

Mattie shuffled her feet excitedly at Miah's touch. Staring at him expectantly, she barked, *"Do you want to go outside? Let's go outside to play . . . let's go . . . c'mon, let's go!"* Miah laughed at the puppy's enthusiastic, noisy yipping. Running to the door, Miah hopped on one foot, pulled on a boot, and tied its lace. After he repeated this same hopping, boot-tying trick with his other foot, the teen opened the door to go outside with Mattie.

"Take it easy with her, Miah. Mattie's recuperating from some serious injuries," advised Jim.

Miah eyed Mattie's fur closely, nodded his head, and walked slowly outside.

After Miah shut the door, Nellie turned to the stove, "Ah, you're in luck, Mr. Wilkins. Miah made some stew this evening. I'll go down to the cellar to find a jar of pears. We'll have stew, pears, and bread for dinner."

"I can't think of anything better to eat," smiled Jim as he removed his hat. He stood inside the doorway, holding his hat, waiting for Nellie to speak again.

"Don't just stand there; go sit by the fire. Relax a bit, take off your boots, if you want. You look like a man who could sleep for days," smiling conspiratorially, "and we wouldn't bother ya if ya did."

He sat down in an overstuffed chair near the fireplace. Tired from his travels, Jim pulled off his boots and exhaled as he leaned back with his eyes closed. "Thank you," he said.

A moment later, Carl leaped onto Jim's lap, making the man open his eyes slightly. To this once-pampered cat, there was nothing more inviting than a warm lap near a fire. "If I didn't know better, Carl, I'd say you were a house cat rather than an alley cat," joked Jim, closing his eyes and patting Carl's fur.

As Nellie finished preparing supper, Miah and Mattie returned from their walk outside. Miah brought in some fresh milk he had stored earlier in an icebox. Before mealtime, Miah served Mattie and Carl a dinner of bread soaked in milk. Afterward, both animals curled up together to sleep on a rug in front of the fireplace, completely content with their new surroundings.

3

ALTHOUGH STARVATION TORMENTED HUGE populations, especially in cities, very few valley residents suffered from hunger. They thanked God for their meals and there was always just enough food to fill their stomachs. Tonight was no exception; Nellie began the meal with grace. As Miah sliced bread and passed pears to Jim, Nellie ladled stew into three bowls. Jim couldn't remember the last time he ate a family dinner but the sheer elegance of conversation combined with a simple meal warmed his exhausted spirit.

"Tell us a little about yourself, Jim," prompted Nellie.

Calmly, he replied, "I'm trying to find my friends. I left the military once PeaceKeepers replaced the U.S. Army." Carefully watching Nellie and Miah's faces, he went on, "I don't trust the world government, especially our 'sovereign leader,' and I didn't want to be a part of his military machine."

"The world government has been in power for a while; have you been keepin' a low profile that whole time?" questioned Miah.

"Yeah. I picked up odd jobs so I could eat but my longest hitch was working on a horse farm in Virginia. Cash under the table, no questions asked."

Nellie sensed his melancholy. "What made you leave Virginia?"

Jim hesitated, "I found out that PeaceKeepers were still looking for me."

"Why are they looking for you?" asked Nellie.

"The world government called me, and many others, deserters. Most of the people I served with refused to join the PeaceKeeping force, so we're all labeled traitors, cowards, or worse. My refusal carries a big penalty, but not wearing their little tattoo guarantees my death sentence;

but what does it matter? Either way, I'm a wanted man." Laying his napkin on the table, "Would you like me to leave now?"

Nellie waved her hand nonchalantly, "Nonsense, Jim, you're no more a criminal than Miah or me, or most of our neighbors. Actually, I can't think of a better person to have next to me in a fight than a soldier. You're welcome to stay with us as long as you like."

Looking at Nellie, Miah asked, "Do you think Jim might be able to help me find my family?"

She touched Miah's hand reassuringly, "It's possible, dear, but let's not get ahead of ourselves. We need to get to know each other better," she answered soothingly.

Jim glanced at the teenager, "What happened? Where's your family?"

Nellie nodded to Miah, "Go ahead—tell him your story."

The teen sat up in his chair, speaking anxiously. "I used to live in West Virginia. About a year ago, I came home from huntin' and my family was gone. Our house was torn up, furniture broken, windows busted, my baby sister's toys were thrown everywhere. My whole family was gone!" Shaking his head, "My mom wouldn't leave me unless it was an emergency. Dad said if we ever got separated, I needed to get to my grandpa's farm in the Smoky Mountains." Frowning, "If my family is alive, we'll find each other in Tennessee. I've been movin' south ever since that day, but I slowed down a bit when I met Nellie."

"Miah was a godsend," added Nellie, patting the young man's hand. "When my husband passed away, I kinda fell apart. I realize now that Jesus called him home but that didn't make life any easier for me." She bit her lip, "Fortunately, Henry kept his Bible on a nightstand, so I started to read it to help me fall asleep. At first, I kinda jumped around, readin' passages here and there, with no real purpose in mind."

"Then I started to read the book of John. The words just seeped into my bones. I thought about things I read while I hoed the garden or fed the chickens." She shrugged humbly, "One day, I fell on my knees and asked Jesus into my heart." She watched Jim's expression, "I was all alone at the time, but for the first time in months, I didn't feel lonely anymore."

Jim remained silent. He nodded his head but said nothing.

Nellie went on, "Farms demand a lot of elbow grease and I couldn't keep up with the work. I needed the well repaired, hay cut and stacked, firewood chopped," waving her hand; "the list goes on forever." Nellie gazed at Miah, "When Miah came here and saw my predicament, he picked up where Henry left off. Before long, everything was back to normal."

Glancing downward, the teen modestly said, "Ah, it's no big deal," but Jim could see Miah appreciated Nellie's approval.

"I knew Miah would leave this farm someday, so whenever I saw a job that needed doing, I asked for his help," Nellie elaborated. "Miah went straight to work and finished everything he started."

The old woman smiled broadly, made eye contact with the young man. Her voice cracking, "I love Miah like he was my own son, but it's time that he finds his own people again." Clearing her throat, "Make me a promise though, if you decide to leave: whenever you get up to these parts again, be sure to stop by and stay a spell with me."

Pursing her lips, Nellie stood up quickly, fussed with a few bowls, and rushed into the kitchen. Jim and Miah watched Nellie leave the room. Neither man mentioned her watery eyes but they knew she was about to cry.

Jim tilted his head toward the kitchen, "Are you sure you want to leave Nellie?"

Miah looked doubtfully at the kitchen, then directly into Jim's eyes, "If I can get someone reliable to help Nellie every day, I really want to look for my family again. Would you like to go with me?"

"Absolutely, I'm headed that direction anyway." Miah shook his head thoughtfully as he pondered this new twist of fate.

Until this evening, Miah didn't know when he'd leave Nellie's farm, but he prayed daily that God would give him guidance. Sometimes Miah was impatient with God's timing; he wanted to search for his family every day, yet he stayed with Nellie because she was so kind. Besides that, the farm was in such disorder when Miah arrived that he couldn't leave Nellie until all the work was done.

Now all her major projects were finished; moreover, Miah made friends with other people throughout the valley. Not only did these people trust Miah, they stayed closely connected with Nellie. Miah felt sure Nellie would get the help she needed because their neighbors always looked out for each other.

As Miah imagined Nellie's life without him, he heard a knock at the front door. "Nellie, Miah, are you okay?" a man called out. Miah reassured Jim with a slight smile and walked to the front door.

Without opening the door, Miah said secretively, "What's the password?"

"Password! Are you kidding me, you little punk?" The door flew open and two armed men stepped into the living room. Jim put his hand on his pistol, but the first man, a Latino, held up his hand, "Chill out, buddy; we know this kid. In fact, we're here to make sure he and Nellie are safe from *you*."

"Yeah, we're just fine," answered Miah. Nellie peered out of the kitchen, waved her hand to the men before retreating into the pantry.

"We saw this strange truck in your driveway this evenin', so we figured we better check it out," said the Latino's tall, red-haired companion.

Jim stood up, walked over to the first man and, following Miah's example, extended his right hand, "My name is Jim Wilkins." The men shook hands.

"Pleased to meet you, Jim. My name is Juan Peña. And this is Sean McFadden."

Jim chuckled, "Is that some kind of joke, Sean and Juan?"

"Yeah, I know it's stupid. I call this huge Scotsman Mac; otherwise, when people say our names together, we sound like some cheesy nightclub act," joked Juan. Juan and Mac carried M4s as they walked over to sit down at the table. "So where did you serve, soldier?"

"How did you know I was a soldier?" asked Jim.

"Huh, are you kidding? One look at the way you move, your cut, how you study the room just screams Special Forces. Mac and I were in the 182nd Airborne, so we rubbed shoulders with you Special Ops guys."

Relaxing, Jim responded, "That's good to know; I like talking with vets."

Before the men spoke again, Nellie returned to the table with three tall steins. "I don't have much to drink around here, but it seemed appropriate to serve three men something other than water or milk."

"What's this, Nells?" asked Mac expectantly.

"Well, it started out as apple cider but I think I aged it too long. It might be hard cider, but I haven't tested it yet. You're my guinea pigs," she proudly announced.

"Well, this calls for a toast," exclaimed Juan. The three men stood up, smacked their mugs together and threw their heads back, taking deep swallows of Nellie's 'hard cider.' Suddenly, all three men were gasping, laughing, and gagging.

Surprised, Miah asked, "What's wrong?"

Wiping tears from his eyes, choking, Jim answered, "Oh, we just swallowed about a pint of apple cider vinegar!" The gaging men roared with laughter.

"Nell's Bells, are you trying to kill us?" coughed Juan, wiping his mouth with the back of his hand.

Unruffled, Nellie replied, "Well, I hear that vinegar is very good for your digestion."

"Oh, in that case," remarked Mac sarcastically, "thank you, Nellie; I feel better already! In fact, I feel so good that I think I'll have another round."

"You and me both, bro," challenged Juan.

Putting his stein firmly on the table, Jim said, "Fill 'er up, Nellie; I can't let paratroopers out drink me."

Laughing, Nellie, refilled the mugs and the men tossed back another helping of vinegar. After swallowing every drop, the men yelled out different words at the same time: "Argh! Nellie's Bells! Have mercy!" Smiling wickedly, Nellie asked if they would like anything else to drink.

Mac wiped his mouth, "I don't know, fellas; what do you think? A chaser of Pepto-Bismol?" The men roared again, still coughing, clearing their throats, blinking away tears.

Undeterred, Nellie returned to the table a few minutes later with five slices of cake. "Just a minute, I have cheroot coffee to go along with the cake," she said.

"What kind of cake is this?" asked Mac doubtfully.

"Applesauce cake," Nellie replied.

"You're killing me, Nellie!" declared Juan. "I've got an idea. You need to write a book, *101 Ways to Use Apples* or *How to Kill Your Friends with Love*."

❦

When the group moved into the living room with their cake and coffee, Jim realized that Mattie and Carl should go outside for a while. As he walked his pets to the door, Juan called out to Jim, "Don't be surprised when you see a friendly set of eyes watching you from the porch. My dog, Happy, is enjoying the cool breeze tonight." Jim nodded, opened the door, and let Mattie and Carl outside.

"*Hello,*" said a deep, kindhearted voice from the darkness.

"Hi," returned Mattie shyly, "who are you?" She walked slowly toward the glowing eyes on the porch.

Carl, who could see much better in the dark, screamed, "Run, Mattie, there's a monster on the porch!"

Happy laughed, "I am not a monster; I am just big-boned." Having said that, Hap stood up, stretched, and wagged her tail.

"Okay, you're not a monster," conceded Carl, "you're a dinosaur!"

Happy's size took Mattie's breath away. "What kind of dog are you?" she asked breathlessly.

"A Newfoundland; my name is Happy, and you are . . . Mattie?"

Looking at the dog towering above her, Mattie answered cautiously, "Uh-huh."

Frizzing his tail, arching his back, the brazen tabby announced, "I'm Carl, and if you hurt Mattie, I'll claw your eyes out!"

"Oh my goodness," reassured the Newfy, "I am not a vicious dog. Juan calls me a 'love dog.' He says my heart is the biggest part of my body."

Relaxing a bit, Mattie tried to assess the dog's size. "It's very dark outside; about all I can see are two eyes waaay above my head," she admitted, her legs trembling.

Smiling, Happy said, "Let us get off this porch; you can see me better in the moonlight." The shaggy black dog led Carl and Mattie down the porch steps, onto the front lawn. Under the glow of a half moon, Happy lay down on the grass in a very unthreatening manner. Carl and Mattie approached her at their own pace, studying the dog's massive size.

"My gosh," remarked Carl, "you're as big as a mountain!"

Happy woofed softly, putting her massive head in her paws. "I will not hurt you. I am thrilled because I love babies. Baby sheep, baby cows, even baby chicks—but to actually see a baby dog is very exciting!" She wagged her tail, "So the last thing I want to do is frighten you, Mattie."

Mattie crept closer to the hairy dog to sniff her nose. As the puppy cuddled next to Happy, the big dog sighed with contentment. Carl stepped closer to the old dog cautiously until he decided that Happy was harmless. From inside the house, the animals heard laughing and talking from their human families. Eventually, they rested peacefully together: a large Newfoundland stretched out on the lawn, a small, Australian Shepherd nestled close to the big dog's tummy, and a fat orange cat dozed in the thick fur of Happy's tail.

⁓◉◎◉⁓

After making sure that Mattie and Carl were safe outside, Jim settled into a soft chair near the fire. He usually didn't spend a lot of time talking with others but tonight was special. He was full, he felt comfortable with these new acquaintances, and he needed some time to relax.

"So tell us, Jim, what's your testimony?" asked Mac.

"Huh? What do you mean by that?"

"I just assumed since you have a clean forehead that you were a Christian," concluded the redhead.

"I don't think I'm a Christian," explained Jim. "I learned about Jesus when I was a kid; my parents took me to Sunday school every week. I tried to do the right things growin' up but when I left home, my life changed." No one said a word; they just listened. "In battle, I did some unspeakable things; they were so terrible that I don't even want to mention them now." He paused, "I can understand Christ dying for righteous people, but not me. I am the worst offender of God's laws." Jim glanced down, surprised he had revealed so much to these strangers.

"Oh, sugar," Nellie spoke gently, "Jesus died for everyone. In fact, Paul tells us that no one is righteous; we've all fallen short of God's glory."[1]

"Even you?"

"Land sakes, especially me; the closer I get to Jesus, the more warts I see in the mirror." Shaking her head, "But I don't beat myself up anymore; I just accept God's grace. I try to be more like Jesus, but I'm a long way from perfect," Nellie gazed into Jim's eyes. "I'm a simple woman with simple faith. When Jesus died on that cross, he took away my sins. All I had to do was confess my sins and accept Jesus as the son of God, and my sins would be gone forever. I wish I knew this a year ago when Henry was still alive."

"You know what keeps me going?" Juan added wistfully. "Jesus promised to give us an eternity in heaven. That's my hope; even when these days are brutal, I'm going home to heaven someday."

"I don't know," doubted Jim.

"Listen," Juan said, "I know where you're coming from. Mac and I both understand your pain; we've been there, probably did some of the same things you did." Mac quietly agreed. "You'll never earn your way to heaven by being good, or religious, or giving money to charities."

Jim said, "Well, I'll think about what you've said. I won't make any promises; not without considering the cost."

---

1. Rom 3:23.

"That's good, Jim," remarked Nellie, "we all have to count the cost. But don't be surprised by our reliance on God throughout the day. We thank him for our food, pray for miracles, and trust in his providence; it's just the way we roll."

"I can live with that," replied Jim.

Just then, the party heard soft rapping on the front door. Miah jumped up to open the door. Standing on the porch was a bald, bespectacled man with a worried expression. "Mr. Myers," exclaimed Miah, "come on in."

Walking timidly into the living room, Thomas Myers took off his hat, and waited for Nellie. When Nellie, Juan, and Mac walked over to him, Thomas spoke haltingly. Wringing his hands, he said in a low voice, "I heard that forty-seven Christians scheduled for execution next week somehow escaped the education center."

Feigning surprise, Juan remarked, "You don't say?"

"Yes. Apparently, the guards were overwhelmed by an organized group who freed the prisoners. None of the Christians have been found."

"Wow, that's really great news!" boomed Mac.

"It is indeed," agreed Mr. Myers, ogling Mac and Juan warily. He emphasized, "I only hope those men will be careful, because I heard that PeaceKeepers want to set a trap using Christians as bait."

"I think anyone helping prisoners escape would expect traps, plan alternative strategies," Nellie responded as she stared intently at her visitors.

"That goes without saying," Juan smiled ruefully.

Uneasy around Jim, Mr. Myers signaled Nellie, Mac, and Juan to follow him outside. Once he felt safer, Thomas said, "I don't know your new friend—he might be an upstanding guy—but I have news for you and this information can't get back to PeaceKeepers." The men shook their heads; they understood. Nellie crossed her arms, listening thoughtfully. Thomas went on, "I heard there will be a train loaded with hundreds of prisoners passing through our valley in a few days."

"Do you know how many troops will be on the train?" asked Mac.

"That's the sketchy part—I'm not sure. This news comes from a reliable source watching the depot in Marshall City. He says the train'll carry supplies and prisoners, so I'd expect a lot of troops will guard the train."

"We'll need better intel before we plan an interdiction," responded Juan. "Do you know when the train's leaving Marshall City?"

"Yes, my friend works night shift on the loading dock. He said the train's scheduled to leave this Wednesday morning, early."

"It's already Sunday night; that's just three days away," replied Mac. "We need to come up with a plan *fast!*"

"I know; I came here as soon as I heard the news," explained Thomas.

Juan asked, "Is your friend reliable?"

"He saved my life and the lives of fifteen other people a few months ago. Yeah, he can be trusted."

"I think," Nellie paused, "I know who you're talking about." Talking faster, "Is he about thirty-five years old, strong as an ox," brushing her cheekbone, "has a scar across his left cheek?"

Thomas widened his eyes, "Yeah, that's him."

Nellie looked directly at Juan and Mac, "Take his word as gospel, fellas. This depot worker will not only give you trustworthy information; he'll fight with you." Thinking ahead, she added, "Whatever you and your fighters need, please let me know quickly. Anything we don't have here, I'll try to collect over the next few days from friends I trust."

4

THE FOLLOWING MORNING, JIM woke up at 3:00 a.m. He couldn't remember the last time he slept in a bed with clean sheets and thick blankets, but the luxury totally renewed him. Jim found Carl nestled by his feet and Mattie curled on the floor next to the bed. He moved his feet carefully to avoid disturbing the animals on his bed or the floor. *This is a good place for you two to live*, he thought. *If you travel with me, you might get caught in the crossfire.* As if she read his mind, Mattie woke up, jumped to her feet, and followed him outside.

As Jim arranged some tools in his truck, he saw Miah step onto the porch. "Where're you going?" asked the curious young man.

"I need supplies, Miah, especially gas if we're gonna find your family."

The teen responded, "Don't leave yet; I'll go with you." Miah disappeared into the house and returned minutes later completely dressed. "I left a note for Nellie so she won't worry, but I can help ya get everything we need."

Jim nodded. Looking at the puppy, he commanded, "Stay." Mattie instinctively sat down, tilting her head as she watched Jim. Addressing Miah, Jim added, "Let's find some fuel while it's still dark outside. Otherwise, someone might get testy when they see me with a gas can." The pair jumped into the Ranger and drove toward Marshall City.

Although the sun hadn't risen over the horizon yet, the two could see relatively well in the moonlight. Jim used his headlights while he drove country roads, but once inside city limits he relied on a sliver of moonlight to navigate. "People must be more cautious with their vehicles around here than in northern cities," the man noted, "because I don't see any abandoned cars."

Staring straight ahead, Miah reassured Jim, "As we drive farther into the city, we'll see more cars." They soon found a parking lot of a large retail store filled with cars and trucks. In contrast to most of the city, the parking lot was well lit and, despite the early hour, people inside the store hustled back and forth past the glass entrance doors.

"What do you think is going on in there?" wondered Jim.

Scoffing, Miah responded, "PeaceKeepers use this building as an 'education center.' There are likely hundreds of people waiting inside to be shipped to the gallows."

Shocked, Jim looked intensely at the teen, lined his brow with concern, then refocused on the store. Narrowing his eyes, "I'm guessing some of these parked cars are full of fuel." Thinking out loud, Jim said, "But in a lit parking lot, siphoning gas is risky business. I'm going to leave you and the truck out in the shadows while I 'liberate' some gas. My dad's old revolver is in the center console if you need it; I have a Glock with me."

Parking the truck out of view, Jim withdrew the two empty gas cans he recently found. He ran in a crouched position to a car parked in a far corner. After he removed the car's gas cap, he smelled the gas; it was good, so he filled both gas cans.

Jim returned with the fuel after he squeezed a small silver coin under the car's wiper blade, payment for the gas. When Jim noticed Miah's doubtful expression, he explained, "The driver shouldn't get too upset when he discovers the missing fuel. The coin will pay for at least two tanks of gas when he deposits silver into his digital account." Studying the store, Jim stated, "Miah, put fuel in our gas tank; I want to get a closer look inside this store. If I don't return in fifteen minutes, drive home on the back roads without headlights. I'll meet up with you later."

Miah glanced at his watch, slipped out the door, and started to fill the truck with gasoline.

Jim crept closer to the store, being careful to remain in the dark or behind storage containers. He watched as guards stood outside a Tire Center door, smoking cigarettes, laughing together. When one guard held the door for his buddy, Jim heard children crying and women murmuring in the store. Jim glimpsed people in ragged clothes moving listlessly inside the building before the door slammed shut.

Incensed, Jim tried to think of a plan to free the prisoners. As he considered his options, a PeaceKeeping soldier approached from behind and poked Jim with the muzzle of his rifle. Jim turned swiftly, grabbed the weapon, and hit the soldier across the face with the rifle stock. Before he made another move, Jim saw five more rifles pointed at him as an angry voice shouted, "Drop the weapon, interlace your fingers, and put your hands behind your head!"

Cursing himself for getting caught, Jim placed the rifle on the pavement and interlocked his fingers behind his head. The guards quickly secured Jim's Glock and conducted a thorough pat-down. Once certain that Jim had nothing of value or additional weapons, they hauled him to the garage's back door and into a semi-converted field office area. Makeshift cubicles with computers filled half the garage, leaving the remainder of the garage jammed with chains, pulleys, buckets of tools, and vats of discarded chemicals. *This looks like some kind of hybrid office/torture chamber*, Jim thought dismally.

Unfortunately, his assessment was accurate. Suspecting Jim knew about the recent prison break, PeaceKeepers began an abysmal interrogation until he lost consciousness. When Jim returned to his senses, the commander studied Jim's bruised face and body. Determining his newest detainee useless, the commander waved his hand nonchalantly in the air, announcing, "This man isn't important to us or our magnificent leader. Put him in the waiting area with the other prisoners. Keep him zip-cuffed to prevent any further disturbance."

Two PeaceKeepers dragged Jim's limp body out of the garage and into a broad open area of the former superstore. Other prisoners gasped at the sight of his bruised, lacerated face. Without speaking, one detainee caught the guards' attention and pointed to a mattress lying on the floor. The PeaceKeepers laughed at the mattress and spitefully dropped Jim on the concrete floor.

A guard kicked Jim once more in the ribs while his friend laughed. Jim wondered silently if that was the soldier he hit with the rifle; if it was, maybe the guy was exacting revenge on him or just recovering a little dignity among his buddies. Pushing through the throng of detainees, PeaceKeepers returned to the garage to eat dinner, resume their informal banter, and forget about the injured man they left on the floor.

A small crowd huddled around Jim. Two men rolled Jim onto his back and a woman tenderly placed his head in her lap. "Elizabeth, please get me some water and rags to clean his wounds," asked the woman. A girl with silky blonde hair ran to a drinking fountain that dripped rusty water and saturated a towel. The wet towel was handed to the woman and she began to wipe dried blood from Jim's eyes and face. "I don't know if you can hear me, but you're still breathing. As long as you're alive, we'll take care of you—so just rest." With those soft words floating in his ears, Jim once again passed out.

⁓☉☾⁓

Faithful to his promise, Miah left after fifteen minutes. As he rolled discreetly out of the parking lot, he saw PeaceKeepers drag Jim into the Tire Center. Miah prayed for Jim's safety as he drove away. Although he felt terrible to leave his new friend, Miah understood that he needed more people to save Jim now.

Once he reached open country, Miah turned on the truck's parking lights and raced back to Nellie's farm. He didn't care how fast he drove because he wanted to talk with Mac and Juan first thing in the morning. He barely slowed down to turn into Nellie's driveway, slamming on the brakes in a cloud of dust.

Nellie ran outside with Miah's note in her hand. Wearing a threadbare nightgown and bathrobe, she seemed unaware of the frosty morning temperature. "What happened?" she looked anxiously at the teen.

Clenching his teeth to keep a steady voice, "PeaceKeepers caught Jim at the education center. We need Mac and Juan's help to rescue him!"

"Hold on, Jeremiah, one thing at a time. What were you doing at the education center?"

"We were getting gas." Nellie arched an eyebrow but listened without comment. "Jim siphoned gas out of a car. Then he paid for it! I don't know why he left money for gas; those 'markers' steal our chickens and corn without paying us!" raged Miah.

"Money doesn't matter, Miah. Go on."

Frustrated, Miah continued, "After we siphoned the gas, Jim took a closer look at things going on inside the store; that's when some Peace-Keepers found him. The last time I saw Jim, they were dragging him into the Tire Center garage."

"Oh, dear Jesus!" exhaled Nellie as she closed her eyes. She prayed, "Lord, please post your angels around Jim. Protect him and keep him safe." When she reopened her eyes, Nellie promptly took control. "Jeremiah, go quickly to the Garcia's house. Juan and Mac sometimes stop there to sleep in the barn if they're out too late. I only hope they haven't started to walk to their houses before sunrise." Miah immediately left Nellie and ran through a meadow to Emanuel Garcia's house.

Neither Juan nor Mac slept well in the Garcias' barn. The accommodations were primitive but acceptable—straw for bedding and horse blankets for cover—but both men kept thinking about the train leaving Marshall City in a few days, so they rested fitfully. After a few hours of sleep, both men felt fairly refreshed and prepared to leave.

As they shut the squeaky barn door, Rosa Garcia stood on the front porch, shouting and waving to get their attention, "Please, come in! Don't leave without having a cup of something hot to drink."

Mac turned to Juan, "Man, I hope Rosa doesn't offer us some of Nellie's hot apple cider." Both men started to laugh.

Juan waved to the beauty on the porch, "We wouldn't miss your company for anything!"

⌒◯◯◯⌒

The following morning produced a new level of torment for Jim. Swollen and discolored, his face resembled a discarded eggplant. One eye was so puffy he couldn't open it, but he could squint with his other eye to discern shapes and light. He assumed that he had a couple of broken or badly bruised ribs, which made breathing an insufferable task. As he gingerly moved each body part, he heard the soft voice that spoke to him throughout the night.

"Good morning," Sara said. "We wondered if you would live to see daylight."

Jim focused his eye on the voice; he beheld a gentle, smiling woman.

"We took turns watching you last night. I'm Sara and this is Dr.—"

The doctor held up his hand, "There's no need for introductions, Sara. This poor man has enough to think about without trying to remember names too." The doctor, a small, wiry man with intelligent, dark eyes, addressed Jim directly, "I did all I could to keep you comfortable in this deplorable place. It seems futile to save a man's life when we're all sentenced to die, but I couldn't leave you on the floor broken, miserable."

"Phanks," groaned Jim through split lips.

"Don't mention it," said the doctor, "and don't bother talking. Just breathing is going to be torturous for a while." Turning to the caring woman, "Sara, I'm going to go visit some other people now that our newest recruit is responding."

"Thank you, doctor," Sara said. Looking at Jim, "Tell me when you want to walk to the bathroom; I'll find some men to help you. This is a terrible place to endure but the inmates are wonderful people." Jim squeezed her hand in reply, closed his eye, and fell asleep.

⌒◯⌒

At the same time Jim met Sara, Miah finished running up the porch steps to the Garcias' front door. Before knocking, he saw Happy wag her tail. He breathed a sigh of relief knowing that Juan was inside.

"Hey, buddy, where's the fire?" bellowed Mac as he opened the door. Miah described the events in Marshall City to Rosa, her grandfather, Emanuel, Juan, and Mac. When he finished, the young man twisted his hands together nervously, expecting harsh words for driving home without Jim.

Sensing the teen's anxiety, Juan remarked, "Don't feel bad about leaving, Miah; you did exactly what Jim wanted you to do. Now we know there's a store full of people and a supply train leaving in a few days. My money says those are the folks that will be on the train headed north—"

"That was my thought too," interrupted Emanuel. Although a short, stocky man with weathered skin and gnarled hands, Emanuel's eyes sparkled with life and energy.

Scowling, Mac said, "We need to pool our resources and make plans. I'll contact all the able-bodied people in my section of the valley, and Juan, you can do the same for yours. We'll bring whatever weapons we have on hand and meet as a group before noon on Tuesday. Where do you want to meet?"

Squaring his shoulders, Emanuel bravely offered, "You and your people can meet here, at our farm. We'll have food and water for everyone. Of course, you may all stay hidden in the barn."

"Thank you, Mr. Garcia," Juan replied. "We understand the risk you take every time we sleep in your barn—"

"And we appreciate your courage," finished Mac.

"My courage comes from the Lord," Emanuel declared simply. "I am a servant of God, just like you."

Juan shook Emanuel and Mac's hands. "It's decided. We'll meet here on Tuesday with as many soldiers and weapons as we can gather in two days."

"May I come too?" asked Rosa. Emanuel blanched as he looked at his independent, brave granddaughter. Determined, she highlighted her strengths: "I am a very capable archer, my eyes are sharp, and can I run quickly. I won't slow you down."

Emanuel bit his bottom lip as he considered Rosa's hasty request. He slowly confirmed to the others, "It's true, Rosa is an excellent archer. I trained her to protect herself . . . and she has the courage of a lion; I only hoped that she'd never test her skills in battle."

Exasperated, she responded, "Grandfather, what would you have me do? The government's executing innocent people that refuse to give up their values. I can try to help free them now, or I can stay home to wait for PeaceKeepers to imprison us later."

The old man nodded his head. "You're right . . . I just don't want to lose you." He understood her reasoning but feared the potential danger. He turned to Rosa, "We have very little time to prepare your weapons and cook enough food for a small army. Can you and I do it in two days?"

Encouraged, she answered, "Of course we can!" Miah immediately added that Nellie and her friends would also prepare meals for the gathering troops.

Mac saw unmasked admiration in Juan's face as the Latino stared speechlessly at the fearless beauty standing in front of them. Amused at his friend's astonishment, Mac proceeded, "Let's not waste any more time talking. I'll see you Tuesday morning!" Mac turned quickly to start jogging across a lush meadow of wildflowers in knee-deep grass to his home on the far side of the valley.

"I'll let Nellie know your plans," said Miah as he pivoted to run in the opposite direction.

Regaining his composure, Juan licked his lips, held Rosa's right hand, and said with a smile, "Welcome to our little band of insurgents." Inwardly, he wanted to kiss her fingers, saying, *What a magnificent woman you are!* Instead, Juan squeezed her hand, called Happy, and turned away breathlessly.

As Juan walked down the driveway, the big dog lumbered faithfully behind her master. Juan discretely looked over his shoulder as he strolled past the Garcia's mailbox to watch Rosa return to her house. As the screen door closed, he glimpsed a blur of burnt orange from Rosa's dress and watched strands of her long black hair float in the breeze, ebony fingers waving goodbye to him.

5

ALTHOUGH HE ONLY SPENT a few days in the education center, Jim regained much of his strength. The pain in his chest was agonizing but the doctor didn't think his ribs were broken. His vision improved as the swelling on his face decreased and Jim didn't mind that he still walked with a limp. His health improved daily.

Despite his height and muscular build, Jim tried to blend into the crowd to learn the prisoners' daily routine. PeaceKeepers woke everyone up by turning on all the indoor lights at 6:00 in the morning. Guards forced prisoners to line up for a breakfast of watery broth with a few grains of rice. After eating, the day stretched into long hours as prisoners talked quietly, washed in stained tap water, slept, or died. Contrary to government propaganda, the center provided no cutting-edge training programs or educational opportunities, just the prospect of eminent death.

To stay alert, Jim met a variety of people and listened to their stories. Regardless of their differences, every prisoner had one common trait: they did not have the beast's mark on their foreheads or right hands. The mark was an outward sign of allegiance to the New World Order. People who feared losing the ability to buy and sell products, or didn't want to live outside normal channels, immediately had the mark branded onto their skin. Many individuals accepted the government's brand to spare their lives, and the lives of their children. Others willingly and excitedly added the mark to their skin; some incorporating the mark into elaborate tattoos or other body modifications in celebration or worship of their savior.

This marking was the government's first step to a dual system of commerce and accountability. The mark was the number that visually gave people access to the world's market. Accompanying the mark was a microchip placed under the skin that contained all the person's metadata. This metadata included everything from personal identification and medical information to employment and emergency points of contact. In real time, this bidding data was used in every transaction. For example, when a mother wanted to buy groceries for her family, she would first have the mark on her forehead or right hand scanned. After acknowledging her allegiance to the New World Order, she could scan her food items, then pay in digital cryptocurrency by using the same microchip inserted under her skin.

This system overcame the weakness of simply relying upon identification from a driver's license or passport. The microchip, being almost impossible to forge, worked in collaboration with nearly unhackable databases (even for advanced machine learning), so there was no way to bluff a transaction. No, world leaders needed something permanent to mark people; thus, the government demanded that everyone be branded on either the forehead or right hand with an identifiable number. Correspondingly, each person also had a biochip inserted into their hands that contained all their personal, medical, and financial records.

Those who believe that the true King of kings lives in heaven refused to receive the mark; thus, they signed their own death sentences. The supreme world leader announced that anyone without the mark would be labeled as an enemy to his authority, to the world at large, and, at best, deserved to die. Consequently, for those unwilling to receive the mark, there was only one way to live: undeceived, unbranded, and underground.

⁓⊙⊙⁓

Although the temperature felt cool and crisp, the sunlight shone brightly on Tuesday morning, the appointed meeting day for the rebel army. Juan and Mac met at the Garcia's farm around 10:30 with thirty other insurgents. Men and women mingled casually, talking in hushed voices. They carried a multitude of weapons, ranging from bolt-action rifles to assault rifles and handguns. Emanuel spoke first to the group, "Ladies and gentlemen! Let's go to the barn where we can sit, eat, and discuss our plans."

The group moved into the Garcia's huge barn for the meeting. Nellie, her friends, and the Garcias arranged hay bales and boxes for chairs, and distributed an assortment of food on tables covered with clean sheets. The guerrilla band helped themselves to preserved wild nuts and berries, roasted pig, campfire biscuits, and canned fruits. Once everyone settled into their seats, Emanuel said grace, then introduced Thomas Meyers.

Thomas began, "I want to thank you for your time, as well as your discretion; we all understand the risks. Not just the risk of meeting together, but our discussion and execution of a plan, which will undoubtedly be considered treasonous. For those of you not prepared to carry this burden, we wish you peace and farewell. We will not think less of you, but we must ask that you leave, now."

No one moved, much less breathed, as the tension and anticipation built.

"Very well. We received credible intelligence that PeaceKeepers are planning to move precious prisoners and cargo from a store in Marshall City to their base early tomorrow morning, in support of a surge effort in that area. Our goal is to interdict the shipment, free the prisoners, and refresh our supplies."

Soft murmuring began within the crowd.

Thomas listed the cargo loaded into Wednesday morning's railcars and the high probability of hundreds of prisoners aboard the train.

"This mission calls for wisdom because we can't blow up the train without killing innocent people," added Thomas.

"Does anyone know where the prisoners will be kept on the train?" asked one soldier.

"All the supplies were loaded into the front cars. We suspect that prisoners will be put in the rear cars sometime tonight," answered Thomas.

"We need to stop this train, disarm the enemy, then sort out prisoners and supplies," reasoned a serious woman. "The guards won't intersperse prisoners among their valuable supplies; starving prisoners will eat their food."

"Good point," observed Mac, "so how do we want to stop the train?"

"I think the best place is the narrow canyon between our valley and the mountains," mentioned a middle-aged farmer. "We could roll boulders onto the track at the far end of the canyon. Once the train completely passes through the entrance, we'll block the entrance with more boulders. Essentially, the train would be stuck in the middle. We would be stationed on the canyon rim. We'll capture the train using our tactical advantage."

"What about the prisoners?" questioned a male voice in the crowd.

"We'll concentrate our attack on the front cars because most Peace-Keepers hate to rub shoulders with rebels. I'm betting there won't be too many guards in the last few cars," a farmer said dryly. After more discussion, the small army agreed to seal the train in the canyon, return fire on PeaceKeepers, and hope for the prisoners' safety during the battle.

Knowing the distance of the canyon from the Garcias' farm, Mac volunteered to lead a group of people to set up blockades. "Anyone is welcome to join me, but I need strong backs to cause a landslide and guards to cover us while we're working." Everyone volunteered to help, so Mac amended his proposal, "We also need a small contingent of volunteers to observe the train in Marshall City."

"I'll lead the Marshall City group," offered Juan. "Since the distance between the city and canyon is too far for our walkie-talkies, we'll be working without communication. Any suggestions?"

"Well, as primitive as it sounds, we could use smoke signals," proposed Thomas.

"Are you serious?" asked a woman with disbelief.

Thomas elaborated, "Once the canyon is blocked, we can start a small fire before the sun sets. The team in Marshall City will see the smoke and know the plan is still on."

"Listen, friends," said Juan, "I appreciate your ideas but let's not do anything that will draw attention to the canyon. The train is going to roll in the morning, whether we have a blockade or not, and unmarked people are going to die when the train reaches its northern destination. It's simple. Let's block the train in the canyon, demobilize PeaceKeepers, free prisoners, and remove cargo without communication. It's risky but if you don't like the plan, again, you're welcome to leave before we say anything else." After more discussion, the group unanimously agreed to send a small group to Marshall City for surveillance, use a larger unit to attack the train in the canyon, and carry out their individual tasks without communication.

"Alright," Mac declared to the assembly, "I need everyone coming with me to finish your meal, then pack some extra food and water for the trip. We'll load into three trucks to make better time." Turning to his friend, "Juan, you're going to have to walk to Marshall City."

"That's okay, bro, I'm taking Miah with me. We can talk along the way," smiled Juan.

"I want to go with you, Juan," Rosa stepped forward.

Juan looked at the single-minded young woman, again surprised by her boldness. Juan turned to catch Emanuel's eye; Emanuel shook his head in support of her idea. Juan responded zealously, "I can't think of another person that I'd rather have walk beside me and Miah." Rosa smiled brightly at Juan, nodding her head with firm conviction.

After a pathetic dinner of watery broth and spoiled potatoes on Tuesday evening, Jim stretched his tall frame and rolled his shoulders. Although his wrists were still zip-cuffed in front of him, he could lift a spoon to his mouth and move his fingers slightly. Jim wasn't sure how he would compensate for his bindings but he decided that he would not die without taking a few of these loathsome guards with him.

Suddenly, the guards began screaming obscenities, forcing prisoners to move to one side of the old store. Before long, prisoners were pushed into tight lines by the store's entrance and given pieces of paper with the numbers four, five, six, or seven written on them in Roman numerals. Jim looked down to find VI on his paper. He wondered what being sixth meant. The imprisoned men scowled at the guards, women looked fearful, and children sniveled, clinging to their parents. Jim realized they were being prepared to move and watched for his chance to execute vengeance.

Large buses pulled up outside the store. The buses were similar to an old Greyhound Jim rode years ago when he traveled across country as a new recruit, except none of these buses contained seats. Prisoners were crammed into the buses by PeaceKeepers. Hot and crowded, the people felt like sardines wedged tightly into tin cans. While he wasn't claustrophobic, Jim could imagine the distress, even terror, for someone fearing enclosed spaces. Each turn or bump in the road caused the sea of humanity packed into the buses to squeeze against or fall onto one another.

After a seemingly endless drive, the vehicles stopped. Disembarking from the modified buses, prisoners were led into a large open area fenced by concertina wire where armed guards and barking dogs patrolled the perimeter. A group of PeaceKeepers began to call for people to line up by their assigned numbers to be loaded into the railcars.

Suddenly panic broke out as prisoners begged and traded with others to get the same number as their friends and loved ones. Some families stayed together, but others were torn apart. Lines of captives were jammed so closely in the boxcars that everyone was forced to stand. Even sick and wounded prisoners stood or leaned against others because there was no room to sit.

Ugh, and I thought the bus ride to basic training was bad, Jim groaned.

Conditions in the cars were deplorable. The fetid smell of body odor mixed with blood and urine permeated the air, gagging Jim. Unlike many of the prisoners who simply gave up, Jim focused his hatred toward retaliation.

Sometime during the night, a pleasant sound interrupted Jim's scheming. It was a song. One prisoner began to sing . . . and then another person started to sing. Soon everyone in the railcar, except Jim, sang. Bewildered, Jim looked around; he saw women, children, and men singing a song of praise to God. People shifted their shoulders so they could reach their hands to heaven as they sang. Jim wondered how everyone knew this particular song, could sing in such discomfort, *and* give praise to God, who had so thoroughly forgotten them![1]

Curiously, the melody didn't stop in their car. Soon, Jim heard the same music echo in other railcars. The men's deep, rich bass notes harmonized with the light, airy melody of women. The longer they sang, the louder and more joyous the music became. People started singing in other languages; melodies fractured into multiple parts that resounded throughout the railway station. The sound was unearthly, a thunder of strength and resilience.

Undeterred by the guards' threats to be silent, the prisoners' music resonated across the landscape and into homes. People living in Marshall City stood outside their houses, listening to the strange choir. Many citizens covered their ears or locked their doors in disgust, but a few people fell on their knees, weeping at the beauty of the sound. Juan, Rosa, and Miah listened to the music from their hiding place on a hillside above the rail yard, captivated by the train and its occupants.

As night deepened, the singing gradually receded but the atmosphere vibrated with reverent power. Once the music ended, PeaceKeepers relaxed, leaned back in comfortable positions, and fell into a deep sleep. Before dawn's first light, Juan, Rosa, and Miah saw three warriors wearing camouflage uniforms and carrying weapons, at the low ready, walk toward the railcars. Each warrior touched the padlocks on the boxcar doors, the locks broke open, and chains fell uselessly to the ground.

When the train car doors slid open, the warriors roused sleeping prisoners. Jim pushed through the drowsy crowd to the opened door of his railcar; he challenged the stranger, "Are you for us or for our enemies?"

---

1. Acts 16:25–26.

"Neither, but as commander of the army of the Lord, I have now come."[2] When the warrior touched Jim's bindings, the zip cuffs ripped open and fell to the ground. Stunned by the man's words and actions, Jim looked at his freed hands with astonishment. Signaling Jim to silence by placing a finger to his lips, the warrior started to help prisoners out of the car.

Before he could speak again to his liberator, Jim realized he was blocking the doorway. Overcoming his confusion, Jim stepped away from the door. Without uttering another word, Jim swiftly passed women and children to the warrior standing on the ground.

As witnesses of the escape, Juan, Rosa, and Miah stared wordlessly at the proceedings in the train yard. When Juan recognized Jim, he motioned for Miah and Rosa to remain hidden while he retrieved his comrade. Approaching the train, Juan realized all the railcars were now empty and each warrior began to lead three large groups of prisoners out of the darkened city.

Juan easily identified Jim's tall frame within the multitude. Juan caught up to Jim, touching his buddy's arm. Jim spun around, ready to attack, but relaxed when he saw Juan's swarthy face. Jim smiled, yet when Juan squeezed his ribs vigorously, he cringed with pain.

Jim croaked, "Bruised ribs, Juan, take it easy."

Juan quickly released his grip, "Sorry!" Pulling Jim's elbow, Juan said, "Let's go, amigo. Quickly."

Frantically searching for Sara, Jim waited a moment. Seeing Sara's dark blonde curls bobbing in the crowd, Jim shoved through the masses to her side, clutching her arm. "Come with me," he pleaded, "I have friends who will help us escape."

"Where's Elizabeth?" she asked frantically as she looked around the rail yard. Spying the teenager, Sara begged, "Can I bring Beth with us?"

"Yes, please bring her, but hurry." Sara grabbed Elizabeth's hand; they quickly followed Jim and Juan back to Rosa and Miah. As they met on the hill above the train yard, cursory introductions followed.

From their vantage point, Juan's small group kept watching the three warriors and the released captives. After being safely guided beyond the city limits, prisoners claimed the mysterious visitors simply faded into the darkness. Exhilarated by their miraculous rescue, prisoners quickly

2. Josh 5:13–15.

scattered into surrounding areas, several hours before the guards awoke to find that three hundred people were missing.

At sunrise, the PeaceKeepers commander was livid after reading the official report. "What do you mean, all the prisoners escaped?" he screamed. "Where were my guards?"

"The guard unit is outside your office with an explanation, sir," a sergeant responded.

"I don't want to see them or hear their excuses, sergeant! Kill them all and double the security around the supply train. If we lose anything else, both you and I will face the guillotine."

The sergeant rushed out of the commander's office. Despite the guards' claim of not being drunk, he scoffed at their lame excuses. *How could so many people flee their notice without being impaired by drugs or alcohol? Nobody sleeps so soundly that three hundred people vanish without a trace!* "Idiots!" the sergeant grumbled to himself. Finding a detachment, he ordered his subordinates to execute the commander's death sentence of the guards before news of the prisoners' escape reached the ears of local gossips and media outlets.

6

MILES AWAY, AT THAT same early hour, Mac and his small army prepared for the coming train. The canyon exit was already blocked with tons of rock and soil. Once the last car passed through the canyon entrance, fighters on both sides of the entrance planned to push tons of rock and debris on the tracks behind the train. After successfully blockading the train on both ends, the battle would begin.

Although the army rested during this lull, no one slept. They were anxious, edgy. Some leaned against rocks and closed their eyes but most just studied the horizon, talking periodically with one another. By mid-morning, a sentry watching the valley identified the train.

"The train's about twenty miles away," he told Mac.

Mac ordered everyone to take positions along the canyon's edge, stay hidden, and prepare for combat. Crouching down behind rocks or laying prone on the ground, each person waited. As seconds passed slowly, their hearts beat rapidly.

❧

While Mac's unit waited on high ground, Juan's group moved through the valley toward Nellie's farm. They stayed off roads; instead they chose to walk on overgrown forest trails to remain hidden. After walking a mile in silence, they began to speak to each other.

"Did you see what happened?" questioned Miah. He thought maybe he fell asleep and dreamt the prisoners' escape.

"Yes," answered Rosa somberly, "my knees kept knocking together."

"I'm surprised I can even walk," agreed Juan. "I'm still shakin'!"

"They were angels," stated Sara assuredly. "They saved us." Elizabeth nodded in agreement.

As the others talked, Jim listened, glancing at his wrists. Confused by the nightly visitors, Jim finally told the others what the warrior said to him. The group listened intently, wordlessly. Although Jim couldn't believe he spoke to an angel, he also couldn't rationalize the experience. Nothing made sense to him; nothing in this upside-down world made any sense to him.

"Do you think angels will go to the canyon?" wondered Miah.

Juan put his arm around the teen's shoulders, "I don't know, guy, but let's pray for them right now."

In the predawn hours, they knelt and prayed. They thanked the Lord for his intervention during the prisoners' escape and asked Jesus to protect their family and neighbors in the canyon. Jim closed his eyes, listening respectfully. Profoundly mystified, he still doubted the existence of an all-powerful God but he would not hinder the belief of his new friends. During his friends' prayer, Jim tried to scientifically explain the night's events, but he remained baffled.

The early morning fog lifted just as the prayer ended. After reopening their eyes, the small group stood up, wiped pine needles and dirt off their clothes, then continued their hike to Nellie's house. Still thinking about the prisoners' miraculous escape and the upcoming canyon battle, Juan reminded everyone, "No matter what happens this afternoon, this is a day to commemorate. By the grace of God, condemned prisoners were set free."

⊛

Until today, Jim never saw the valley in its entirety. When he first arrived on Sunday to help Nellie with her fence, afternoon shadows already stretched across the landscape. The following morning, Jim and Miah drove to Marshall City in the dark. After Jim escaped the train early Wednesday morning, he realized that all his dealings in the valley had occurred in dim light, or moonlight.

But now, standing on the edge of a forest in the morning, Jim understood the residents' passion for their valley. The nameless Virginia glen, a ten-mile-by-five-mile cove completely surrounded by the Appalachian Mountains, spread out before him. Golden fields spotted with clusters of late autumn wildflowers, split-rail fences, and farmhouses built of logs or stones filled the grassy cove.

From his vantage point, Jim identified Nellie's farm as he took note of other landmarks nestled within the secluded glen. Hay neatly stacked in rows, livestock grazing within fenced fields, a railroad track snaking through pastures. But the crown jewel, a sapphire in a setting of gold, was a shimmering lake in the valley's northeast corner, nestled in a field of yellow grass. Created by runoff from rain and snow in the mountains, the lake beckoned residents to drink its cool, fresh water or swim beneath its sparkling surface.

Looking beyond its unparalleled beauty, Jim studied the valley for access. *How did people move through the valley?* Dirt roads ran along the valley's perimeter. These roads provided three entrances: Jim accidentally found one entrance in the southeast corner near Nellie's house; two other entrances lay in the southwestern and northwestern corners. Depending on which western road was taken out of the valley, people could travel into the mountains toward Marshall City or, for the more daring, across the mountains into Kentucky.

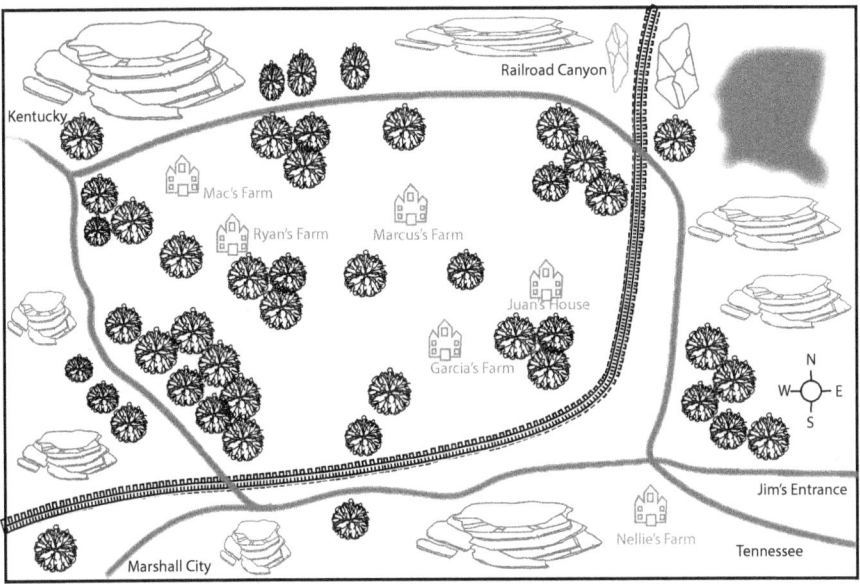

The only other visitors passing through the valley rode in railcars. Since trains didn't stop in the valley, sightseers simply looked out their windows at farms as they traveled to other destinations. Trains traveled over the southern mountains from Marshall City, ran along the lower border, and bent north, passing through a picturesque canyon. The track followed a twisting path through more mountains north of the valley, ultimately ending in a faraway northeastern city.

On this specific fall morning, no one, except Jim, admired the valley's rustic beauty. Today, valley residents riveted their total attention on the canyon in the rugged northern mountains. For Mac's seasoned fighters, the canyon's beauty was its sheer walls, high ledges, and loose boulders. Just before he dispatched his troops along the canyon's rim, Mac said to them, "Be strong and courageous. Don't be afraid; don't be discouraged, for the Lord your God will be with you."[1]

⤳◌◔◌⤳

Mac kept his eyes focused sharply on the train as it passed through the glen. With his army carefully hidden, Mac watched the train slowly roll into the canyon's entrance. Suspicious of a rebel attack, the train's engineer proceeded into the canyon with apprehension. Despite the tactical danger of moving through a narrow, strategically vulnerable corridor, the engineer proceeded forward with the assurance of safety from the extra troops onboard.

When the last car passed through the entrance, Mac signaled his rear detachment to wait. He paused until the train's engine reached the middle of the canyon; then Mac ordered his strongmen to release a cascade of boulders and debris onto the track behind the train. Rocks, uprooted trees, and loose soil thundered down the hillside, settling upon the tracks, sealing the canyon's entrance, trapping the train.

Without knowing that the track was now blocked in the rear, the engineer continued moving through the canyon. Fear gripped the engineer's heart when he approached the canyon's exit and saw a blockade of rubble at least a quarter mile long in front of the train. A PeaceKeepers captain screamed to the engineer, "Back up! Get us out of this canyon!" The engineer reversed the train but his heart sank even lower when he discovered a new mountain of rocks and trees on the track behind them.

Panicking, the engineer stopped the train. Before he could consider his next move, his eyesight instantly vanished! His world turned black; he couldn't see the instruments in front of him or the conductor beside him. He waved his arms frantically touching gauges, rubbing his eyes, to no avail.

---

1. Josh 1:9.

His world disappeared, yet he was not alone; government troops on the train were also blinded. He heard terrified screams from guards experiencing the same complete blackness. PeaceKeepers now anticipated facing a battle of unseen power, helpless to inflict casualties upon their enemies, useless to defend their cargo, and powerless to protect themselves.

Puzzled, Mac's army listened to the commotion in the train, but remained still. Valley soldiers reacted differently to the disorder; inexperienced fighters watched the scene with wide eyes, confused, while former vets became more intense as they assessed the situation, formulating new tactics in their minds. Mac raised his hand in the air to hold their attack. Before issuing orders to the entire army, he sent four soldiers down to inspect the train. The remainder of Mac's unit watched the train through scopes on their rifles, ready to attack if, or when, Mac gave the order.

The four soldiers crept to the train warily. They found guards bumping into each other, falling down steps, shouting wildly, and mistakenly hitting one another.[2] Some guards blindly shot their weapons inside the train to resist imaginary attackers. As PeaceKeepers died by their own hands, Mac's army remained in their protected positions, listening, watching.

Eventually realizing the folly of his forces' actions, the PeaceKeepers commander ordered his detail to stop firing their weapons. One or two panicked guards continued to shoot their weapons, but even they relented as the commander repeatedly screamed his orders, "Halt! Cease fire!"

After the shooting stopped, Mac immediately took command. He ordered his soldiers to approach the train cautiously but to subdue the enemy by whatever means necessary. Once Mac's troops disarmed the enemy, they led PeaceKeepers off the train and demanded the blind men to lie on the ground. Several valley soldiers bound the captives' wrists and ankles with twine or baling wire while others gathered weapons.

"What are we going to do with these prisoners?" asked Alicia, a tall, no-nonsense Iraqi veteran. She brushed some stray blonde hair off her sweating face as she gazed intently at the helpless PeaceKeepers.

Mac ordered, "I want you and two others to guard these men while we unload the train. Railroad comptrollers will soon realize the train isn't moving. They'll send a crew to check out the problem in a day or two. I

---

2. 1 Sam 14:18–20.

want your unit to leave before government reinforcements arrive; make sure the prisoners remain bound, but give them water and shelter until their relief comes."

Mac studied the prostrate prisoners and a train bulging with cargo. He continued to talk with Alicia, "We need to concentrate on unloading this train without interference; but if any PeaceKeeper tries to overtake you, shoot him. This battle belongs to the Lord; he deserves the entire honor for this victory. I only hope we'll have enough time and strength to secure these supplies before more government forces arrive." Alicia nodded; she quickly chose her team, placed guards around the blinded captives, and watched everything closely.

Mac turned away from the PeaceKeepers to examine the train's contents. His army confirmed a wealth of supplies but no one found any civilian prisoners. "I don't know what to tell you about the supposed detainees, Mac," a farmer said. "There aren't any prisoners, but we sure have a lot of supplies."

Mac announced, "Let's get this train unloaded as quickly as possible. Put as much as you can in the trucks; we'll take the supplies to Emanuel's house. If we run out of time, hide the remaining supplies in caves along the canyon. I'm betting that more PeaceKeepers will arrive within a few days, so we need to work smart, and fast."

Mac chose two men to oversee operations. One man led the shipment to Emanuel's house and the other organized unloading the train. "Our main goal is to get these supplies transferred to Emanuel's farm. Once the first convoy is unloaded, return for the next load. It's more trouble to carry supplies to a cave, but right now we're short on both time and trucks. I don't want to lose valuable cargo because of our limitations," Mac directed his colleagues.

Mac looked at another female vet, a lithe Asian American, "Monica, I'm putting you on the canyon rim as our overwatch. I know you won't let anyone get close to our operation." Monica nodded and swiftly turned to climb the mountain. Before she started her ascent, she secured her worn, but extremely accurate, hunting rifle over her shoulder, smiled at Mac, and winked her approval.

As the morning progressed, the need to hide freight in caves disappeared because Mac underestimated the community's "call to arms." Valley residents heard gunfire in the canyon, then later watched heavily laden trucks race to Emanuel's house. Without exception, every able-bodied person rushed to the canyon to help. When Mac saw dozens of people with horse-drawn wagons and handcarts waiting at the entrance of the canyon, he quickly improvised a new plan.

Mac pulled aside his two neighbors, "Marcus and Ryan, I need your help." The men stopped working and followed Mac to a quiet place to talk. "Each of you has farms with large storage barns, and I trust you." Both men looked at Mac earnestly, waiting for further instructions.

Mac continued, "With all the people wanting to help us, I'd like to divide the supplies into three equal divisions. We'll store a third of the supplies at the Garcia farm and the other two thirds at your farms—that is, if you're willing." The two men shook their heads in agreement. "Both of you, and Emanuel, will distribute food and medicine to our neighbors. This gives us the added security of spreading supplies to three separate locations rather than one. There's less chance of losing everything to a fire or a government attack."

Mac studied his two friends. No two men looked so completely opposite on the outside but had the same heart inside: Marcus Washington, forty-five years old, weathered skin the color of dark chocolate, short, nappy, salt-and-pepper hair, and an easy grin; and Ryan McGuire, thirty-eight years old, ghostly white, freckled skin, shaggy auburn hair, and sky-blue eyes. Both men immediately agreed to Mac's plan. "Excellent!" exclaimed Mac. "I'll make the announcement to our soldiers and the residents outside the blockade."

After Mac gathered the small army and valley residents together, he explained his idea. "We have so much to be thankful for this morning. The PeaceKeepers' train did not carry any prisoners, so no innocent victims were hurt today. We have a train full of cargo that we'll share with everyone. We'll separate and transport the cargo to Emanuel Garcia's, Marcus Washington's, and Ryan McGuire's farms. Emanuel, Marcus, and Ryan will help distribute the goods to everybody in the valley."

He continued, "Once government officials realize their train is missing, PeaceKeepers will come down on us hard, so we can't waste time. Don't minimize the danger we now face; once you receive your supplies, you may want to leave the valley for a while. If you're willing, we need all the help we can get to move this cargo today. Once you have your supplies, I'm sure Marcus, Ryan, and Emanuel would appreciate your help delivering food to our neighbors that are too crippled, old, or sick to get supplies on their own."

The crowd agreed with Mac's plan with shouts and whistles. Determined to move the cargo to each of the homesteads as quickly as possible, valley residents worked tirelessly. Without one word of complaint, the assembly moved an entire trainload of heavy crates filled with fresh and canned foods, medicine and bandages, and automatic and semiautomatic weapons safely to barns and outbuildings on the three farms by nightfall.

7

As Mac's army secured provisions, Juan's group moved slowly back to Nellie's house. Although the doctor wrapped Jim's ribs firmly with torn sheets, he still felt pain when he walked, and he tired easily. By Wednesday evening, hours after the miraculous prisoner escape and train attack, the walkers finally reached Nellie's door. Mattie and Happy scrambled out of Nellie's house when they heard familiar voices. The dogs woofed and pranced in circles around the group, especially the worrisome Mattie. The weary travelers laughed as they reached down to pet their lively dogs.

"Hap, I'm so glad to see you again!" said Juan, bending down to stroke her long, thick hair.

Happy barked, *"Juan! Juan! Juan!"* Juan laughed at Happy's incessant barking. He grabbed his big dog by the waist, playfully rolling her to the ground.

Rosa smiled as she watched the man and dog wrestle together. She said with wonder to Sara, "I never saw a dog more devoted than Happy."

Holding the big dog's face between his hands, Juan replied, "Yeah, she's a 140-pound marshmallow, isn't she?"

Meanwhile, Jim sat on the ground to let Mattie jump into his lap. As she kissed his face, her whole body wiggled with excitement. Jim stroked her fur, murmuring weakly, "You're a good dog, Mattie. Such a good dog."

Mattie whimpered, *"I was so afraid I'd never see you again!"*

All the noise in the front yard drew Nellie and Carl out of the house. Standing on the porch, Nellie shouted her greeting, and Carl, now even fatter, walked over to Miah, rubbing his head on the teen's legs. *"Welcome back, sport,"* purred the tabby.

After the animals' raucous homecoming, greetings followed. Jim introduced Sara and Elizabeth to Nellie; Nellie welcomed both of them with a hug. Smiling broadly, Nellie motioned enthusiastically for two strangers to come out of her house. A young married couple walked onto the porch, waving shyly. "I'd like you to meet Brant and Toynell," she added, "people who were mysteriously freed from a train leaving Marshall City early this morning."

Sara ran to the dark woman with an exotic, braided hairstyle, squeezing her tightly. "Toy, I never thought we'd see each other again!"

Toynell's husband, Brant—a handsome black man with an easy smile—rushed toward Toynell and Sara, embracing them in his arms. "We were saved by God's grace . . . again," he exclaimed. Crying, Elizabeth joined the group; the four friends laughed and wept together.

Missing his own family deeply, Miah felt tears well in his eyes. Embarrassed, the teen picked up Carl, nuzzling his face in the cat's fur to hide his unwanted tears. Carl didn't mind the subterfuge; he considered himself a man's cat anyway.

"What a glorious day!" remarked Nellie. "We hoped you'd stop by here before going to Rosa's house. I just need fifteen more minutes to finish dinner. If you don't mind delaying your trip awhile, we'll all eat together."

"Dinner would be great, Nells, but we need water first—lots of water," coughed Juan. Miah hurried to the well and pumped several gallons of water from the hand faucet. Dipping a ladle into the bucket, each walker drank slowly, savoring the refreshment. After his third helping, Juan wiped his mouth, "Now we can talk again without tasting dust in our mouths."

"Come inside; tell us what happened to you," urged Nellie. "We have lots of catching up to do."

After a few awkward minutes of getting comfortable with each other, the conversation flowed easily. The former prisoners described their arrests, life as detainees, and their release in the train yard. Rosa and Juan explained what they saw from the hill above the train station; Jim related his experience with the commander of the Lord's Army.

Both Miah and Beth listened closely but didn't talk. Beth looked shyly at her folded hands in her lap, occasionally glancing in Miah's direction. She was completely captivated by this tall, unassuming young man. Not only was he strong and good-looking, but his thoughtful words and quiet disposition absolutely intrigued her.

Miah responded in kind. *She is so beautiful,* he thought. *Sixteen years old, pale skin, rosy pink cheeks; she looks like a porcelain doll.* Unable to stop staring, he noticed that when she tossed her blonde hair away from her face, he saw dozens of different colors shimmering in the light. *Her hair even looks like spun gold.* When Beth noticed Miah studying her hair, their eyes met; Miah smiled self-conscientiously, and Beth quickly looked down at her hands again.

Jim noticed the unspoken exchanges between the two young people. He smiled as he thought wryly, *Even in the most extreme situations, love can surprise us.* Jim leaned back in his chair, listened to the lively dinner chatter, and felt a closeness with his new friends that he hadn't experienced in years.

After dinner, Rosa and Juan excused themselves to finish their walk to the Garcia farm. Jim said, "Let me go with you. I need to pick up my truck; besides, there's safety in numbers." The three walked slowly through the fields to compensate for Jim's sore ribs. Despite their unhurried pace, Jim still struggled to keep up with the couple.

Turning to Jim, Juan asked with concern, "Are you sure you want to walk tonight?"

"Yep, there's a lot to do. I want to keep moving so my muscles don't tighten up. Don't worry, I'm fine."

Understanding Jim's need to press on, Rosa and Juan continued their dinner conversation, trying to ignore Jim's labored breathing. Strolling toward Rosa's house, they enjoyed the cool evening air, laughing as they watched Happy romp playfully in front of them. By the time they reached the Garcias' house, the yard was peaceful; valley residents had already safely hid all the supplies and returned to their own homes for dinner.

"Grandfather!" Rosa called to the old man rocking in a chair on the front porch. Emanuel stood up, hobbled over to his granddaughter, and threw his arms around her. "I have so much to tell you, Grandfather!" she said breathlessly.

"And I have a lot to tell you too, rosebud," he beamed. Holding her close, smelling the soap in her hair, Emanuel acted like a man who hadn't seen or held his granddaughter in years. "I was worried when we didn't hear anything from you." Stumbling with words, "Well . . . this late at night, I thought maybe . . ." clearing his throat, "I prayed throughout the day for you and your friends." He sighed, "Thank God you're alright."

After Emanuel finished hugging Rosa, he turned to face Juan and Jim again, still keeping one arm protectively around his granddaughter's shoulders. Emanuel described the battle, at least as he understood it from secondhand reports, and he recounted the cargo transfer. Everyone liked Mac's idea of dividing the provisions among valley residents. They also agreed with Mac's choices of Emanuel, Marcus, and Ryan to oversee the distribution of goods.

"But Mac's afraid for the safety of our people, especially those who can't walk very well," Emanuel added. "PeaceKeepers won't tolerate our disobedience; they'll label us as traitors."

After thoroughly discussing battle tactics and supply logistics, the group grew quiet, thoughtful. Uncomfortable with the silence, Jim switched subjects, "Miah and I plan on leaving soon to find his family in Tennessee; do you know anyone who'd like to come with us?"

"I'll pass the word along," Juan replied. "There'll probably be a lot of people running to the mountains now. What about you, Emanuel? What do you want to do?"

"This is my home. I want to stay here," Emanuel patted Rosa's hand, "to take care of my friends and family."

Rosa looked anxiously between her grandfather and Juan, an old man she loved intensely and a young man who captured her heart. "I will stay to help grandfather deliver all the food in storage." *But after that job is done, what will I do?*

Her hesitation prompted Juan to say, "I'll help with the food exchange too." Then, looking straight into Rosa's eyes, he said boldly, "And after that, we'll see what happens."

⸎

Jim returned to Nellie's house before sunrise on Thursday morning, only four days since his arrival to the valley. He parked the Ranger in a secluded place filled with thorny shrubs and dense vegetation. Having returned from Emanuel's house with provisions for several families, Jim hid the truck because he didn't want anything stolen by persistent looters wandering the countryside. As he walked wearily to the front porch, he heard Mattie bark expectantly.

"Company!" the puppy yipped.

Sitting on a porch rocking chair, Nellie said, "Be still, Mattie; it's just Jim." Addressing Jim in her relaxed Southern drawl, "Hey there, darlin', how're ya doing?"

"I'm exhausted, but I wouldn't trade the last twenty-four hours for all the money in the world."

"Atta boy!"

As Jim stepped onto the porch, he noticed a shotgun resting on Nellie's lap. "Do you need relief from guard duty?" he asked.

"Naw, I'm fine. This is the best time of day, between 3:00 and 5:30 in the mornin'. I watch the sky change color, birds start to sing, and roosters and cows begin rustlin' around." Gesturing for Jim to sit down, "I'll brew coffee in a few hours and get some breakfast going, but until then, I just like listenin' to the mornin' sounds."

Jim sat on a chair next to Nellie. He breathed deeply, felt a hitch in his ribs, gritted his teeth, then tried to relax again. *Remember to take shallow breaths*, he scolded himself. He looked idly over the fields, listening to the steady, rhythmic creaking of Nellie's rocking chair. Within minutes, Jim rested his chin on his chest and started to snore.

✧

When Jim woke up, the sun was well over treetops and people were talking in the kitchen. Standing up to work kinks out of his back and shoulders, the tall man glanced down to see Mattie's stubby tail wiggling furiously. He scratched her ears, "Good morning, sunshine. Whatta you say? Should we go see what everybody's doin'?"

Stepping into the house, Jim encountered cheerful banter. Although she spent most of the night guarding her house, Nellie was bright-eyed, energetic. "Jim, we have a few jobs that we'd like you to do today."

"Whatcha need?" he asked.

"Well, Brant and Toynell decided to stay here with me instead of traveling through the mountains. But they're city folks and they want to learn some things before you take off."

"Arright," Jim replied. Turning to Brant, "What can I help you with?"

Brant stepped forward, "I wanna learn how to shoot a gun. A few years ago, I used to be a computer analyst, but without computers, it's like we stepped back in time a hundred years." Glancing at everyone in the room, "I know this isn't news to you but we're still going through culture shock. Instead of driving cars, we walk or ride horses. Without the mark, Toy and I can't shop in grocery stores. We rely on others to milk cows, grow vegetables, or shoot game for food. We try our best to help, but we still have a lot to learn." Toynell put her arm around Brant's waist, a quiet gesture of support for her husband.

"No problem, Brant," Jim clapped the young man's back. "I'll teach you basic weapon handling and cleaning today. With practice, your skill will improve."

Miah added, "I'm going outside now to take care of the cattle; I'd really appreciate some company. Do you want to learn how to milk cows?"

"Yes," Brant said eagerly.

"Great! I'll show you what to do. It'll take some time to remember all the steps, but we'll work together. After a while, you'll get to know the girls and they'll feel comfortable with you."

Relieved by the easy acceptance from these new friends, Brant thanked everyone for their understanding. The former computer analyst stepped onto the front porch to put on a pair of Henry's old rubber boots that Nellie gave him. Afterward, Brant and Miah walked together to a barn as Miah started giving Brant some pointers on caring for milk cows.

After Miah and Brant left, Sara switched the conversation from farm work to domestic concerns. "This morning, Nellie, you mentioned that Jim brought back supplies for several neighbors." Nellie nodded. "Well, Beth and Toy would like to help you deliver these goods today. I'd like to stay here to clean and mend clothes before we leave."

Jim widened his eyes with pleasure, "Before you leave? Are you going with Miah and me?"

"Yes, if you don't mind, Elizabeth and I would like to go with you." She watched Jim's expression carefully, "But before we leave, we want to make sure Nellie, Toynell, and Brant have everything they need."

Jim grinned, "Sounds good. We won't leave until Nellie's farm is buttoned down." Jim put on his hat and started to walk outside, trying to disguise his limp, "Let's get rolling because there's a lot to do."

"Hold on, Jim," said Nellie. "Eat your breakfast, let Miah and Brant take care of the animals, you can supervise us as we load supplies into the wagon. While we're delivering food and medicine, you can get your truck ready for the trip." Noticing his careful movements, she reminded him, "Just take it easy; we'll get everything done."

"That sounds like a plan to me," admitted Jim. "This afternoon, anyone who wants to practice shooting can go with Brant and me. We'll make a lot of noise in that gully south of the farm; we should be far enough away from the cows that we won't be a problem."

"What are you saying, Jim?" asked Sara. "Does noise affect a cow's milk?"

"Oh yeah, if we make too much noise, we'll be drinking sour milk tonight instead of fresh cream," Jim winked slyly at Nellie, sitting down at the kitchen table.

Sara walked slowly outside with a worried expression on her face. Nellie smiled as she filled Jim's coffee mug, "Well, Jim you may be a good man, but I'd wager there's still a lot of devil in you."

8

His earlier wanderings with Juan, and last-minute plans to organize an army, kept Mac away from home for almost a week. Finally, on Thursday morning, Mac and Marcus rolled into Mac's driveway in a horse-drawn wagon. On the ride home, Mac stretched out on top of crates in the back of Marcus's wagon and slept. Expecting the typical sounds in his yard, chickens clucking and dogs barking, Mac was instantly aware of the unusual silence. "Slow down, Marcus; something's not right." Marcus stopped his horse, set the wagon's brake, grabbed his rifle, and carefully slipped to the ground.

Both men crouched down, moving swiftly toward the house. Peering into a living room window, Mac saw the darkened room; listening carefully, he heard his dogs whimpering inside. Motioning for Marcus to go to the back door, Mac stepped lightly onto the front porch, sidestepping creaky boards. He turned the doorknob, slowly. When he cracked open the front door, two dogs ran frantically past his legs to get outdoors.

He was greeted inside by the dank smell of decay, sickness. As flies circled filthy dishes piled haphazardly in the sink, he noticed spoiled food sitting on the countertop; his wife never left such a mess. Fearful, Mac hustled into the boys' room first, but saw nothing.

He opened the door to his bedroom to find his wife and two young sons in bed together. Mac ran to the bedside, placing his hand on the forehead of his youngest son, a two-year-old toddler. No fever, but also no pulse. Panicking, he touched his older, five-year-old son's forehead. Although Mac confirmed the older child's raging fever, he also felt a weak pulse and listened to the child's faltered breathing.

Mac gently lifted his son from his wife's arms, placing the boy in a bathtub. "Marcus, please start carrying cold water from the well. There's a bucket next to the well house. We need to get his temperature down, fast!" Marcus turned abruptly and rushed outside.

Mac returned to the bedroom to touch his wife's forehead. Her eyelids fluttered, she gazed groggily into her husband's face, then closed her eyes again. "Mac," she said weakly, "how are the boys?"

"Not good, Pat. What happened?"

"I think it's the plague," she gasped. "I traded some chickens for blankets from a traveling salesman a few days ago," her voice cracked. "That evening the baby started to get fussy. The next day, all three of us were sick."

Mac closed his eyes with grief. Another plague, pandemic, whatever. No one knew much about this new disease because it struck suddenly, killing tens of thousands of people living close to each other. Doctors and nurses in hospitals contracted the pandemic while caring for patients. Unfortunately, the few researchers investigating the disease, using sterile technique, still had not identified a pathogen. Valley residents had been isolated from this dreadful infection because the mountains served as a major obstacle to most homeless people searching for food, water, and shelter. Until now.

Since Mac knew very little about the disease or its mode of transmission, he applied all his medical understanding to ease his wife and son's suffering, without exposing others. When Marcus came into the house with two buckets of cold water, Mac shouted, "Marcus, leave the buckets by the door! Don't touch anything. Put your hand over your mouth."

Marcus backed up quickly, stepped off the porch, placing a handkerchief over his nose and mouth. Mac stood in the living room speaking loudly to his friend, "Tell everyone in the valley that this house is quarantined. My wife bought some things from a tradesman and somehow caught the plague. Maybe a germ was in the cloth, or on the man; who knows?"

Vaguely recalling the history of the Black Death during the 1600s, Mac made an impromptu decision, "I'll leave a note in our mailbox so you'll know if we need anything. Check our mailbox every Monday. If there isn't a note, you'll know we're all dead." He paused before making his next request, "Don't risk your lives to give us a funeral. Destroy every living creature on our farm. Don't touch anything without gloves. Keep your faces covered, then burn everything! Burn the animals and our house, with our bodies inside. Do not let this disease spread!"

Marcus swallowed hard at the grisly thought of a fire consuming Mac's entire household. Marcus's sad brown eyes looked directly into Mac's blue eyes; he replied solemnly, "I understand."

After issuing these orders, Mac waved for his friend to leave. Mac choked back tears as he thought about his dead son, but he remained determined to stay alive to care for his surviving son and wife. As he watched Marcus walk back to the wagon, Mac whispered to himself, "So long, Marcus." He shut the door, took a deep breath, and returned to his wife's bedside.

Marcus retreated to his wagon. After he sat on the seat, he bent his head in prayer. Once he finished praying, fear suddenly gripped him. What if that same salesman went to his house? His family could be in danger too! Without a moment's delay, Marcus prodded his horse to trot home. Despite its fatigue from yesterday's supply runs, the trusty animal kept a steady pace until they reached the Washington farm.

Upon arriving to his farm, Marcus sighed with relief. Instead of finding the desolate quiet of Mac's farm, he saw people moving purposefully in and out of his house, chattering busily, laughing loudly. Thinking that the busy activity was related to the supply redistribution, Marcus held his hand in the air, waving enthusiastically. His sixteen-year-old son waved back but did so with reluctance.

When Marcus stopped the wagon, he jumped down to hug his son, TJ. "What's everybody doin'?"

"Packing up to leave," his son said haltingly.

Marcus stepped back, looked his son in the eyes, "Who's leaving?"

"We are. Mom, Talia, me . . . and a bunch of neighbors."

"What?"

Marcus marched up the porch to speak with his wife, who stood at the front door. "Constance, what are you doing?" he demanded in a voice mixed with anger and confusion.

"I'm leaving you and taking the kids with me." Marcus took one step toward her but Constance held her palm up to stop his advance. "Before you say anything more about the trials Christians will endure in the last days, I want you to listen to *me*." She stood ramrod straight with determination, "I'm *tired* of living like a pioneer. Now that the world government controls this country, I heard that everything's returning to normal. I want to go to stores to buy food using a scanner, I want to see a doctor if we're sick, and I want to turn on a light using a *light switch*." Waving her arms to emphasize her frustration, "I want to live like a regular human being again."

"But where will you live?"

"I'm going back to my parent's home in Ohio. Some of our neighbors here are going to different places but we'll all travel together over the western mountains. Afterward, we'll split up to go our separate ways."

Marcus stared at his wife, numbed by her callousness. "Don't take our children, Connie," he pleaded. "They'll perish if they receive the mark."

Constance sniffed, "I don't believe that nonsense anymore. I told them they can stay with you if they want, but they both decided to go with me. They also want a normal life, among *normal* people."

Marcus turned to his son, "Is that true? You want to go with your mom?"

Imitating his mother, TJ said, "Yeah, Dad, there's nothing here for me. I wanna see my old friends, hang out on the street, maybe even play basketball again."

"That isn't going to happen, son," Marcus replied. "Don't be deceived; life is different now. Nothing's the same as it was before."

"Before what? We don't even know *why* the U.S. fell apart," whined TJ. "Anyways, I don't care anymore, Dad. I'm tired of chopping wood, planting vegetables, or praying to a God I can't even see."

Realizing TJ wouldn't stay with him, Marcus spied his daughter as she listened to their argument. He turned to her, "Don't leave, Talia." Marcus knew his thirteen-year-old daughter's heart; she was a kind, gentle soul. She would never disobey her mother, even if it meant risking her life, but she had to choose between him and Constance.

Not meeting his gaze, she sniffed her runny nose, "There's nothing for me here, Daddy; I want to go with Mom."

An idea struck him, "If you go, I want you to take something with you." Marcus brushed past his wife's body blocking the door and marched into the house. He rummaged through a desk drawer until he found a pocket-sized Gideon's Bible. Returning to his daughter, he said with conviction, "Here, take this Bible. Read it."

"Oh, Dad," she groaned, "You know I can't understand the Bible. It's just a bunch of mumbo jumbo."

"It's the living word of God," corrected Marcus. "You read books about wizards, magic, and dragons but the Holy Bible is filled with *actual* supernatural events: a man who collapses a temple with his bare hands, people being raised from the dead . . . a virgin birth."

Talia rolled her eyes—a show of disrespect for her mother's benefit—then held out her hand apathetically.

Marcus had another idea, "Wait a minute."

Pulling a pen from his pocket, he drew a map on the back cover of the Bible. Speaking as he sketched, "If you ever want to come home, follow this map. It shows you the names of roads you'll need to take to return to this valley." Marcus handed the open Bible to his daughter. Talia glanced at the map, closed the Bible, and slipped the small book into her coat pocket.

Looking at his wife, Marcus said abruptly, "Go ahead, finish your packing. I have some supplies for you and your friends in my wagon; it's food and medicine from the supply train. Just take a crate for each family; put our box with your other belongings."

"Humph!" Constance balked and stomped away.

She never even asked about the battle, thought Marcus miserably, *or thanked us for the food.* When Marcus returned to his wagon, he noticed Ryan McGuire's wife, Shirley. She and her children stacked suitcases and trunks into another wagon.

"Does Ryan know you're leaving?" Marcus asked.

Shirley laughed, saying, "He'll find out as soon as he reads my letter." Overhearing what Constance told Marcus, she added her own complaints, "And there's another thing that's driving us away from this disgusting valley, I want to talk with my family again, in person or with a *cell phone.*" She punctuated the last two words for emphasis.

As Shirley lifted a chair into the wagon, she thought of something else that bothered her. "You know what else I want? I want to know the exact date, and year, of *any* day. I want to celebrate my birthday! I don't want to live according to four seasons like a farmer anymore. I want a daily planner again; I want to control my own schedule!"

Marcus heard this complaint from his own wife countless times. Because the supreme leader hated to enumerate years as B.C. (Before Christ) or A.D. (After [Christ's] Death), he created a new system of naming and recording days and years. Predictably, the new calendar began when the supreme leader assumed control of the world's financial and political structures. Key holidays marked new religious festivals established by the New World Order but Sabbaths dedicated to the Lord were unlawful.

Very few people continued to document days under the former Julian calendar. Most people just wanted to live to see the following day without worrying about next week, or even next year. So birthdays, wedding anniversaries, Christmas, and Easter were forgotten dates. Interestingly, Halloween still found its way into the new calendar, but the supreme leader enjoyed the revelry and debauchery that revolved around this pagan holiday. Yes, Halloween was still a day to celebrate ghouls and witches; it was a day of great importance.

As Marcus considered criticisms about calendars or communication, he shook his head in disgust, unhitching his horse from the wagon. Leading the animal to its barn, Marcus thought about his family, friends, faith. He refused to compromise on several matters: he loved Jesus unreservedly so he would continue to obey God; he loved his family, so he wouldn't force them to stay with him; and he loved his friends, so he wouldn't abandon them now.

He put his horse into a stall, adding clean straw on the floor for bedding. He gave the docile creature fresh hay. He brushed her coat as she ate. Separated from the others outside, Marcus pressed his face against her neck to weep for his family. The horse bent her head down in submission, nickering softly, *"Thank you, kind man."*

Marcus looked into his horse's dark eyes as he ran his hand over her coat, "You have such a sweet disposition." Sighing ruefully, "I only wish more people acted like you."

Marcus remained in the barn to brush his horse until he heard Constance yelling, "Marcus, we're leaving now!" He walked reluctantly out of the barn, placing a hand on his forehead to shield the sunlight; he saw four wagons filled with his neighbors and their household items. Constance walked over to her husband, saying without apology, "It just got too hard." She turned away, climbed into the last wagon, and never looked back.

"It just got too hard." Those few words rolled around in Marcus's head for days. When he woke up in the morning to start a fire in the stove, he heard, "It just got too hard." The words mocked him as he stacked hay in the barn or carried firewood into his house. By Sunday, just four days after their victory in the railroad canyon, he figured he'd go mad if he thought about the difficulties his family had endured this past year.

But in truth, it wasn't his fault. He didn't create the fall of the United States, an event he still couldn't completely fathom. He didn't cause natural catastrophes; those were the acts of God. Nor did he demand that everyone worship a one world government; that was the scheme of the supreme leader.

Marcus knew the situation wasn't his fault but he missed his family desperately. Suddenly, he remembered Ryan. How was Ryan coping without his family? He needed to reach out to his pal; he needed to talk with someone friendly. Marcus locked his house, put a bridle and saddle on his horse, and hoisted himself onto the saddle. By the time he reached his front gate, his two dogs joined him and trotted happily in front of him.

Because Ryan lived close by, Marcus reached his friend's house early Sunday afternoon. Sitting in his saddle, Marcus called, "Hey, Ryan, are you home?" Ryan stuck his head out of a sturdy wooden barn built a year ago; he waved to Marcus. Three families were collecting their rations from the train, and Ryan was talking with them.

"Come on over, Marcus," invited Ryan. Marcus tied his horse to a tree and walked over to the gathering. "How're you doing?" asked Ryan.

"Fair to middlin'," answered Marcus. "Constance and the kids left me."

"Yeah, I know. My family's gone too," Ryan empathized. "You know what my wife wrote? No God was worth all the pain and suffering she and the kids endured every day." Ryan shook his head, "Jesus died for her." Making a dismissive gesture, "I guess not being able to access social media or get a manicure seemed more important than the crucifixion of an innocent man on a cross."

Pitying Ryan and Marcus, members of the three families gathered around the two lonely men for encouragement. During their conversation, one woman offered to bring them loaves of bread weekly; another woman volunteered to wash their laundry. Ryan and Marcus easily accepted their neighbor's gifts and thanked the families for their generosity.

After securing their supplies in wagons, the families prepared to leave. Seeing a little girl struggle to reach her mother seated in a wagon, Marcus lifted the child into her mother's arms; he ruffled her hair when she smiled at him. Ryan stood next to another wagon to chat about the upcoming growing season with an interested farmer. Eventually, the wagons rolled out of Ryan's yard. The two men took note of the dwindling supplies left in the barn, relieved that people were receiving their allotted provisions promptly.

Marcus asked Ryan, "Do you want to go with me tomorrow to Mac's house? His family has the plague. He's staying there alone to care for them. I promised to check his mailbox every Monday." Steeling himself, he added solemnly, "If there isn't a note inside, it means he and his family are dead. I'm supposed to kill every living creature on his farm, then burn all the buildings, including his house, so the disease won't spread."

Ryan stepped back, staring wide eyed at Marcus. "Really?" Shifting his gaze toward heaven, Ryan spoke softly, "And I thought my life was bad. At least my family was healthy; that is, they were when they left me."

Ryan scratched his chin, "Listen, why don't you stay the night here? We'll ride over to Mac's house tomorrow to see how he's doing. If there's no letter in the mailbox, I'll help you keep your promise to Mac."

Marcus exhaled with relief. Grateful that Ryan was willing to help him, Marcus agreed to stay the night. Before dinner, the men moved Ryan's livestock into a secluded field with a pond, and made sure the chickens had enough food and water to last several days. Once the animals were snug, they ate dinner; later, they sat outside to watch the sunset.

As the men talked, they watched the sky change color gradually: canary yellow to flaming orange, deep burgundy to the velvety blackness of night. They chatted about families, cars they once owned, even the barter rate of grain. It really didn't matter what they discussed as the sky darkened and stars appeared; they simply needed someone to talk to and someone willing to listen.

Winter

9

LESS THAN A WEEK after the train incident, blustery winds began to blow. With the onset of winter, four rickety wagons carrying supplies and families from the valley, including Marcus's family, proceeded slowly up a winding mountain pass. As the travelers climbed higher in elevation, the temperature grew colder. The passengers wrapped themselves in moth-eaten, threadbare blankets while the wagons rumbled forward. When snow blew around their thin bodies, the passengers pressed together closely, but the oxen seemed oblivious to the weather and plodded steadily onward.

At the end of the first day, a disreputable man with dark, snarled hair named Ennis found an acceptable site to set up camp. A large bend in the road provided room to circle their four wagons near a fire pit created by another band of disheveled wanderers. Ennis, a lazy man, wanted to use the modest fire the other wanderers started. He cunningly thought, *Maybe we can finesse an extra meal or two from these strangers while we're at it.*

"Do ya mind if we unhitch our wagons here with you?" asked Ennis.

"By all means, join us," answered an outgoing man with sandy blonde hair. "There's safety in numbers."

Ennis commanded his crew of women and children, "Let's unhitch the wagons for the night." Emboldened by his self-acquired authority, he ordered, "Somebody take care of the oxen; I hate touching those stinkin' brutes!"

Without offering any protest, Marcus's son, TJ, began to unfasten harnesses and yokes. He roughly pushed the oxen into a group and hobbled their feet, muttering to the weary creatures, "You know, someday, when I'm back in civilization, I'm never gonna look at another stupid ox again." He slapped an ox's rump; the beast flinched. Still unaware of living conditions outside the cloistered valley, he mumbled as he secured ropes, "Maybe I'll drive a car, go to a fast-food place, buy a burger, probably see a movie with my friends. Hey," kicking another ox harshly, "I might even eat you in one of my burgers!"

"Listen to you, Mr. Gangsta," chided Talia with her arms crossed. "I don't like living like a farmer either but at least you can show these poor animals a little respect." She stroked an ox's massive neck while the brawny animal placidly chewed grass. "Without them, we'd be stuck up here on Mt. Whatever, trying to stay warm." Softening her tone, "I'll help you with these guys, then we'll see what's cooking for dinner, I'm starving!"

Looking sheepishly at his sister, "Yeah, I'm hungry too. I wouldn't hurt the oxen too much; I was just talkin'."

"Yeah, I know, you're always 'just talkin'.' I get so tired of your endless gripes." Thinking about the home she left, "At least Daddy had nice things to say at the end of each day."

TJ hardened, "Well, 'Daddy' isn't here and we're not ever going back to that stinkin' valley. Mom told me so." TJ shoved passed his sister, saying over his shoulder with disdain, "Get some water for those ugly brutes or else they may drop dead pulling our wagons tomorrow." Talia stared at her brother's back, unconsciously touching the Bible in her coat pocket.

꿨

The valley wagons carried meager supplies for eighteen people: canned food, two rifles, a box of shells, tools, furniture, various kitchen utensils, suitcases filled with clothes, and four crates from the supply train. The group consisted of three mothers, eight children, and six men. Two of the men were very old; the other four were deemed shiftless, unreliable men by most valley folks. To everyone's dismay, one of those shiftless men, Ennis, tried to establish his leadership within the group.

Ennis's decisions caused dissention among the women; in fact, the mere presence of the four younger men concerned the women. Initially, the mothers discussed the strengths and weaknesses of including two decrepit and four undesirable males in their company; ultimately, they allowed the men to join them. Although none of the mothers trusted the younger men, the women knew the four malcontents could repair wagons and hunt for dinner. The mothers decided the men could provide some protection from wild animals and, more importantly, the even wilder human beings wandering the country, so they grudgingly allowed the men to join them.

Although the men weren't the most ideal traveling companions, the women were desperate to leave the valley. The women, and their teen-aged children, habitually grumbled about country living. A few years ago, before the fall of the nation, they were hip suburban mothers. They once drove new SUVs loaded with luxurious gadgets, attended music recitals, enrolled in local colleges, even chaired special committees. They were the movers and shakers in their homeowner associations, the women that others regarded highly, the ones whose opinions mattered.

What were they in the valley? Harassed farm wives: their weekly coifed hair now sun damaged and brittle, their beautiful nails chewed off or broken, and their extensive wardrobes reduced to a few hand-sewn cotton dresses made from feed sacks. Country living was detestable!

Not only did the women resent their incredible fall from social grace, but they hated their husbands for dragging their children into a ruthless life of subsistence. How could their husbands sleep at night knowing their children were stacking hay with pitchforks and gathering eggs rather than going to dances and playing varsity football? It made no sense at all! When the women met weekly to quilt, shell peas, or grind grain, they discussed their displeasure and finally plotted their escape.

Once the mothers decided to return to old neighborhoods—falsely presuming their previous lives even existed anymore—they hid their schemes from their husbands. They slowly began to gather supplies: extra tools here, discarded clothing there; it all added up over time. A few days before their departure, each woman talked with her children about leav-ing the valley. Most of the children agreed wholeheartedly to accompany their mothers but a few faltered when they thought about leaving their adopted homes in the secluded glen.

Some of the children, especially the younger ones, cried. These youngsters didn't want to leave fathers, close friends, or beloved animals. Incensed, one mother called her daughter a fool. Ryan's wife turned away from her fifteen-year-old son, Jason, and said spitefully, "Go ahead and live with your father; see if I care!"

Halfheartedly, Jason left with his mother and siblings the following morning, but he was remorseful. Throughout the day, Jason worried about his siblings tagging along with his misguided mom, but he remained si-lent. Once the four wagons stopped on the first night, Jason decided to return to his home, and his dad, in the valley. He told his brothers and sister his plan before he talked with his mom because he knew she would belittle him in front of everyone, which, of course, she did.

"You're an idiot, just like your father!" screamed Jason's mother, Shirley. She reached into a toolbox, grabbed a rusty hammer, and flung it at him. Jason blocked the hammer with his forearm as she ranted, "Get outta here! I don't ever want to see you again!" Jason stood erect but remained silent. As a final insult, she screeched, "And stay away from the food because we'll need everything for *our* survival! You can eat grass like the horses."

Jason bowed his head. He asked if anyone else wanted to return with him but no one stepped forward. Embarrassed, Jason stood between the friendly, outgoing man's camp and his mother's company, trying to maintain some measure of dignity. Mercifully, the outgoing man stepped forward to lead Jason away from the two camps.

The tousle-haired man encouraged Jason to follow him into a forest clearing. When he turned to face Jason again, he introduced himself, "My name's Greg. Pastor Greg."

"Jason," the teen said sadly.

The pastor sat on a log, then waited for Jason to sit somewhere. Warily, the teen sat down on a fallen tree. Jason watched the pastor with red-rimmed eyes, but said nothing. Eventually, Pastor Greg said, "Do you want to talk?" Ashamed of his mother's display, Jason shook his head no, discretely wiping tears from his eyes.

Despite Jason's unwillingness to speak, the pastor started talking about innocuous subjects: native plants, forest animals, even the abundance of poison ivy growing in the woods. Eventually, Jason corrected the pastor on several points of discrepancy. As their conversation drifted casually into the evening, the pastor listened calmly as the young man shared his knowledge of plants and animals. After the sun set, they took turns identifying different constellations and night sounds. Around midnight, Pastor Greg asked Jason, "Do you want to go back to camp, maybe sleep a few hours?"

Jason stood up, nodding his head. "Thank you. I . . . uh, really enjoyed talking with you."

Pastor Greg and Jason returned to the two quiet campsites. Alarmed that no one was awake to guard either camp, the pastor sat down on a stump, holding his rifle firmly. He told Jason to get some sleep. Jason knew Pastor Greg's group was traveling toward the valley, so before he retired Jason asked if he could join the pastor in the morning.

Greg responded, "You're welcome to join us. We could use another strong man to help us."

When Jason returned to his mother's campsite, he rummaged through their wagon, found his bedroll, and settled down to sleep near the fire. He saw one of his younger brothers sucking his thumb while he slept; Jason pitied his brother because the boy hadn't sucked his thumb in years. *Poor little guy*, thought Jason, *his whole world is falling apart. He's scared and helpless*. Jason pulled a blanket over his brother's exposed shoulders, then prayed for his family, including his mother.

Early the following morning, seventeen valley people prepared to leave the camp in ox-drawn wagons. While the women repacked each wagon, the four younger men shouted orders to the children and old men. Talia looked anxiously at Jason as the wagons rolled away from their campsite. She waved to Jason, smiling apologetically. Jason understood her gesture and returned the wave.

10

RYAN AND MARCUS DELAYED their trip to Mac's house on Monday to care for a wounded cow in Ryan's herd. They applied an herbal poultice to the cow's injury and monitored her for a day; consequently, Ryan and Marcus proceeded to Mac's farm on Tuesday. Instead of following the road, the pair passed through the forest. They suspected government troops would now scour the valley for "unmarked insurgents" that seized their supplies; their assumption was correct. When the pair heard heavy trucks rumbling along dirt roads, they slipped even deeper into the forest for cover.

"I hope Mac's okay," whispered Ryan.

Remembering the smell inside Mac's house and their somber farewell, Marcus concluded, "His life is in God's hands."

Around noon on Tuesday, the two men found a campsite with embers still flickering in the fire pit. On the ground lay a coffee cup, a woman's jacket, and a child's shoe. "Someone left this place in a hurry," noted Ryan. Picking up a discarded doll, "I think we frightened some homeless people away."

After looking intently at the doll, Marcus announced in his stout, bass voice, "Hear, O Israel: the Lord our God, the Lord is one. Love the Lord your God with all your heart and with all your soul and with all your strength."

Staring at the plastic doll, a toy with one closed eye and a missing arm, Ryan completed the scripture softly, "And love your neighbor as yourself."[1]

Once they stated their creed, Marcus and Ryan stood patiently waiting for a response. Several men, women, and children stepped hesitantly from behind trees and bushes. Ryan bent down to give the doll back to a

---

1. Matt 22:37–39.

small, filthy toddler who held her chubby hands up to the freckled Irishman. "Baby," she garbled.

"Here you go, angel," Ryan said gently.

"Dad?" an anxious voice called out.

Ryan spun on his heel to see the face of his son peering from behind a tree. "Jason!" Ryan remarked with surprise. Ryan ran to Jason and hugged his son tightly. "I didn't know if I'd ever see you again! Where are your brothers and sister?"

"They're gone." Raising a hand to the bedraggled people in the clearing, Jason explained, "Our group met these nice people two nights ago in the forest. Pastor Greg invited us to eat with them. They also let us sleep by their fire."

Chagrinned, Jason added, "The pastor asked our group to travel with them but Mom said they didn't want to return to the valley, or have anything more to do with Christians." Remembering his mother's behavior, he looked at the ground, "The pastor gave Mom and the others some food and water; then Mom's group left. Mom didn't even say thank you to them; none of the valley folks did." He added quietly, "I didn't want to live without you or Jesus, so I stayed. When I said I wasn't going to go with her, Mom talked to me like she hated me."

Ryan braced his son in his strong arms. "She doesn't hate you; she's fighting with God. And with me."

Pastor Greg, a handsome, young man sporting a rugged six-day-old beard, stepped forward to shake Ryan's hand. "My name's Greg. We actually escaped from a train in Marshall City several days ago." Extending his arm toward the group of escapees, "We've been living by our wits and my novice survival skills ever since."

Marcus broke the ice with a hearty laugh, "We know a few things about that train!"

Before Marcus could elaborate, Ryan interrupted, "Thank you for taking care of my son and sharing your food with our families." Gesturing toward Marcus, Ryan said, "Meet my good friend, Marcus." Marcus stepped forward and offered his bear-sized hand to the stranger. As Greg and Marcus shook hands, Ryan said, "We're on our way to see another friend who's taking care of his sick family."

Without reservation, the pastor asked, "May I go with you?"

Surprised, Ryan informed the bold man, "Our friend's family has the plague. We don't even know if they're alive anymore."

"That's all the more reason for me to go with you," explained Greg. "If they're sick, I'll anoint their heads with oil and pray for them. If they're dead, we'll bury them properly."

Remembering his oath, Marcus said firmly, "We'll discuss funeral plans later." With a pained expression, Marcus asked, "Do you understand what you're asking? The risk involved?"

Smiling humbly, the pastor responded, "I do. Surviving every day is a process of overcoming risks, but the Holy Spirit is telling me to go with you."

"Then . . . I guess . . . you're welcome to join us," Ryan answered, thinking the man might be half mad.

"Dad, take me with you," begged Jason. "I was coming back to the valley to find you. I don't want to lose you again."

Ryan studied his son. He knew the potential dangers ahead but he also understood his son's desire to stay close, "You can ride our horse; I'll walk beside you. When we get near Mac's house, do exactly what I say."

Jason recognized the warning tone in his father's voice. He nodded his head compliantly.

Considering their mounts, Marcus said, "With the dense growth in the forest, I think it's best that we lead both horses anyway." Looking at the pastor and teen, "You're welcome to come with us." Addressing the bedraggled women, children, and old men standing near the dying fire, Marcus advised, "Stay here; we'll return for you as soon as we can. We should be back by nightfall." The adults murmured their consent, holding their children close as the foursome walked toward Mac's house.

꠸ꕷꕷ

Just before they reached Mac's farm, Ryan's group spied a government truck outside the McFadden's front gate. Several soldiers were talking with a lieutenant. After Marcus motioned for the others to remain hidden, the big man crept closer to hear the ensuing conversation.

"The sign is freshly painted, sir, so I think the disease is still inside the house," explained a private.

The lieutenant studied a word Mac painted in black on a rough piece of wood and hung on his gate: Pandemic. Knowing the devastation of this virulent disease, the officer backed up, ordering his men to return to the truck. The truck slowly pulled away from Mac's driveway and rumbled down the road.

Marcus watched the government vehicle lumber over several hills at an idle pace. Once the dust from its wheels drifted away, Marcus stood up and walked to the mailbox. He slipped on his work gloves to avoid contact with any germs on the envelope, then removed a letter. Its message read:

Hey Marcus,

Pat, William, and I are still alive. I don't know how much longer either of them will live but I'm okay. We have enough food for another week. Thanks for checking on us.

Your friend,
Mac

Marcus inwardly thanked God for sustaining his friend's life. Marcus crumpled Mac's letter in his left hand while he pulled off his right glove. He reached into his coat pocket with his ungloved hand to retrieve a match. Marcus flicked the match's head with his thumbnail, igniting a spark, then he lit the corner of Mac's letter. Once flames completely engulfed the note, he dropped the burning paper on the ground. He watched the blackened sheet wither and blow away as harmless ash. He returned to his friends to relate Mac's message.

"I still want to pray for the family," insisted Greg.

Marcus pushed his straw hat back, wiped his forehead, "Are you sure?"

"Yes. You don't have to come with me. I'll introduce myself outside his house and hope that he'll open the door for me."

Gravely, Marcus shook his head, "No, I'll come with you. Mac knows me. I doubt if he'd open the door for you but he might open it for me." Turning to Ryan, "I need you to return to those poor folks waitin' in the woods. Since we're going inside Mac's house, we'll stay quarantined with him until the Lord tells us it's safe to return."

Marcus added, "Remember to check the mailbox next Monday. Take my horse with you; I don't want her to get sick. Oh, and look after my farm while I'm gone, okay?"

"Of course," answered Ryan, "Jason and I'll take care of everything." Marcus squeezed Ryan's shoulder reassuringly. Without saying another word, Marcus and Greg left the father and son standing by the side of the road.

Ryan and Jason McGuire watched as Marcus and Pastor Greg walked down the driveway to Mac's front door. As the two uninvited men approached Mac's porch, the door opened. "Marcus, don't come any closer," warned Mac.

Although Mac stood in the shadows, Marcus and Pastor Greg could see red splotches on the tall man's face and hands. "You know me, Mac," answered Marcus. "I'm not a careless or foolish man. But I want you to meet someone who says the Holy Spirit told him to pray for you and your family." Pointing to Greg, "This is Pastor Greg, a man miraculously released from the train in Marshall City."

Mac stepped closer to the door's opening to look at the two men through puffy, runny eyes. "I've been praying all week for God's help . . . maybe you're the answer to my prayers." Mac opened the door wider, he said obligingly, "If you're willing to take the chance—please, come inside. We need help."

When the McGuires saw Mac welcome Marcus and Pastor Greg into his house, they turned to leave. Taking the two horses' reins, the father and son retraced their path through the forest toward the refugee camp. With Pastor Greg's blessing, Ryan McGuire assumed temporary leadership of the refugees; Ryan accepted this new responsibility with grace and the refugees followed his guidance respectfully.

↜◉↝

Marcus and Pastor Greg walked purposefully into Mac's house. Despite oil lamps flickering in the living room, the house felt gloomy, cramped . . . foreboding. Without showing any concern about touching diseased skin, Pastor Greg shook Mac's hand, "My name is Greg. Thank you for inviting us into your home."

Still unsure about his new guest, Mac tilted his head as he looked at Pastor Greg, "You're welcome," he said stiffly. Remembering his manners, "Please sit down; I'd offer you something to eat but I'm afraid our kitchen is contaminated."

"No hospitality is necessary," Greg responded. "May I ask you a personal question?"

"Of course."

"Are you and your family Christian?"

"Yes."

"May I anoint your heads with oil and pray for your healing?" Greg asked.

Mac bowed his head, "By all means."

The young man reached into his pocket and brought out a small vial. He put a touch of oil on Mac's head, placed both his hands on Mac's face, and began to pray in a strange language. Marcus stepped forward, laid his right hand on Mac's shoulder, praying in English. Mac shut his eyes, as he silently received their prayers.

When the prayer ended, Mac reopened his eyes and said, "Come with me to my bedroom. You can pray for Pat and William there."

The men followed Mac down the narrow hallway until they entered a dark, nasty-smelling room. Curtains drawn to protect their light sensitive eyes, Patricia and William looked like two small bundles under blankets rather than two sleeping people. Sitting on the bed next to William, the pastor saw an emaciated child with sallow cheeks and oozing sores. His heart broke with pity; Greg gently gathered the five-year-old boy into his arms, anointed his hot forehead with oil, and began to pray. Marcus and Mac followed Greg by laying their hands on the child to pray.

When the prayer for William ended, Pastor Greg tenderly tucked William back under some blankets, then moved over to Pat's bedside. Dark circles under her eyes, thinning hair, and skeletal arms revealed the effects of this deadly disease upon her body. Choking back tears, the pastor bent down, anointed her forehead, and the three men prayed fervently for her. The men ended their prayer when Patricia opened her eyes, squeezed Mac's hand, and smiled faintly.

Remembering that Mac's note didn't mention his youngest son, Marcus asked delicately, "Where's little James?"

"He was dead when I got home on Thursday," Mac struggled to say.

"Where is your dead son now?" inquired Greg kindly.

Bowing his head in shame, Mac explained that the demands to care for William and Pat didn't give him the time, or strength, to bury his toddler. "I tried to bury him the first day I got home, but the frozen clay outside was hard as cement. Even when I used a pick, the hole was too shallow to bury James."

Mac continued, "After a few days with Pat and William, I got the disease; by then, I was too weak to lift a shovel, let alone dig a grave." Mac sighed, "I finally wrapped little James in a sheet and placed his body in the root cellar for safe keeping." The memory brought a flood of tears to Mac's eyes.

Marcus put his arm around Mac, pulling the bereaved man close to his side. "We're brothers Mac; there's no shame in cryin'."

Unhurried, Pastor Greg waited for Mac to stifle his sobs. When Mac cleared his throat, Greg politely requested, "May I pray for your dead son?" Mac gazed at the pastor through filmy, crusted eyes, trying to measure this stranger; afterward, Mac shook his head doubtfully, yes. He no longer felt like fighting.

Mac stood up unsteadily and slowly shuffled to the door. "Please, Mr. McFadden, stay here and rest. I would like to pray for James alone," Greg said.

Although exhausted, Mac insisted on leading the others outside. The three men put on their coats and walked to the underground root cellar. Mac unlatched the cellar's heavy, oaken doors and motioned the pastor forward. Pastor Greg stepped down into the depths carrying a candle for light.

Marcus closed the solid doors to keep cold winds from blowing down the cellar stairs. Mac found a knitted wool hat in his coat pocket, pulled the hat over his ears, and stuffed his hands into his coat pockets. Marcus pulled his coat collar up to his ears, scrunched his shoulders up, and crossed his arms in front of him to stay warm. They waited outside the door, stamping their feet, exhaling frosty breaths.

Ten minutes passed, then fifteen. Marcus arched an eyebrow to Mac, pointed his chin toward the porch, as if to say, *Do you want to go back into the house to get warm?*

Before Mac responded, their silence was broken by the sound of footfalls on the steps. The cold men watched the doors expectantly, saying nothing. As the heavy doors groaned open, Pastor Greg grinned and reached down into the darkness to lift up Mac's frail little boy, James.

The child was alive![2] Although ashen colored with dark circles around his eyes, James was awake and breathing! Unable to fully grasp the enormity of the miracle, Mac's eyes flooded with tears. He reached hungrily for his child, wrapped his arms tightly around James, and kissed the little boy's face over and over again.

Suddenly a terrifying thought entered Mac's brain. Gasping in horror, Mac screamed over the wind to Greg, "Did I put my living baby into a dark underground hole for a week?!"

---

2. John 11:38–44.

Alarmed by Mac's despair, the pastor grabbed Mac's arm, "No, Mac, your son was dead and very, very cold when I found him." Turning to the child, Greg said with tears in his eyes, "But look at him now; he's warm and very much alive!"

"Daddy," James said softly.

Awestruck, Marcus exclaimed, "Praise be to God in the highest! Jesus . . . Jesus, you are the great I Am. My God . . . my God, My God!" Marcus fell to his knees, covered his face with his hands, mumbling praises to God.

Pastor Greg stood back to watch the men; it felt as if he was dreaming. He didn't know what to expect when he went underground; he only obeyed a prompting by the Holy Spirit to pray for James. He read in the Bible of people being raised from the dead but he had never witnessed such a breathtaking event in his life, until today. Humbled by God's mercy, the pastor fell to his knees, placed his head on the frozen ground, and thanked the Lord for hearing the prayers of his people.

Although reeling from the shock of his son's resurrection, Mac jolted back to reality when he felt James shivering from the cold. The brawny man swiftly ran to the house carrying his son. Mac kicked his door open, rushed into the living room, and carefully placed James on a couch.

Sitting James near the fireplace, Mac threw more logs on the fire, and covered his son with thick blankets. As he picked up firewood, Mac noticed that the red splotches on his hands seemed to be fading. *What is happening to me? Am I losing my mind?* Thinking of Patricia and William, Mac tucked one more blanket around James, turned quickly, and raced down the hallway to check on the rest of his family.

When he entered the room, Mac saw his wife sitting up in bed and William looking groggily around the room. Mac crawled carefully onto the bed, pulling his wife and son into his arms. He squeezed them tightly, weeping with unbridled joy.[3]

Pat spoke with a weak, tremulous voice, "Mac, you're going to break us in two."

Mac sat back slightly, looked into his wife's eyes, and started kissing her face, her hands, her arms. "You're talking," he uttered. Raising his voice, "You're alive, William is alive. Patricia, James is alive!" Mac started shouting with all his might, his tears flowing freely.

---

3. Matt. 8:16–17.

Standing at the bedroom door, Pastor Greg and Marcus stared dumbly at the McFaddens. Both men felt completely astounded and utterly exhausted by the day's experiences. Despite his fatigue, Marcus enthusiastically embraced the young pastor in his arms, picked Greg up effortlessly, and proclaimed, "Thank you, Lord of heaven and earth, for letting me live to see this day!"

⁕⊙⊙⊙⁕

The next few days passed quickly on the McFadden's farm. Mac, Marcus, and Pastor Greg cleaned everything. They burned whatever they thought might harbor the plague pathogen: blankets, towels, clothes, pillows, bed linens, even bedroom furniture. While the fire raged outside, they scoured the house with harsh lye soap and boiled cooking utensils. By the time the house was sanitized, Pat, William, and James regained enough strength to eat their meals with the industrious men.

Throughout the process of cleaning the house and watching his family heal, Mac changed. As he remembered the miracles of the past week, his heart and mind filled with awe and wonder. In addition to the pastor's story of angelic deliverance from the train, Mac witnessed the blinding of PeaceKeepers, his family's healing, and his youngest child's resurrection. Overwhelmed by the magnitude of God, Mac would never be the same.

Neither would Marcus nor Pastor Greg. Both men now knelt as they prayed. When they spoke the Lord's name, they did so with great fear and trembling. There was nothing nonchalant about their reference to Jesus; their words reflected reverence and awe.

After a week, Marcus and Pastor Greg finally decided to leave Mac's house, but they did so reluctantly. The Lord's Spirit rested peacefully upon Mac's family and their belongings. Although difficult to leave this sanctuary, Marcus and Greg knew they needed to resume their responsibilities elsewhere.

As they walked through the forest, they discussed many things. The primary subject that piqued Marcus's curiosity was God's Spirit. "Tell me more about the Holy Spirit," urged Marcus. "I saw miracles that I thought were dead, but you speak freely about the Holy Spirit. You seem really comfortable with God."

Smiling, Greg pondered aloud, "Is anyone ever comfortable in the presence of our Holy God? I'm not." Staring upward, "I love Christ with every fiber of my being. I seek his face daily but when the Lord draws close to me, I'm usually too weak to stand. Most of the time, I'm speech-less." Noticing Marcus's confused expression, he continued, "I'm sorry for rambling; I'll gladly tell you what I know about the Holy Spirit."

As they walked, Pastor Greg described the two baptisms covered in the Bible. "There was water baptism demonstrated by John the Baptist and the baptism of the Holy Spirit given to us by God. Water baptism was a public display of seeking repentance and a cleansing of sin."[4]

"The baptism of the Holy Spirit occurred first at Pentecost.[5] This second baptism, the baptism of the Holy Spirit, was God's gift of super-natural empowerment to believers. It's given to us so we can effectively complete the work God wants us to do."

"But I was saved as a child and baptized with water in my church," explained Marcus.

"That's wonderful," the pastor said. "Many Christians stop there and go on with their lives thinking that there's nothing more . . . but they're mistaken."

"Really?"

"Yes, when Jesus returned to his Father, he told his followers not to leave Jerusalem but to wait for the gift his Father promised. Jesus con-firmed that John had baptized with water but they would be baptized with the Holy Spirit. Jesus also said that they would receive power when the Holy Spirit came on them so that they would be his witnesses to the ends of the earth."

"Yeah, I remember hearing about that in church. Our pastor told us that spiritual gifts were given to the early church, but there was no more need for spiritual gifts today," replied Marcus.

"Why aren't spiritual gifts needed today? Do you know people who are sick . . . hungry . . . depressed?"

Marcus nodded, yes.

Greg reasoned, "People still need a savior. An honest person will tell you that they don't know all the answers, they've been hurt, and they've made a lot of mistakes."

"I get that we need a savior but why do we need to pray in tongues? Why do we need to see miracles? Why do we need to look weird to the rest of the world?"

4. Mark 1: 4–5.
5. Acts 2:1–13.

The pastor shrugged, "Because we believe in a supernatural God. Think about it; *everything* about Christ was supernatural: he was born of a virgin, healed the sick, cast out demons, fed thousands of people, and rose from the dead. His life made people believe that he was truly the son of God."

"Okay . . ."

"Now, Jesus is seated at the right hand of the Father, interceding for us with prayer, and encouraging us to go out into the world to preach the good news."

"I understand that too, but why do we need spiritual gifts?" Marcus persisted.

"Because some people need to witness a miracle to believe in Christ. Some people need an inexplicable healing to know that there's a God in heaven that loves them. The Holy Spirit empowers Christians to effectively do the work that our Father designed them to do."[6]

"So praying in tongues . . . does what?" Marcus asked.

"A tongue is an outward sign of the Spirit within a believer. It's the coolest thing," answered Pastor Greg. "When I pray in English, I mention all the things I can think of, but after five minutes, I'm usually done. I can't think of anything else to say. But when I pray in the Spirit, I speak in another language, and I can pray for hours. The words are distinctly foreign; I actually speak in a different cadence. I've even heard people praying in primitive clicks and groans but they're still speaking somebody's language."

"But what's the point?" pressed Marcus.

"Instead of me fumbling with my own words, the Holy Spirit takes a language and sends my prayers directly to God." Trying to find a suitable analogy, "With English, I feel like I'm delivering my messages to heaven by carrier pigeon, but when I pray in the Spirit, my prayers skyrocket to God's ears. The Holy Spirit knows exactly what needs to be said, and he says them." Struggling for an explanation, "He uses my lips to speak an unknown prayer while my very human mind observes the results of those prayers. Sometimes, I even understand what I'm saying."

Pastor Greg offered further clarification, "The Holy Spirit is God, and he is talking with God, so results happen. I see people healed, sometimes I can interpret a tongue, and . . . this week . . . I saw a child raised

6. 1 Cor 12:1–11.

from the dead. In a nutshell, being baptized in the Holy Spirit allows believers to further God's kingdom supernaturally."

Anxiously, Marcus asked, "How can I receive the baptism of the Holy Spirit?"

"You have to allow the Spirit to move through you; this requires humility. After I lay my hands on you and pray, give the Spirit permission to rise up inside you, to speak through your lips. Sometimes people don't open their mouths to let the Spirit speak, but if you earnestly seek the Spirit, he will come to you."

"Pray for me, pastor. I want to do the work that God called me to do."

Pastor Greg laid his hands on his friend and prayed in the Spirit. Within minutes, the muscular, dark man began to mutter words that were unfamiliar to him. Marcus laughed robustly while he continued to speak haltingly in this new, foreign tongue. As Marcus became more comfortable with the realization that *someone within me is speaking,* his voice grew louder. Soon the pastor joined Marcus in prayer; subsequently, both men spoke simultaneously in two unknown languages to a God that understood every word each man spoke.

11

AFTER OVERTAKING THE TRAIN, people in the valley began to divide into smaller splinter groups. During the week that Marcus, Ryan, and Mac cleaned house, Jim and Miah prepared for their trip to Tennessee. Furthermore, because they decided to stay in the valley, Brant, Toynell, and Nellie learned to share daily farm tasks and quickly coalesced into a family. Nellie hated to see Miah leave but she understood the young man's desire to find his own family.

One evening just before their departure, Miah charged into Nellie's house, yelling, "There's a huge fire a couple miles away. I think it's the Garcias' farm!"

Everyone ran to the Ranger. Jim, Nellie, and Sara squeezed into the cab; Brant, Toynell, and Beth leaped into the bed; and Miah grabbed a side mirror, his feet balanced on a running board. Jim drove the truck at a furious pace. He didn't slow down until the vehicle skidded into Emanuel's driveway, throwing rocks and gravel in its wake.

By the time they arrived, the house, barn, and haystacks were completely engulfed in a raging firestorm. Ignoring his sore ribs, Jim flung his door open and ran toward outbuildings. Before he reached the first shed, he hit a wall of blistering heat that immediately stopped him. Jim instinctively covered his face, turning away from the scorching flames.

"Is anyone alive?" screamed Sara.

"I can't tell," Jim yelled over sounds of screeching animals, popping timbers, and raging wind. "Wait a minute," he peered through the smoke, "I see some movement to the right."

Running into a field on one side of the house, they found Rosa sitting on the ground, cradling her grandfather in her arms. Crying, Rosa bent her head over the old man's face, her shoulders shuddering.

Rushing to the young woman, Sara dropped to her knees. Sara briefly examined Emanuel, took his pulse, then turned to Rosa. Placing her hand on Rosa's shoulder, Sara talked to the shocked young woman in a calm, steady voice. "Rosa, are you okay?"

"He's dead," moaned the young woman, "my grandfather is dead!" Sara nodded her head knowingly yet said nothing.

Jim looked back and forth, searching for movement within the flames, "Is Juan here?" he asked Rosa.

"Yes, he ran over from his house. I . . . I don't know where he is now," Rosa answered anxiously. Her eyes widened, "Find him, Jim! Please find him!" A fresh wave of fear gripped the young woman. She frantically looked from side to side hoping to see the brash Latino somewhere outside the flames.

When Jim limped back into the smoke-filled yard, he saw Juan pulling a terrified horse from the barn. Using a thick lead rope attached to the horse's halter, Juan dodged the horse's flailing front hooves; the animal swung its head, kicking wildly to escape the rampant inferno. Following Juan's example, Jim, Brant, and Miah ran fearlessly into the barn to save other animals.

When he entered the barn, Jim discovered empty burlap feed bags piled in one corner, untouched by sparks. Understanding an animal's instinctual fear of fire, he threw a burlap sack over a frightened cow's head and the cow relaxed slightly. Jim tossed the bags to the other men to use with the cattle, horses, and goats. The sacks prevented livestock from seeing encroaching flames so the men were able to hurry animals out of the barn with less resistance.

Throughout the chaos, Jim, Miah, Brant, and Juan tied livestock to fence posts in a field upwind of the fire, then ran back in the barn to retrieve more animals. Some animals were badly scorched but none died. By the time the cattle, horses, and goats were safe, very little was left of the house or barn. The roof of the house collapsed while the barn continued to burn furiously, flames devouring straw, hay, and weathered wood.

While the men focused on large stock, Sara, Beth, and Toynell concentrated on saving smaller animals. They grabbed terrified ducks and chickens squawking and limping away from the fire, gently placing the birds into the back of the truck. Once inside the truck bed, Nellie covered the birds with damp bed sheets; sheets she found packed in the truck, which she moistened from the well. The sheets cooled the animals' hot bodies, soothed their singed feathers, and kept the terrified creatures from flying away. As Nellie sat on a wheel well, she stroked the frightened birds, singing softly to them.

After accounting for all the livestock, Juan searched feverishly for Rosa. He ran to each charred building screaming her name in desperation. When he heard nothing inside a building but groaning and snapping timbers, he ran to the next structure. His sight blurred from hot ashes, but even after he blinked his watery eyes he couldn't see the exotic beauty anywhere.

Jim caught the sweating, fearful man by the arm and yelled, "Juan, Rosa's okay."

"Thank God," exhaled Juan, as he wiped a sooty hand across his brow. "Where's Emanuel?"

"Emanuel's dead . . . I'm sorry, Juan."

Juan searched Jim's face for answers, "What happened?"

"Maybe a heart attack, smoke inhalation," shaking his head; "I don't know."

Juan sighed with regret. After a brief moment, he thought of someone else, "Happy. Where's Happy?"

Looking in each direction, Jim's eyes widened and he answered with renewed alarm, "I haven't seen her!"

At that point, Jim and Juan started to call for Happy. "Come here, girl!" "Happy!" "Dinnertime, Hap!" "C'mon, buddy!" Soon everyone in the area called the old dog's name, but there was no sign of Happy.

Worried, Jim shouted and whistled until his throat hurt. He recalled seeing a black blur run blindly after Juan into the barn but he never saw her in the field after they left the barn. Rather than say anything to anyone, Jim only called louder for the shaggy dog, poking his head into dark recesses that would camouflage a Newfoundland.

While people searched for Happy, Juan spotted Rosa, still sitting on the ground next to her grandfather. He ran to her, fell to his knees, and held her tightly in his arms. When Juan finally loosened his embrace, he brushed Rosa's hair out of her eyes, kissing her forehead lovingly, "I thought I'd lost you," he confessed openly, without reservation.

Rosa sniffed, wiped tears away with her hand, and looked into Juan's concerned face. She didn't say a word. Juan said, "I'm so sorry about Emanuel, Rosa."

As Juan stroked Rosa's tangled, smoky hair and spoke tenderly to the small woman, he felt a hot, slobbery tongue on his neck. "Happy?"

Juan turned around to see Happy standing behind him, her tail wagging, her bright eyes smiling.

"Hap!" he choked hoarsely. "My big girl . . . you're okay!" Relieved to see his faithful friend, Juan's breathing wavered. He turned his head away from Rosa because he didn't want her to see the burning tears falling down his cheeks.

Afterward he thought, *Who cares if I'm crying?*

Juan threw one protective arm around Rosa and the other around Happy. Despite exhaustion and sorrow, Juan felt a resurgence of strength. In between the two lives that now mattered most to him, Juan tossed his head back, shouting with exhilaration, "Thank you, Jesus, for keeping Rosa and Happy safe for me!"

⸲⊙⊙⸱

As the fire's smoke cloud bloomed, families from neighboring farms hurried to the Garcias' homestead to help fight the blaze. They pitched buckets of water onto the house, barn, and adjacent buildings. By the end of the day, they completely extinguished the fire. As weary firefighters shoveled soil onto dying embers at dusk, they talked about the tragedy with each other. Was everyone safe? Did anyone bring ointments to treat the animals' cuts and burns? And most importantly, how did the fire start?

How indeed? The sergeant of a small PeaceKeepers detail smiled. He heard this question while he and his soldiers observed the smoldering barnyard from their hiding place.

"Serves them right for stealing *our* supplies," he whispered to his unit. "I hope that spy was right when he said the old man hid our goods somewhere on his farm. I don't care about the man; I just don't want our food getting into their worthless bellies."

He signaled his men to proceed quietly back through the evening twilight to their vehicles, parked a few miles down the road. Without speaking another word, the group crept away from the Garcia farm. Once confident that they were sufficiently cloaked by darkness, the sergeant ordered his people to move quickly. The unit slipped away without detection through the smoke-filled gloom of night.

⸲⊙⊙⸱

The morning after the fire, many valley residents came to Rosa's aid. They sorted through ashes and debris in search of anything valuable.

They retrieved pots and pans, steel feed buckets, assorted pieces of hardware. The fire destroyed almost everything flammable: leather harnesses, wooden furniture, cloth garments, and staple food; but some metal items, not too badly twisted from the heat, were redeemed.

Rosa appreciated her friends help but she was tired, numb. Her grandfather, her last living relative, died in the fire. She was thankful that she and the animals survived, but she remained detached, in shock.

Rosa sat down under a tree to watch the activity in the barnyard. When she felt a warm presence near to her, she turned around to find Happy sitting behind her, panting, wanting to shake hands. Rosa threw her arms around the kindly dog and buried her face in Happy's fur. Rosa cried into the dog's shaggy coat. Happy remained as motionless as a statue to show Rosa that Newfoundlands are strong, composed dogs. Enduringly faithful.

Happy mumbled, *"I will protect you,"* but all Rosa heard was a strange guttural sound deep within the Newfy's chest.

"Oh, Happy, I don't know what I'll do," wept Rosa. "Everything is gone—everything."

"Not everything," a voice replied. Startled, Rosa glanced up to see Juan's worried face. Juan admitted, "When I saw the fire, I was so afraid you were hurt. I ran here as fast as I could. I know you lost everything . . . but, you didn't lose me."

Bending down on one knee to squeeze her small hands between his rough hands, Juan declared, "Rosa, I love you. I don't know when I started to love you, but even as a teenager, your beauty broke my heart."

"Wha . . . ?" she looked at him, dazed.

He pressed on, afraid that he might lose his courage, "By the time you volunteered to help with the prisoner rescue, I was a goner. I was yours. Now all I want to do is spend my life with you." Catching his breath, Juan asked solemnly, "Rosa, will you marry me?"

Rosa stood up to look down at Juan kneeling before her. Her mouth twitched nervously with emotion as she put her arms around Juan's neck, sliding gracefully into his sturdy, loving arms. She started to laugh and cry at the same time; maybe it was a combination of grief and joy, but the young woman couldn't stop smiling as tears rolled down her cheeks. It didn't matter to Juan; he just rocked Rosa gently in his arms, letting her do whatever peculiar thing she was doing with tears, and laughter.

He said, "You don't need to answer my proposal right away; you have a lot to think about. Just know this: I will *always* love you, and I will always be ready to help you."

Pulling back from Juan's embrace, Rosa looked deeply into his eyes. "I love you too. I fell in love with you the first time I saw you."

"Huh?"

Smiling, she reminisced, "I was just a skinny teenager when I first saw you, a handsome soldier in his uniform who stepped off a train, greeting his friends with loud jokes; I couldn't take my eyes off you."

Puzzled, Juan admitted, "I don't even remember seeing you at the train station. I remember you as a teenager, but that was months after I came to this valley."

"When you stepped off the train, I hid behind Grandfather so you wouldn't see me staring at you. I remember thinking that you moved with the confidence of a lion."

Juan gazed at Rosa in wonder. "Will you marry me?" he asked again, more assertively.

Without wavering, she replied, "Yes!" Smiling widely, her eyes glittering with tears; she added thoughtfully, "Just give me some time to sort out my life."

"I will give you all the time you need; my life is yours." Juan pulled Rosa into his arms. They kissed for the first time—an open, honest pledge to seal a lifetime of commitment to each other.

Several neighbors helping Rosa smiled at the happy couple; they diverted their eyes and continued to pick up trash. Bending down together with their heads close, one woman spoke to her friend, "Isn't God good? Even in the midst of tragedy, love prevails." Her friend grinned and shook her head in agreement. They walked away inconspicuously, leaving the young couple alone to dream of their future together.

જ⊚Ꭰ

A few days after the fire, Marcus and Pastor Greg found the escapees' camp still hidden in the woods. Ryan and Jason McGuire offered housing to the refugees but the wanderers preferred to stay outdoors after their stifling confinement in the education center. The McGuires visited the camp daily but they understood the refugees' need for fresh air and open space. Several refugees snared birds or rabbits for dinner while they waited for their pastor, but after a week of living outdoors, the small party was finally ready to find more significant shelter and clean water.

When Marcus invited the group to his farm, everyone readily accepted his offer. By nightfall, the entourage arrived at Marcus's place. Unfortunately, while absent, his farm was ransacked. Instead of seeing his well-tended gardens and freshly painted barn, Marcus noticed boarded up windows on his house and outbuildings burned. As Marcus led the company into his barnyard, he met Ryan and Jason carrying their rifles low as they patrolled his property.

Apparently, the devastation looked worse when Jason encountered the damage two days earlier. The young man went to Marcus's farm to complete routine chores when he found clothes strewn over the yard, windows broken, and graffiti painted on the house. Jason cocked his shotgun and began to walk slowly around the property, looking for looters. He moved cautiously through the house but didn't see anyone.

After finding no one in the house or barnyard, Jason decided to search for Marcus's livestock. Eventually he found the animals grazing lazily in a secluded meadow, undetected by vandals. Knowing the animals were safe, he latched the meadow gate and returned to Marcus's house.

Saddened by the sight, Jason started to clean and repair the damage. He picked up dishes, furniture, and clothing laying outside on the ground and carried everything back into the house. Afterward, Jason went to the barn, where he found plywood, nails, and a hammer to patch windows. Because he couldn't find a saw, the young man simply nailed spare pieces of wood across window frames. The finished product looked terrible but at least the shuttered windows prevented rain or snow from coming indoors.

Just as Jason finished the windows, he saw his father approach.

"Hey, Jay, what's going on?" asked Ryan.

Jason showed his dad the destruction caused by intruders. "I sealed up the house and found Marcus's animals, but I couldn't find any paint to cover the graffiti." Both men stared silently at the hateful words sprawled across the clapboard siding. The words made no mention of Marcus's age, gender, or skin color; they ridiculed his faith: Bible Basher, Jesus Freak, Jew Lover.

Ryan sighed, shaking his head in disgust. As he turned away from the siding, Ryan looked at Jason's repairs, "You're a good man, Jason. Let's move Marcus's animals to our farm for safekeeping. From now on, we'll take turns guarding his property along with our own."

Jason responded, "I locked his cattle and horses in the lower field. Should we drive them back to our place tonight, or wait until tomorrow?"

"What would you want Marcus to do if he found our house all torn up?" asked Ryan.

"I'd want our animals to be safe."

"Me too." Ryan nudged his son, "Let's go home, get our cattle ponies and sheepdogs; we'll get his stock into our pens tonight."

A few days after the vandalism, Marcus returned home with the band of refugees; that's when he saw the damage to his home and met Ryan and Jason finishing their walk around his barnyard. After their greetings, Jason described what he found to Marcus as the tall, dark man surveyed his property. When Jason finished speaking, Marcus clasped his hand on Jason's shoulder, thanking him. "It looks like I have some work to do to get my farm back in order." He motioned to his new friends, "But at least I have a lot of hands to help."

As the refugees clustered around Marcus, they immediately volunteered to start the cleanup. Touched by their concern, Marcus said, "We'll worry about straightening things out tomorrow. Let's get these kids into a bathtub; then we'll find places for y'all to sleep tonight."

Marcus led the weary travelers into his house. Together, Marcus, Ryan, Greg, and Jason made beds for everyone on couches, floors, even in dresser drawers for the smallest children. After brief baths, the refugees collapsed into their makeshift beds, falling asleep quickly. Within hours of his return, Marcus also slept soundly. Maybe it was habit, maybe it was weariness, or maybe Marcus just felt comfortable knowing that, once again, his house was filled with people he truly loved and wanted to protect.

12

As Marcus slept peacefully at home, his wife, Constance, and their children, TJ and Talia, slept fitfully at camp. In the mountains, travel was a hardship during the winter. Although graveled, the road was still steep and treacherous. The oxen slowly pulled the wagons uphill, but without snow removal the wagons slipped dangerously close to cliff edges or got stuck in slushy ruts. By nightfall everyone was ill-tempered; they quarreled over everything: their rations, crying babies, and even the pettiness of where to sleep.

The four idle men increased the group's problems. Unwilling to help gather firewood or hunt for food, the men drank homemade liquor, screamed profanities at children, and spoke lecherously to the women. Several mothers feared for their daughters' safety, so they kept the girls separated from the men whenever possible.

After a week on the road, Constance finally ended the struggle as the group began making preparations for the night. When Ennis made another rude remark to Talia, Constance lifted a shotgun to her shoulder, saying, "Get outta here now before I blow your miserable body off this mountain!"

"You won't last two days out here without us," growled the short-tempered man.

"We'll take our chances," declared Constance. "Grab your things and leave before I shoot your ugly face!"

Grabbing his bedroll and backpack, Ennis stepped away from the infuriated woman. "Come on, fellas, let's get outta here."

The three other men pushed women and children aside as they scrounged for their belongings in the wagons. Insolently, they tossed the women's possessions on the ground haphazardly and stuffed extra portions of food into their backpacks. Without asking permission, they led four horses away from the resting livestock, tying their packs on the horses' backs. One man kicked snow into the sputtering fire and spit contemptuously on the ground.

"You'll see us again," threatened Ennis, "and you'll beg for our forgiveness."

"I'll never beg for anything, especially from you," snarled Constance, grinding her teeth. She pressed her finger tighter on the trigger, "Now go!"

The four men glared at the women as they cursed, storming out of the camp. Silence followed. One of the remaining old men stirred the fire's coals then placed more wood on the embers. The old man didn't look up because he feared that he and his friend might also be cast aside. He worried that without the women they might die in the mountains.

"Connie, I'm afraid," confessed Gloria, an anemic-looking woman with thinning, mousy brown hair. "What if they come back?"

Constance turned abruptly, staring harshly at the pathetic woman, "What if they stayed? What if they abused your daughter or slit your throat while you slept? No one said this trip was going to be easy!"

"I know," whined the woman, "I just didn't think it would be *this bad*."

"Well, think again because we still have a long way to go before we reach civilization. Go back to the valley if you want, or call Ennis; he'll probably come back for you, and your kids, especially your daughter."

Staring at Constance, horrified, Gloria shook her head vehemently. "No! I couldn't do that; you know I couldn't do that."

"Then shut up! I don't have time for your bellyaching!" After humiliating Gloria, Constance turned to her children. She pointed to the remaining horses, ordering TJ and Talia, "Stop gawking and hobble those horses."

She turned to face the remaining travelers, throwing words at them like poison darts. "I'm so tired of this stupid group of idiots! From now on, we'll need to have a guard at night because those shiftless men will come back to steal whatever they can from us." Still shaking with fury, Constance held her rifle tightly and marched away from the campsite, "I'm going to see if I can find something to kill for dinner. Somebody has to feed this sorry outfit!"

ᘒᗺᗺᘐ

At the same time, miles away in the valley, Sara and Elizabeth finished loading supplies into Jim's old Ranger. They stayed at Nellie's house an extra week to help disperse train cargo to neighbors and prepare for their departure, but now they were ready to leave. Placing her hand on the girl's arm, Sara asked, "Alright, sweetie, tomorrow we start on a new adventure. Are you ready?"

"Yes, ma'am," answered the shy girl.

Sara's heart melted. She couldn't help herself; Elizabeth was the gentlest, kindest girl she ever met. And Sara knew children; she had three children of her own. She didn't know where her children were now, or if they were even alive, but she was a mother. The last time she saw her sweet children, they had their hands and faces pressed against car windows, staring at her while her husband drove away in anger, dropping the clutch and spinning the wheels.

It was all her fault. As a younger woman, she experimented with drugs. Working as a server in a fine-dining restaurant, she dealt with coworkers and restaurant patrons who routinely drank and took drugs. Gradually, she slipped into a lifestyle of making terrific money and spending some of that money on cocaine. Her husband didn't approve but she didn't care. Instead of going home after her shift ended, many times she went out with her new friends to get high.

One night, another server introduced her to methamphetamine. Without question, after her first experience with this new drug her life changed dramatically. She no longer dabbled with drugs—"dabbled" a euphemism to salve her conscience—she abused drugs, and meth became the driving force of her existence.

She lived to get high. Her children and responsibilities at home disappeared. Nothing mattered more than getting high. Her husband pleaded with her to seek professional help but she wouldn't listen to him. Her body screamed for more meth. Food-crusted dishes in the sink, dirty diapers on the baby—nothing else mattered except getting high again.

Eventually her husband packed the children into their car and drove away. Sara still remembers that sight: three forlorn little faces with round, imploring eyes staring at her while her husband threw bags into the trunk, slammed car doors, and ignored her hollow promises. She cried, but later, when the craving to get high overrode her despair, she went out to score more meth. Sara's life spiraled into a trap of stealing money to buy methamphetamine, getting high, and needing more drugs later.

One night as she wandered through the city streets, looking for her drug dealer, she saw an attractive storefront window. Amber light glowed from a lamp sitting on a desk covered with a brightly colored tablecloth. Books sat on the desk alongside a tea kettle with a matching teacup. The window dressing enticed her. In her fuzzy, addled mind, she decided to look at books when the store opened the following morning. Satisfied with her plan, the skinny, drug-ravaged woman curled up on the front doorstep to take a nap.

The following morning, Sara felt a frail, distorted hand shake her. "Wake up, honey," an elderly woman said. Sara focused on a face that looked more like a dried apple than a person; lively green eyes sparkled from the deeply lined face. Startled, Sara tried to get up quickly but fell against the door's threshold. "It looks like you need a little nourishment," remarked the old woman as she clutched Sara's arm. The stooped woman helped Sara stand up as she led the meth addict into her bookstore.

The old woman ushered Sara to an office in back of the store. The office wasn't much bigger than a bedroom closet but it contained a small dining table, an ancient school desk with papers piled on it, and one bookcase lined with business ledgers.

Pointing to the table, the woman said in a scratchy voice, "Sit here; I'll make you some toast." The kindhearted matron shuffled into an apartment attached to the bookstore and started banging around in a kitchen. Sara considered leaving the musty bookshop, but she was starving; before long, she smelled an orangey, cinnamon aroma wafting from the kitchen, making her stomach growl even louder.

Ten minutes later, the old woman shuffled back into the room with a tray of toast and biscuits, a teapot, two slightly chipped teacups, honey, and dried creamer. Smiling pleasantly, the woman said, "I'm sorry I can't afford butter anymore but here's a little something for you to eat." Sara helped the woman set the table and the two of them sat down. *Two misfits*, thought Sara, *a junkie and a geriatric. Pathetic.*

The old woman bowed her head in prayer, gave thanks, then looked up at Sara. "Go ahead and eat now, love. You're no bigger than a minute."

Sara devoured the food. She tried to eat with some degree of delicacy but she couldn't remember the last time she ate; moreover, the food was delicious! Speaking with crumbs on her mouth, Sara said, "Are the biscuits and bread homemade?"

The old bookworm grinned, "Of course they are, sweetie. It's amazing what I can bake with a little sourdough starter and flour." With a spark of mischief, she added, "Let me get you some more food before you eat my tablecloth." The woman placed her arthritic hands on the table, lifted herself from her chair, and tottered back into the kitchen.

Scanning the disheveled bookstore from the office, Sara asked loudly, "How can you find anything in this store?"

Laughing heartedly, the old woman explained, "I have a system. It drove my husband crazy when he was alive, but I can find any book you want. If I don't have it, I'll get it for you and have it wrapped when you return in a week."

Sara stared blankly at the woman's flippancy. *Have a book wrapped in a week? What about electronic books? How can she keep this business afloat? Do people even read hardback books anymore?* The questions whirled in Sara's head as she considered this train wreck of a business. "May I help you organize some things? Even though I usually serve tables, I have a degree in business management."

After she sat down again, the old woman placed her hands in her lap, looking straight into Sara's eyes, "I have no money to pay you."

"That's okay; I just want to thank you for this terrific breakfast."

The woman stood up slowly, brushed some crumbs off her lap, "That sounds wonderful. I start everyday with devotions. I learned that lesson late in life, but I read the Bible daily now. You can join me this morning."

With that simple plan, Sara began her slow retreat from drug addiction. Sometimes she still thought about methamphetamine, but rather than desiring its enticement, she dreaded its enslavement. Meth destroyed her family, damaged her future, practically killed her.

In the beginning, the old woman took care of Sara, but during the last few months Sara took care of the old woman, until she died. Before she passed away, the old woman traded her bookstore with a dentist to repair Sara's drug-damaged teeth, a gift Sara could never repay. Sara still mourned for that generous soul who showed her mercy and taught her forgiveness. That old woman was the mother she never had. In her quiet times, Sara still wept for her children, who lacked a mother's guidance, but maybe her children found someone else to take her place; maybe they found an old booklover too.

Shaking these thoughts from her head, Sara now looked at the young woman standing in front of her. Lithe and comely, one day Elizabeth would make her own decisions. Sara wanted to offer Beth the same wisdom and peace the old woman gave her, to give Beth the guidance she longed to give to her own three children; or maybe just do something good for another person to redeem her otherwise miserable, selfish past.

Shifting her thoughts back to her current life, Sara said, "Let's help Nellie and Toynell with dinner. I have a feeling we'll leave early tomorrow morning."

❧◎◎☙

The women at Nellie's house prepared a large meal because they expected, and received, extra company. Seated at the large oak table were Nellie, Miah, Sara, Beth, Jim, Brant, Toynell, Rosa, and Juan. Nellie not only took extra care preparing this meal; she also spent a lot of time talking with each individual. She feared that tonight might be the last time she would see some of these good people on earth.

"We'd like to travel with you," Juan explained to Jim, "but we still have some things to do here before we leave."

Intuition overriding diplomacy, Nellie asked abruptly, "Are you two going to get married?"

"Yes," Rosa said blushing.

"Mac and his family want to visit soon and they're bringing some new guy named Greg who can marry us," added Juan. "In the meantime, we can finish passing out food to our neighbors and packing our things." Juan shook his head, "You know, it's so weird every time I think about it, but Emanuel hid all the train's cargo in his root cellar; the fire never touched anything!" Everyone just sat quietly; no one spoke.

Rosa broke the silence, her voice trembling, "We'll also trade all of Grandfather's livestock before we leave."

Nellie glanced over at Brant, "If you and Toynell are interested, Brant, I'll help you buy some of Rosa's livestock, with whatever she wants in trade."

"That would be great!" exclaimed Brant, holding his wife's hand, looking at both Nellie and Rosa.

Then Nellie hugged the young Latina sitting beside her. "Congratulations on your wedding, Rosa; you found a wonderful man. And remember, whatever you need, just ask and we'll do our best to help." Smiling at the betrothed couple, Toynell and Brant also agreed quickly.

"Thank you so much," said Juan. Uncomfortable with Nellie's compliment, he quickly changed the subject, "So Jim, are you ready to leave tomorrow morning?"

"Everything's packed, ready to go. Sara and Beth will ride in the cab with me and Miah will ride in the back with Mattie."

"What about Carl?" asked Beth. "Is he—?"

"Carl wants to stay here," interrupted Nellie. "He can't tell me what he's thinkin' but I swear that cat talks with his twitchin' tail!" Explaining further, "During the packing hubbub, he just looked at me like I should know what he wants. I think he wants to sit by the fire and drink fresh milk every day rather than ride in a dusty old truck. So unless he jumps into the Ranger tomorrow, that big orange cat's stayin' here."

"Is this true?" gasped Mattie as she looked at the purring tabby.

"Yep, I like being a kept cat. I can tease geese, hunt in the meadow, or sit on Nellie's soft lap if I want. I'm not going anywhere!"

"Speaking of animals," ventured Juan, "could you take Happy in your truck tomorrow? She's getting pretty old and I'm afraid walking behind our horses would be hard on her."

"No problem," answered Jim. "We'd be glad to bring Happy with us."

"Thank you," Juan said in a relieved voice. "We'll leave Hap here with Mattie tonight. She'll be a little concerned that she's not walkin' home with me this evening, but she'll get over it. Happy can play with Mattie every day and she *loves* to ride in trucks."

Upon hearing her name, Happy stood up, wagging her tail. Happy gazed at Mattie, *"Truck?! Did he say 'truck'? I love trucks!"* she whined.

Mattie wagged her tail, *"Yeah, when we ride in the truck, we'll bark at cows in the fields, let our ears flap in the wind—"*

"Let my lips flap in the wind," slobbered Happy with anticipation.

"Oh, good grief!" moaned Carl. Looking sideways at the puppy, *"One bit of advice, Mattie: don't stand downwind of that big dog's floppy, drooling lips."*

Happy panted joyfully. Suddenly she gave Carl a big, juicy kiss on top of his head; she loved him so much! *What a joker*, Happy smiled. Ears flat, drool dripping off his head, Carl cringed while everyone around the table laughed at his pitiful expression.

Jim's caravan left at an opportune time. Although winter, travelers passing through the valley assured Jim that mountain roads remained open. They would miss Juan and Rosa's wedding, but both Sara and Jim felt uneasy about staying in the valley. Something was going to happen soon, so they wanted to leave as quickly as possible. Their work at Nellie's farm was done, the truck ran okay, and everyone seemed excited to start something new.

When evening approached on their first night of travel, Jim found a secluded campsite near a river, but off the main road. The travelers got out of the Ranger, stretched to work cramps out of their backs and legs, then unloaded a few things from the truck. Miah and Jim erected a canvas tent while Sara and Beth made a small fire to cook dinner.

This pattern became their routine in the days ahead. After securing a perimeter, the men erected the tent and the women prepared dinner. Jim didn't push his group too hard because the rocky roads were usually rutted and snow covered. Even on a good day, travel was slow, but the unhurried pace allowed everyone time to get familiar with each other without unnecessary stress. They had plenty of opportunities to talk and admire the scenery together.

After leaving Virginia, they drove up a winding mountain pass into Tennessee. Jim followed the path Juan highlighted on a map because Juan knew the less-traveled mountain roads; later, the newlyweds would follow the same route to join Jim's group. Approving Juan's choice of roads, Jim soon discovered they only passed local traffic: farm wagons, pedestrians, and horseback riders. Consequently, as they journeyed deeper into the mountains, Jim and Sara felt less anxious about accidentally running into PeaceKeepers or gun thugs.

As they traveled, Jim appreciated Miah more every day. Without prompting, Miah did the work of two men, accomplishing his tasks quickly and proficiently. Not only was Miah a capable handyman, Jim trusted him.

Because of that trust, Jim gave the young man his M4. "Miah, I feel better knowing that you have a rifle in case we ever have trouble. Besides, we're going to need game to eat. Both jobs require a good weapon." The rugged young man straightened his shoulders, nodding his head.

Jim wasn't the only person who admired Miah. When everyone sat by the fire at night, Beth stole glimpses of the strapping young man. Despite her best efforts to appear uninterested, Miah noticed her furtive glances at him.

Miah didn't mind the young woman's attention; he enjoyed Beth's company. Once they helped set up camp, the two teenagers wandered through the woods with Happy and Mattie. They hunted for game together, but most often they simply explored an area and talked.

After the first day of travel, Beth insisted on sitting in the back of the truck with Miah and the dogs because, as she explained to Jim and Sara, "It gives you guys more room in the cab." Sara and Jim accepted her explanation without comment but glanced at each other with knowing looks. They knew Beth adored Miah.

Within days, Jim's group bonded into a tight unit. They related honestly, relied on each other, and prayed together. Although Jim remained uncommitted in his faith, Sara always led their meals with a prayer. During grace, Jim respectfully closed his eyes, bent his head, and listened to her words.

Sometimes as Sara prayed, Jim's mind wandered. He thought about tasks he wanted to accomplish the next day, tried to name birds singing in the trees, or listened for approaching footsteps. Despite his wandering thoughts, Jim secretly acknowledged that his unplanned stop to help Nellie was one of the best decisions he had ever made in his life.

Jim was glad to belong to this new group of people but he really didn't know who to thank. *Is there a God in heaven that hears prayers? Or am I just a lucky soldier that fell into the right place at the right time?* Jim didn't care. All he wanted to do was shut his eyes, listen to Sara's calm voice, and daydream for a few minutes.

13

LIFE IN THE VALLEY ebbed and flowed during the winter. Everyone had different priorities. Mac and his family grew stronger, physically and spiritually; Ryan and Jason repaired tools; Marcus established order within his new "family"; Nellie and Toynell sewed clothes; and Juan and Rosa prepared for their marriage.

One winter day, probably sometime in January on the discarded calendar, Juan saw Mac riding his horse alongside another rider. Juan rushed outside to greet his friend, "Welcome back, amigo! Ryan told me about your brush with death." Looking at Mac with an exaggerated grimace, Juan said, "You still don't look very good but you never were very good-looking anyway."

Mac stopped his horse, turned to his companion, and remarked, poker-faced, "Why did we ride over to see this guy?" Mac dismounted. He and Juan embraced heartily and slapped each other on the back. "Juan, I want you to meet my friend, Pastor Greg." The pastor dismounted and the two new acquaintances bumped fists.

Juan led the men into his small house for a hot drink. The clapboard house had a combined kitchen and living room, one bedroom, and a bathroom with just enough room for a bathtub and sink. Despite its compact design, Juan's home radiated manly warmth and comfort: an overstuffed sofa draped with an olive green poncho liner, rifles hanging on walls, galvanized metal dishes drying by the sink, and oil lamps sitting on tables throughout the house. Without any pretense, Juan's house looked and felt like a hunting cabin.

Stepping into the house, Mac taunted Juan, "So are you ready to take the matrimonial plunge?"

"I'd marry that beautiful woman in a New York minute," Juan said. Turning to the pastor, "So would you like to marry us today?"

"Uh . . . I guess I could," Pastor Greg stammered; "I really just came over to meet you. I'd like to talk with you and Rosa before you take your vows, but there's no reason to drag our feet either."

"I'm just teasing you, Greg." Juan pulled out a chair by a heavy oaken table, "Sit down, have some coffee." Juan glanced at Mac, "I'll ride over to our neighbor's house, the place where Rosa's living right now. We should be back in less than an hour."

Mac nudged the pastor, "See? I told you he was a man of action. Once he made up his mind, wild horses couldn't drag him away from Rosa."

Juan flashed a pirate's smile, slid a baseball cap on his head, and walked out the door. "I'll see you two before your coffee gets cold."

True to his word, Juan returned with Rosa before Mac and Pastor Greg even finished one pot of cheroot coffee. The foursome enjoyed an afternoon of conversation over a simple meal Juan and Rosa prepared together. As they ate tamales and beans, Pastor Greg talked about the blessings and challenges of marriage referenced in the Bible. To answer specific questions, Mac related his own experiences with Patricia.

As twilight approached, Juan insisted on returning Rosa to her temporary home but offered to let the men stay the night. Mac and Greg agreed to stay. As he helped Rosa with her coat, Juan said to the pastor, "Hey, do you have a place to live?" When Pastor Greg replied that he lived with Marcus, Juan said, "Why don't you take this house? Rosa and I plan on moving to Tennessee to meet up with Jim's group, so my house'll be empty soon. This is a great place for a single guy."

"Thank you," gasped the young man. "I'd like that very much!" Smiling with a roguish grin, Pastor Greg replied promptly, "So do you want to get married tomorrow?"

⚜

Although the couple didn't marry the next day, they didn't dawdle either. Within a week all their neighbors gathered to celebrate the wedding. Rosa and her friends decorated Nellie's covered pavilion with bouquets of dried herbs and evergreen boughs. Under the pavilion, they draped faded sheets over tables, placing heavy bowls of roasted nuts on the tablecloths to keep them from blowing away. A stiff winter wind blew throughout the day but Juan stacked a pile of wood for a bonfire near the pavilion so everyone could stay warm outside.

Several hours before the ceremony, Juan walked around Nellie's yard, marveling at the beautiful setting. He sat down in a corner of the pavilion and prayed. Juan prayed for his upcoming marriage, his friends, his future family. As Juan thanked God for the current blessings in his life, he also remembered his past—his checkered, questionable past.

⁂

Once he left the army, Juan didn't know where to go or what to do. All of his family died during the early destruction of the United States. Stationed overseas when the U.S. government collapsed, Juan couldn't return home until he found a flight that landed near New York City. Because city riots disrupted airports, Juan flew into a New Jersey county airport and hitch-hiked to his parent's house in Brooklyn.

Juan saw the same level of devastation in his old neighborhood that he saw in Afghanistan. Burned-out buildings, cars abandoned on streets, garbage littered on sidewalks, and the ever-present smell of decay. When he found his family's old apartment building, Juan pulled his Glock from its holster, stepping carefully over broken glass and charred rubble.

He cautiously walked up one flight of stairs, then another. On the third-floor landing, Juan looked through the broken door of his parent's apartment, assessing the damage. He turned the doorknob, pushed the ragged door open, and entered slowly. He hoped that he still might find his parents or younger sister hiding in the apartment but the rooms lay empty, ransacked.

"Mr. Peña?" a hesitant voice broke the silence behind him.

Juan turned quickly to confront a middle-aged man standing by the threshold. Relieved to see a familiar face, Juan asked, "Do you know where my family is?"

The neighbor looked at his feet, "They're all dead." The man shook his head sorrowfully, "A gang of brutes broke down their door and started to scream at your father. Your dad gave them all his money and told them to leave, but they wouldn't go. They pushed your mother and sister from one man to the next, saying all kinds of unspeakable things." He exhaled deeply, "Your dad grabbed one of the men's guns and shot him, but the others instantly turned on your family." He waited, remembering the moment, "They killed them all."

Juan inhaled, then noticed the bloodstained floor. Scowling, "Did the murderers get away?" he asked quietly, menacingly.

"Well, yeah, at first. They ran out of the building dragging their wounded friend with them."

"Do you know who they were?"

"Nah, I've never seen them before." The man said hurriedly, "But when they rushed out of our building, they ran right into a troop of American forces still patrolling the streets. The idiots started shooting at the soldiers. The soldiers fired back, killing the whole gang on our front steps."

"Good," Juan said without remorse—compensation for killing his family. After fighting battles overseas and later seeing the same war-torn devastation in his old neighborhood, Juan's sense of justice was decisive, deadly. Juan looked at the neighbor, "Are you alone? Do you need anything?"

Shrugging his shoulders, "Oh, you know, I get by. I'd love a clean glass of water, but there's no clean water or glasses anywhere in this city," complained the neighbor.

Stifling tears, Juan nodded, and turned away from the man; he abruptly left his parent's apartment, planning never to return. He walked the mean streets scanning the damage everywhere and hoping to find a group of looters, someone wreaking havoc. Juan was so angry he wanted to kill anyone he saw mistreating another person, but his old neighborhood mocked him with silence. As he passed shuttered businesses, his heart seethed with hate.

Undeterred, Juan paced up and down avenues looking for a fight. When he turned a corner, he saw a disheveled man with a scraggly beard, wearing rags, shouting, "Repent, for the kingdom of God is at hand!"

"What a wacko," mumbled Juan. He walked down the street, drawing closer to the screaming maniac, but Juan ignored the man's outbursts.

"Hey you, man with the gun, are you saved?" the evangelist yelled.

Juan strolled to the corner, looked at the man without uttering a word. Staring at the sorry excuse of humanity, Juan grumbled, "Why do you care if I'm saved?"

"Because it matters to God."

"I know a little about God, but today I just want to send a few people to hell. First-class ticket. No waiting to ride on this train," he snarled.

Across the street, a window broke and three teenage boys ran out of the store carrying a widescreen television. The boys laughed and screamed curses at a beleaguered storekeeper. Juan ran in front of the boys, aimed his gun at them, and said menacingly, "Put the TV down—now."

Two boys ran off, leaving their friend alone holding the gigantic widescreen TV. The boy grunted and put the television on the ground but he never took his eyes off of Juan's pistol.

"Get on your knees and put your hands behind your head," ordered Juan. The teen dropped to his knees, clasped his fingers together, and placed his hands on his head; he'd done this before. Furious, Juan raged, "Why are you doing this? Why are you stealing from this helpless man?"

"Hey, we're poor and everybody's doing it. Why shouldn't I?"

Juan pressed the barrel of his pistol to the teen's forehead, "What is wrong with you?! You're stealing a television and there's no electricity in the city!"

"Well, uh . . . we, uh . . . we need to eat."

"What're you gonna do? Eat this TV? What's wrong with you?" Juan clenched his teeth and pressed the gun even harder into the teen's head.

Behind his back, Juan heard a slow, steady voice, "Put, the gun . . . down." Recognizing the evangelist's voice, Juan didn't turn around but continued to stare at the looter.

"Why should I, reverend? This punk's a criminal. A thief!" His voice as hard as stone, "He deserves to die."

"We all deserve to die, but that wasn't God's plan," countered the voice.

Juan scrutinized the terrified teen's eyes; he looked over the boy's shoulders and saw the shopkeeper watching from a distance. Juan moved slightly to keep the evangelist in his peripheral vision. Three people: the storeowner, the kid, and the crazy man; he could see them all at once; he could take them out in a matter of seconds. This was his training. This was *his* specialty.

Considering his options, Juan said to the street preacher, "Give me one reason why I should let this piece of garbage live."

"Because he was made in the image of God," answered the man. The silence was deafening. Juan considered his options. The preacher added, "And so were you."

Slow to relent, Juan finally lowered the pistol to his side. Still very dangerous, Juan controlled his temper in spite of his internal fury. The teen looked back and forth between Juan and the preacher, his eyes filled with fear.

"Get outta my sight!" hissed Juan. The looter fell to the ground and crawled hastily forward. After stumbling a few feet away from Juan, the teen stood upright, snuffling tears, bawling curses. When Juan glanced at the shopkeeper, the man held his arms up in surrender and backed into his store, never breaking eye contact with Juan.

Juan turned to confront the itinerate preacher, "What about you?"

"I'm still here if you want to talk."

Juan goaded him, "You're not afraid to die?"

"No. I'm not."

Curious with the man's response, Juan slowly holstered his weapon. Although feigning a laidback demeanor, Juan's muscles remained tense. He expected the outrageous man to do something unpredictable, something weird. "Why aren't you afraid to die?"

The preacher replied, "I'm going to heaven; and let me tell you, brother, it's a lot nicer than earth."

Juan scratched his head, "You're crazy, man. You can look down the barrel of a gun and say you're not afraid to die?"

Slumping down to sit on the sidewalk, the street preacher exhaled heavily, "Well, no—the gun thing? My knees are so weak I can't stand; you scared me to death!" Grabbing his knees to control the quivering, the man stayed seated. His voice cracked, "But when I die someday, I know I'm going to heaven."

Intrigued, Juan sat next to him, "Yeah, how can you be so sure?"

Taking a deep breath to regain some composure, the scruffy-looking man talked haltingly at first, then became more relaxed when he realized Juan wasn't going to kill him. He started to describe the gospel of Jesus in a thoughtful, rational manner. Unlike his outward appearance, the man was actually articulate; as a result, the two men sat on the curb for over an hour discussing retribution and salvation. The stranger answered all of Juan's questions, even lingering doubts that had haunted Juan since childhood.

Even before talking with the preacher, Juan knew that he wouldn't find peace on his own; he needed a savior. He never thought about a personal relationship with God; Jesus was just a bloody man hanging on a cross in the cathedral. He stared at the crucifix when his mother took him to mass but he never understood what the priests said. He just sat quietly, watched the rituals, and copied his mother when she did something religious. The whole exercise was hollow, empty; therefore, as soon as he was old enough to stop going to church, he did.

Afterward, he did whatever seemed right to him. He used his own moral compass—his broken, corrupted compass—to guide his decisions. Juan sometimes felt remorse for his actions; but until the evangelist told him that everyone had a broken compass, he didn't realize that no one could achieve righteousness on their own.

Nobody could work their way into heaven by doing good deeds, because the preacher said, "Even the best deeds of man are as filthy rags to the Lord."[1]

Eventually, Juan told the stranger about the atrocities he committed as a gangbanger; the evangelist listened without condemnation. Juan knew he lived a vain, wretched existence. He wanted to change—no, he had to change; he needed a new life, but until today he didn't know how to make that adjustment.

Juan admitted, "I know what things I've done wrong." He paused to find the right words, "And I don't want God to count them against me anymore." He sat motionless on that forlorn city street sidewalk with his hands clasped in front of him.

Patiently, Juan listened to the preacher's life-giving words. With guidance from a grungy evangelist, Juan confessed his sins to God and accepted Jesus as his personal savior. The preacher put his hand on Juan's shoulder and prayed that Jesus would enter Juan's heart. Juan bowed his head submissively, humbly submitting his life to the Lord.

After they prayed, Juan sat still, breathing deeply. Eventually, they stood up, but Juan wasn't ready to leave the evangelist. Juan asked the man impulsively, "Hey, I have some things in my pocket worth trading; would you like to get something to eat?"

The preacher looked around at their stark surroundings, "I don't think there are many restaurants open anymore."

"Who needs a restaurant? I remember a great little shack down by the waterfront, where the owner always sold seafood. It's a rough place, with a shady crowd, but if Rocky's there, he'll feed you as many fried fillets as you can stuff into your mouth." Smiling as he thought about haggling with his old buddy, Juan added, "And even if Rocky doesn't like what I have to trade, he owes me a favor anyway. He'll feed us if he's still around."

Starving, the preacher agreed. As they walked down the block toward Rocky's seafood shanty, the two men bantered affably.

"Man, when I first saw you, I thought you were a lunatic," confessed Juan.

"Yeah, a lot of people say that."

---

1. Isa 64:6.

"Well, maybe you could comb your hair, or trim your beard," suggested Juan.

"Whoa now, let's not get crazy . . ."

⁓◌⊙◌⁓

Juan smiled as he remembered that conversion. Nellie roused him from his reverie when she asked him about the wedding. "Huh? What did you say, Nells?"

She repeated, "Do you have the rings?"

Patting his shirt pocket, he said, "Right here. Are we ready to start?"

"Not yet. I'm just taking care of a few final things. You might want to find Mac; he's been looking everywhere for you."

Juan stood up, flexed his back, and extended his arms overhead. He looked down at the cheerful woman and impulsively hugged her. "Thanks for all your help, Nellie; you're such a beautiful friend!" She turned her head aside; despite her advanced years, whenever she was given a compliment, Nellie still blushed like a schoolgirl.

14

As Jim's entourage pressed deeper into the Appalachian Mountains, he knew they needed to find better lodging. The tent provided some protection from the weather but with freezing winter snowstorms occurring, he wanted to find better housing; moreover, they were almost out of fuel. Jim scrounged through every dilapidated shack and abandoned RV they found along the road, searching for gas. He stopped the truck whenever he noticed a possible shelter but after closer examination, nothing satisfied their needs.

His search ended when they found a deserted gas station nestled in the woods. The timing of their find was perfect. When the four travelers pushed the Ranger into the station, the truck's fuel tank and extra gas cans were empty. Although the gas pumps no longer worked, Jim hoped they could overwinter in the abandoned buildings.

Everyone got out of the truck to investigate the property. Besides gas pumps, the site contained a mechanic's garage, a convenience store, and a small house connected to the rear of the store. Previous scavengers knocked over shelves and furniture in the store and house, but the damage was minimal. The advantages of shelter and warmth far outweighed the inconvenience of repairing the service station.

"This is our lucky day," remarked Jim.

"It is," said Sara.

Jim opened his palms, "What do you say? Shall we set up short-term living quarters here until spring?"

As she stood upright from pushing the truck, Sara laughed, "I don't think we have much choice, do you?" Relieved to sleep in a house with a fireplace, Miah and Beth quickly approved the gas station.

"Then let's get started," urged Jim. "We'll roll the truck into the garage and set up housekeeping."

Although the store and house contained very few valuable items, the group found enough supplies to improve their living conditions. Miah cobbled together a semi-level table from four discarded two-by-fours to use as legs and a chunk of linoleum for the tabletop. To complete the table, Beth and Sara carried in four tree stumps, partially rotted but still useable, for chairs.

Without question, the best discovery was cleaning products. After Jim broke the lock to a nondescript, vine-covered shed behind the store, they found a small storage room with scouring products and paper supplies overlooked by foragers. By nightfall, the tired wanderers cleaned the house well enough to sleep on the floor and planned to finish sanitizing the house another day.

Once the house was somewhat organized, Miah and Jim gathered firewood from the forest and killed two rabbits for dinner. Afterward, they roasted the meat over a fire in the living room's large stone fireplace. The smell of sizzling fat nearly drove the dogs wild. *"Roasted meat,"* whined Mattie. Happy looked at Mattie with her droopy, twinkling eyes. The mere thought of seared meat made the poor dog continuously lick her lips and drool excessively.

"It looks like we're going to have to share our dinner with the girls," noted Miah as he watched the dogs. "Either that or we'll have two of the saddest dogs you ever saw!"

Jim said, "I wouldn't have it any other way." He sliced off a chunk of meat while it hissed over the fire. Jim blew on the meat to cool it, then said mildly, "Sit." Both girls sat politely in front of him—Happy's bushy tail swept the floor repeatedly—and he gave each dog a bite of food.

That night, the dinnertime prayer differed slightly from previous evenings because everyone spoke. Miah thanked God for providing a generous meal, Beth mentioned the warm, dry house, and Sara added traveling mercies. At the end of grace, Jim surprised the others when he simply said, "Thank you."

The rest of the day simply became a time to rest. Throughout dinner and into the evening, the group's mood remained relaxed, easy. For an exquisite moment in time, peace blanketed the house and all its inhabitants; no one worried about anything.

The following day, Miah and Beth set out to hunt for larger game. They dragged a plastic sled, found in the garage rafters, through the snowy woods in case they shot a deer. Despite the cold temperature, the couple enjoyed their time alone to explore the forest and hunt. Although they talked intermittently, they mostly used silent hand gestures to communicate. Time passed quickly. Before they knew it, the afternoon sun cast a bronze shade over the mountains, yet they did not find any game or wild vegetables to bring back for dinner.

"It's getting late. We better head back," said Miah.

"You're right. Sara'll worry if we don't get back soon."

As they backtracked, they spied a moving object in the distance. Miah made eye contact with Beth and put his index finger to his lips; then the two hunters crept slowly toward the suspicious movement. When they drew closer, they saw a young girl sitting on the ground talking to an animal she held.

Drawing close to the girl, Beth said softly, "Hi." Bending down to the child's level, she asked with concern, "Are you okay?"

Startled, the girl looked at them with tears in her eyes, "It's my goat; she's hurt." Clearing her throat, she cried, "I'm afraid she's going to die."

Miah bent down next to the girl. When the frightened animal jumped from the girl's arms, he noticed it limped away with pain. Miah examined the young goat's leg, "I'm not sure but I think her leg's broken." Looking at Beth, Miah added, "Jim can probably help her." Trying to comfort the little girl, he continued, "Would you like to come back to our place to see if someone can help your goat?"

Without pausing, she said, "Yes. But she hurts awful bad, mister."

"I know; I'll be gentle with her." Miah shook his head, considering his ironic situation. He would've happily brought home a young goat for dinner, but now he handled this wounded animal as if made of glass. As his stomach growled he thought, *Well, if Jim can't help the goat, maybe we'll eat her for dinner anyway.*

Miah picked up both the little girl and her goat, placing them carefully on the sled. "It's gonna be a bumpy ride but this is the fastest way to get you and your goat down the mountain."

The girl shook her head, holding the goat close to her chest. Both Beth and Miah grabbed the lead rope to pull the sled together. Yanking the sled over bare rocks and sliding over the snow through steep gullies, they approached the gas station in less than an hour. Jim saw the sled.

He poked his head into the kitchen, updating Sara, "Miah and Beth are bringing something down the mountain. I'm going up to see what they're doin'." Sara wiped her hands on a towel as she stood in the doorway watching Jim stride up the incline.

The long-legged man met the young people on the trail within minutes. As he looked at the dirty waif on the sled holding her wide eyed goat, Jim said to the teenagers with amusement, "Hey, what did you two find?"

Intrigued, Jim stood next to the sled, bending at the waist with his hands on his knees. Miah explained the goat's symptoms as Jim started to stroke the young goat's fur. Lowering one knee to the ground, Jim felt the goat's leg and confirmed Miah's diagnosis, "You're right, Miah, this little lady broke her leg."

As tears welled in her eyes again, the girl sucked in her breath, looking anxiously at Jim, "Can ya'll help her?"

"I can," answered Jim, "I hear goats recover nicely from broken bones. Let's get your friend to the garage. We'll bind her leg down there."

Jim carried the young goat to the garage and placed her on a workbench. "We'll just put a splint on her leg, wrap everything up snug, and keep her quiet for a while." As Jim splinted the goat's leg, Miah held the animal still. Throughout the process, the girl watched Jim's movements with great interest while she continued to stroke her pet's coat. Afterward, Jim mentioned, "It might be hard to get your goat back up the mountain until her leg gets better. Is it alright if she stays here with us a while, just 'til she gets stronger?"

The girl quickly consented. Just as quickly, she cried, "I was so afraid someone would say that she was just some dumb baby goat, and shoot her because she couldn't walk." Looking up at Jim with sorrowful eyes, "I couldn't eat her, mister. She's my best friend."

Miah cleared his throat and looked up toward the ceiling.

"She'll be fine," assured Jim. "We'll make a small pen for her outside; you can visit her whenever you like."

Embarrassed by her tears, she briskly wiped her nose with both hands, blinking her eyes a few times. "I don't know what to say, doctor; my family don't have much."

Chuckling, Jim said, "Don't worry about payment; it's on the house. And I'm not a doctor; I'm just a guy that knows a little about triage."

Lifting her chin up and swallowing, she stated, "I'll be by ever' day to give Posey some leaves. She kinda likes it for breakfast." She shook Jim's hand firmly, once, "Thank ya kindly, doc." Repeating her staunch promise to visit every day, she pulled a stocking hat over her matted hair, turned, and ran up the mountain as if she were a goat herself.

Sara watched the ragamuffin run uphill, "What a funny little girl."

"Yeah, but it feels good to help others," said Jim as he watched the girl disappear into the woods. Turning to Miah, Jim asked, "So what's for dinner tonight?"

Miah threw out his arms expansively, radiating a dazzling smile, and said, "Dandelion soup and cattail muffins."

Jim clapped Miah's shoulders with good humor, "Thank goodness for dried plants!" Gazing down at the goat, "Well, Posey, let's get you settled in for the night." Stroking her face, he thought, *Who knows? You might help open a few doors for us with our new neighbors.*

⁓᠊ᡋᠥᡊ᠊⁓

Little did Jim know that his passing thought quickly became reality. True to her word, the girl returned the next day. Afterward, she returned every morning to bring food for Posey and a small gift for Jim. On the first day she brought Jim preserved carrots; the following day, she brought a handful of potatoes; on the third day, she brought a rock she thought looked just like President Lincoln, hat and all.

On the fourth day, she brought her younger brother. "Ya cain't keep my brother but I wanted ya'll to meet him anyways."

The boy was even more interested in Jim and his family than the girl. After Sara greeted the boy, she gave both children water and stale crackers. The children sat by the fireplace to warm their hands, staring wide-eyed at all the "neat stuff" in the house.

It didn't matter that the boy sat quietly, nibbling his cracker, because his sister talked enough for both of them. "Where did ya'll come from?"— "Do you have any kin in these parts?"—"Whoa, that's a ginormous black dog; what's his name?"—"We have us a cat named Buster but he's real mean."

As the girl chattered, Sara listened. Wanting to join the conversation, Beth walked casually into the living room, idly brushing her long, silky hair. Sara asked Beth, "Do you want me to braid your hair?"

After Beth said, "Yes, please," Sara worked a comb through Beth's blonde hair. Afterward, she started to braid it. The mountain girl's jaw dropped open as she ogled Sara's nimble fingers create a fancy braided hairdo for Beth.

Dumfounded, the girl said, "I ain't never seen nothin' so beautiful in all my growed days!" Touching her snarled hair, the girl asked, "Can you do that to my hair?"

"Let me finish with Beth and I'll run a comb through your hair," replied Sara.

The boy finally spoke, "You'll probably need a pitchfork to get through Patsy's hair." He started to giggle, but stopped suddenly when the girl pinched him.

"So your name is Patsy, huh? I wondered what to call you. I was beginning to think I'd have to name you myself," teased Sara.

Patsy reddened. "I figgered you had better thangs to remember than ma name; but anyways, I's Patsy and this here," indicating her brother, "is Ralphie."

"Hey," Ralphie said bashfully.

Sara's heart melted. She was braiding a beautiful young woman's hair, listening to tall tales from two boisterous children, and relying on the skills of a strong young man outside. Once again, Sara ached to see her own children. Fighting back tears, Sara decided that until that time came, whether on earth or in heaven, she would thank Jesus daily for bringing others into her life, people she could love unconditionally.

Despite all the tribulations, Sara had to admit, she was happy. She was starting to carve out a home in the wilderness with some remarkable people. She knew conditions were primitive, life was precarious; in truth, this could be her last day on earth. But it didn't matter anymore. Sara knew the dangers and uncertainties in life, yet she was happy.

After Sara finished braiding Beth and Patsy's hair, she sat on a bench and read a story to Ralphie. When she closed the book, she relaxed as she stared at burning embers in the fireplace. Unaware of her beauty, Sara stood up, dusted cracker crumbs off her lap, and turned to see Jim watching her, admiring her. Sara smiled openly at him. *This is the man that helped change my life.*

Without hesitating, Jim strode over to Sara, gathered her into his arms, and kissed her passionately on the lips. When they finished kissing, he looked down at her surprised face, "I wanted to kiss you from the first day I saw you, you gorgeous, amazing woman." He loosened his embrace but still cradled her in his arms. "I love you."

With flushed cheeks, Sara confessed, "I love you too!"

A small voice behind them said, "Ya mean you two ain't married?" Jim and Sara still held each other as they turned around laughing. They saw Patsy and Ralphie looking at them in bewilderment.

"No," answered Jim, "but if this fine woman will have me, I'll change that situation as soon as possible!"

"Is this a marriage proposal?" Sara asked coyly.

"Yes, it is!" Holding Sara's hand, Jim looked deeply into her eyes, "Sara, will you marry me?"

By this time, Miah, Beth, Patsy, and Ralphie gathered around closely, gawking at the laughing couple with expectant, nervous smiles. "I would *love* to marry you, Jim," responded Sara. Sara's answer brought down the house: Miah and Beth cheered; Patsy and Ralphie jumped up and down holding hands, giggling; and the dogs barked, wagging their tails because they sensed something very special just happened.

Jim scooped Sara into his arms and kissed her again. Afterward, Jim held Sara closely and whispered in her ear, "I promise you that as long as we live, I'll kiss you first thing in the morning. Every day." Sara turned her head into Jim's chest, leaned into his arms, and wept with joy.

15

While Jim and Sara fostered love in the southern mountains, Constance and her party restrained hate as they plodded painfully over the western mountains. No one in Constance's group found relief. In less than two weeks of travel, several children died from dysentery, the women argued bitterly, and the old men suffered frostbite.

Whenever they crested a mountain, everyone raised their chins and strained their eyes in search of grasslands again, but so far all they saw were mountains. More mountains, more trees, more snow, and more rugged roads. In desperation, Gloria finally screamed her dismay, threatening to kill herself.

"Go ahead, kill yourself," taunted Constance. "That would be one less mouth to feed."

Despondent, Gloria relented, pouting. She stopped her tantrum but she never forgot Constance's vile words. Gloria buried Connie's rebuke deep inside her heart; rather than forgive Constance, Gloria let those words fester into a cold, hard bitterness that she nurtured with hate. *When we get out of these wretched mountains,* Gloria promised herself, *I will make Constance eat her words. If there's any justice in this world, she'll die.*

Besides their mutual dislike for each other, the group routinely lost supplies. Posting an evening guard rarely helped because the guards usually fell asleep. Constance beat the children that slept during their watch but when she raised a stick to hit Shirley McGuire—another bone-weary mother—Shirley drew her pistol, tightening her mouth, "Don't try it, Connie. I also don't mind having one less mouth to feed."

Constance lowered her stick, unaccustomed to being challenged. Ashamed of her own cowardice, Constance refused to look at anyone. She stormed out of the camp yelling furious vulgarities, chastened by Shirley's threat.

"I'm afraid we're going to die up here," one grizzled, old man told his friend. "If the weather, wild animals, or outlaws don't kill us, those angry women will."

Nodding his head, his friend whispered, "I have guard duty tonight. Instead of staying here, let's take off while everyone sleeps." The two friends quietly agreed. The old men performed their regular duties: harnessing livestock, gathering firewood, and securing wagons; but whenever possible, they stayed out of the women's way for the rest of the day. While the women ignored them, the old men waited until nighttime to execute their escape.

That night, Constance repeated her daily custom of highlighting their slow progress and criticizing each person's contribution to their difficulties. "You call this a fire? I couldn't boil water with these pathetic embers," she scolded Talia. "TJ, give the oxen more to eat; if they die, we die!" Looking sternly at the elderly gentlemen, "Get away from me, you smelly old men! Who asked you to join us anyway?" After tripping over a child's rusted metal truck, the irritable woman heaved the toy down the mountain, "Do I have to clean up after everybody? What's the matter with you all?!"

As the boy cried over his lost toy, the old men looked at each other with an unspoken understanding. *Let's get out of here as soon as we can.*

Foolishly, Constance maintained her tirade for the rest of the evening. When she retired to her bedroll, everyone breathed a sigh of relief.

TJ broke the silence, "I hope we find that road to Ohio soon."

Talia looked at him in wonderment, "We're *on* the road to Ohio, stupid. We're just not through the mountains yet."

TJ viciously hit his sister across the face, slamming her to the ground, "Don't call me stupid again or I'll knock you out!"

Talia rubbed her cheek, stood up defiantly, and walked to her bedroll, pretending not to care. *I will not let TJ see me cry. I will not cry.* Stifling her tears, *Do not cry!*

A slight smile curved on TJ's lips as he thought, *That'll teach her who's boss.* He dropped another log on the fire, sneered at the old man guarding the camp, and said pointedly, "Don't fall asleep or you'll have to deal with me in the morning." Then he stomped off to find his blanket, feeling superior now that he was the only real man left in the camp.

෴

Talia woke up early the following morning. The campsite was eerily quiet; she didn't even hear the old men snoring on the other side of the fire pit. Her stomach churned and her insides felt terrible. *It must've been somethin' I ate*, she thought. Talia wrapped her thin coat and blanket tightly around her shoulders. Thinking she might get sick, she slipped out of the camp to splash cold river water on her face. She flinched when she touched her bruised cheek, remembering the cruel glint in her brother's eyes when he hit her.

As she pushed through the dense undergrowth surrounding their wagons, Talia plotted revenge against TJ, but before she reached the camp's perimeter, she heard unusual voices. Sensing more discord, she slipped behind a bush to watch the camp. Walking around the dying fire were five men she'd never seen before. *Where was the guard? Who are these people?* Talia sank lower behind the bush, watching the drama unfold.

"Who're you?" Constance barked at the strangers.

"Your new neighbors," growled a man's voice. A rough looking character: the man's hat, boots, and chaps were mud spattered and worn; his beard unkempt and dirty; and his eyes looked dark and vacant, dead—fish eyes.

"Well, I don't feel very neighborly," countered Constance belligerently. She straightened to her full six-foot height, putting her hands on her hips.

"Neither do I," answered the man.

Without thinking twice, he pulled a revolver out of his holster and shot Constance in the forehead. Constance fell flat on her back, her eyes wide open with surprise. While women and children stared at her lifeless body, her head began to saturate the soil with blood. A toddler cried but everyone else watched the newcomers with dazed, shocked expressions.

"Shut that kid up or I will," warned the man.

Gloria wrapped the boy in her arms. She buried his head against her chest, stroking his hair. She whispered soothing words into his ears, never taking her eyes off the man in control.

Turning to his partners, "Take whatever food and supplies we can carry with us. Grab the horses too."

"Hey, boss, can we take some women with us?" asked an excited outlaw, leering at the teenagers.

"Nah, they'll just be more trouble than they're worth." As the men ransacked wagons searching for food and weapons, TJ stood up to watch.

The leader stopped, looked suspiciously at the tall, slim teen, and asked, "Are you gonna be a problem?"

With false bravado, TJ answered, "No, I wanna join your gang."

Four men laughed at the arrogant young man but the leader held up his hand to quiet his gang. "Why should we take you?" he asked, slanting his eyes.

"Because I'm strong, I can shoot a gun, and I don't want to babysit a bunch of women and kids anymore." The men ridiculed the brash teenager; they couldn't imagine inviting a kid to join them. They were a group of hardened criminals; this kid was just a pup.

The leader silenced his men with a slight wave of his hand. "Okay, junior, I'll tell you what: gather up all the weapons and ammo, then saddle a horse for yourself. You can tend our fires and cook our meals. If we like ya, you can ride with us; if we don't like ya, we'll kill ya. How's that sound?" dared the leader, a nasty glint in his eyes.

"Sounds good to me." TJ jumped into a wagon, tossed aside extraneous items, pots, toys, anything he considered worthless; and pulled out rifles and pistols. He handed the weapons to a man standing by the wagon, then he found some boxes of ammunition and held the ammo in his arms. After he stepped off the wagon, TJ walked over to the valley horses and chose the best mare in the herd. Afterward, he put his bridle and saddle on the mare. While the men continued to paw through the women's supplies, TJ tied his bedroll to a saddle and led his mare over to the leader. "I'm ready."

"Okay, men, it doesn't look like there's much more to take. Let's go."

"Wait a minute," said Shirley McGuire. "What about us? You took everything we had!"

Bending down in his saddle to look directly at Shirley, the man said dismissively, "Lady, you're lucky we didn't kill y'all." As Shirley withered, the thieves rode out of the camp, laughing as they yelled insults at the women. TJ followed the men on his horse; he didn't bother to look over his shoulder at the mournful women and children staring after him.

Good riddance, brother, thought Talia. Before Talia stood up, she heard Shirley and Gloria arguing again. She decided to watch the confrontation from her hiding place before she returned to camp.

"What are we going to do, Shirley?" Gloria shrieked. "No guns, no food, no horses, no men; we're doomed!"

"Shut up, Gloria! We keep moving west." Counting on her fingers, "Kentucky first, then Ohio." Trying to pacify Gloria, Shirley continued,

"We're going to find our old homes again. If we're lucky, we'll resume the lives we left two years ago."

"Are you sure?"

"No, I'm not sure about anything! All I know is, I have three children to feed and my wealthy parents once lived in Ohio."

Gloria responded, "We could return to the valley—"

"Fat chance. I'm tired of slogging out a life in the valley: hiding from PeaceKeepers, birthing livestock, gardening 'til my fingers bleed—nope, I'm never going to return to my husband or that miserable farm."

Always a follower, never a leader, Gloria dropped her head in resignation. "Well, let's get the children dressed and fasten the oxen to our wagons. Maybe we'll find another group traveling west so we can join them."

Noticing a missing girl for the first time, Shirley glanced to the right, then the left, "Hey, where's Talia?"

"I don't know," Gloria looked around for the soft-spoken girl. "Maybe the gunshot scared her away."

"Well, she might join us down the road but I'm not going to wait around for her," huffed Shirley. "Let's get busy."

"What about Constance? Should we bury her?

Shirley snorted, "No, I have neither the time nor the inclination to bury her miserable body." With that final decree, they turned away from Constance in an effort to redeem the rest of their day.

The two women picked up trampled clothes, unbroken dishes, and scraps of food they found on the ground. They packed the remaining supplies and placed their traumatized children into wagons. Shaking her head at their bleak prospects, Shirley coaxed her oxen team onto the snowy, treacherous mountain road. As the remaining families continued to head west, the two teams easily pulled the nearly empty wagons over the mountain.

Talia watched the wagons roll away without her. Disheartened, she murmured, "Mom's dead, and TJ's nuts. Who needs 'em anyway?" Talia had no desire to join the two grouchy women with their whimpering children. *What'll I do now?* Still sitting in the bushes, Talia thought, *I can go back to Dad's house. I may not have much to offer him but at least I can milk cows or weed gardens.*

She pulled the Gideon's Bible out of her coat; something she'd done countless times the past few days. She looked at the crude map drawn on the back cover. In one corner of the map, Marcus had written in small print, "You're always welcome at home, sweet Talia."

I may not have much but at least I have enough sense to know when I'm wrong, reasoned the girl. *Dad won't let me starve.* Desperate to find safety, Talia turned east and started her long walk back to the valley.[1]

1. Luke 15:11–32.

16

UNKNOWN TO TALIA, SOLACE in the valley diminished. After receiving their share of supplies from the PeaceKeepers train, many residents fled. They feared retribution from the government and their fears were well founded. Within days of the train attack, small bands of government forces raided and burned numerous farms in the cove. Following these raids, wandering urban gangs that heard about the fertile valley began to loot farms that escaped the government's wrath. The once flourishing, isolated valley residents now faced starvation and imprisonment, just like everyone else in North America. They hurriedly left their homes hoping to find safer locations, but safety was now a bygone word in this New World.

Despite the danger, a few residents remained in the valley. Nellie, Brant, and Toynell continued living on the farm because whenever they spotted wandering groups, they hid. Brant kept the livestock nestled in a secluded meadow where he found a massive cave in a sandstone hillside. When danger approached, he prodded his herd into the cave; a cave with an entrance camouflaged by overgrown shrubs.

Using the cave as a hideaway, the three escaped death many times. Brant, Toynell, and Nellie discussed making the cave their new home, yet they weren't ready to share their living space full-time with all their livestock. As a result, they never completely relaxed when they returned to the farmhouse; they watched their surroundings constantly, and they kept a low profile when unwanted visitors came near.

Mac, Marcus, and Ryan used an alternative method of survival. Because their farms were close, they guarded the outlining perimeter of their combined properties. They approached any suspicious intruders, and fought those who wished to harm them. Eventually, their reputation as a stronghold against aggressors grew beyond the mountain ranges, and the battles decreased.

Within the consolidated boundary of the three farms, many refugees found sanctuary. The men built two new houses for incoming residents or found room for newcomers in existing houses, but everyone shared guard duty and farming tasks. Although the men deferred to Mac for final decisions concerning the whole community, each man still retained leadership of his own farm.

Mac asked Nellie's family to join them but Nellie chose to remain on her own property. Regardless of the increased dangers, she lived comfortably in her home with Toynell and Brant. Faithful to Nellie, the young couple quickly adapted to rural life. In fact, once they understood the daily routines, they continuously made improvements on the farm, but they maintained a constant vigilance of strangers to protect Nellie and their possessions.

After witnessing the couple's integrity, Nellie amended her will to name Brant and Toynell as sole heirs to her farm once she died. When Nellie gave the couple a copy of her will, she said, "I don't know what the future holds but this farm is yours once I pass away. Honestly, I doubt if the New World Order will even honor this document, but my personal will and property deed are yours anyway."

Touched by Nellie's generosity, the couple gaped at her, speechless. Toynell gasped, putting her hands on her cheeks, and Brant simply hugged the kindly woman. From that day forward, whenever Nellie considered changes on the farm, she always conferred with Brant and Toynell before making decisions. Nellie trusted and loved Toynell and Brant as if they were her own family; similarly, the young couple referred to Nellie as Grandma. Ironically, these three decent people crossed cultural and racial norms that once severed the nation; as a result, they created an authentic, robust family that now only death would separate.

Unfortunately, death was common. Government detachments forced Christians to denounce Jesus and receive a mark of allegiance or face execution. Some people opted to receive the mark and were set free; most Christians chose death.

This was not an easy decision to make because it was not death by injection in a secluded room; no, it was a public beheading using either a guillotine or a saber. Very often the blades of either instrument were dull, making executions even more excruciating to victims. The sentence was bloody, gruesome, and vindictive. It was exactly the bloodlust that the supreme leader desired.

Besides beheadings, people of all ethnicities and religions died from multiple causes. Starvation, murder, and pestilence afflicted the global society, but in addition to these disasters the earth also provided unmitigated misery. Seas raged with fury, dormant volcanoes erupted, rivers turned to blood, and earthquakes leveled large land masses.

Residents of Tennessee and Virginia were not immune from these earthly devastations. On a fair day in late winter, possibly February or March, Jim noticed that Happy and Mattie disappeared. *Strange*, Jim reflected, *the dogs never miss breakfast.*

On that same day, miles away from Jim, valley residents also noticed animals behaving strangely. Talia heard all the forest birds suddenly fall silent, then watched them fly away swiftly, panic stricken. In Mac's compound, the penned livestock tried to break through fences: cows bellowed, pigs ran in circles grunting nervously, and horses tossed their heads, snorting in terror.

"What's the matter with these animals?" Mac said aloud. Marcus scratched his head, shrugging his shoulders. Joining his friends, Pastor Greg listened to their discussion but offered no ideas.

And then the ground started to move.

Although the earthquake surprised people, it didn't happen suddenly, and it didn't surprise animals. Days earlier, animals heard a low rumbling beneath their feet; the animals that could run and hide disappeared long before the quake arrived. Seismographs recorded tremors deep within the earth's crust, an ever-present reverberation, a sound that resembled the tumultuous roar of an oncoming train. Scientists issued alerts to people living along fault lines but with the spotty communication among government agencies and local communities, most people didn't receive any warnings. Now it didn't matter.

The cataclysmic motion tore the valley in half as the fault split the western and northeastern mountain ranges. A gigantic, quarter-mile-wide chasm ran through the once-pristine glen; houses, animals, and people fell into the dark crevasse, disappearing forever. The violent heaving of the earth caused everyone to fall helplessly to the ground. Reflexively, people frantically grabbed for something solid—anything—to save themselves from falling into the ever-widening fracture.

As the earth convulsed violently, the crescendo of its destruction defied the listeners' imaginations. The explosive sound of granite splitting apart, the screams of animals and people, the thunder of demolishing buildings intensified the earthquake's horror, a cacophony of sound straight from the bowels of hell.

And then, fifty-five seconds later, the earth stood still. A deadly silence followed. Not even a breeze blew. Against all logic, it seemed the earthquake, with its magnitude and ferocity, actually disrupted the sky's tranquility and strangled the wind's voice.

After regaining consciousness from a blow to his head, Marcus stood up on wobbly knees, surveying the devastated landscape. Mercifully, none of the five farms in their community fell into the abyss. Even more remarkable was the pattern of the newly created crevasse. The fracture surrounded more than three quarters of the perimeter of their community, leaving only two miles of land still attached to the remaining valley. They now lived on the edge of a steep cliff with only a small section of land accessible to outsiders.

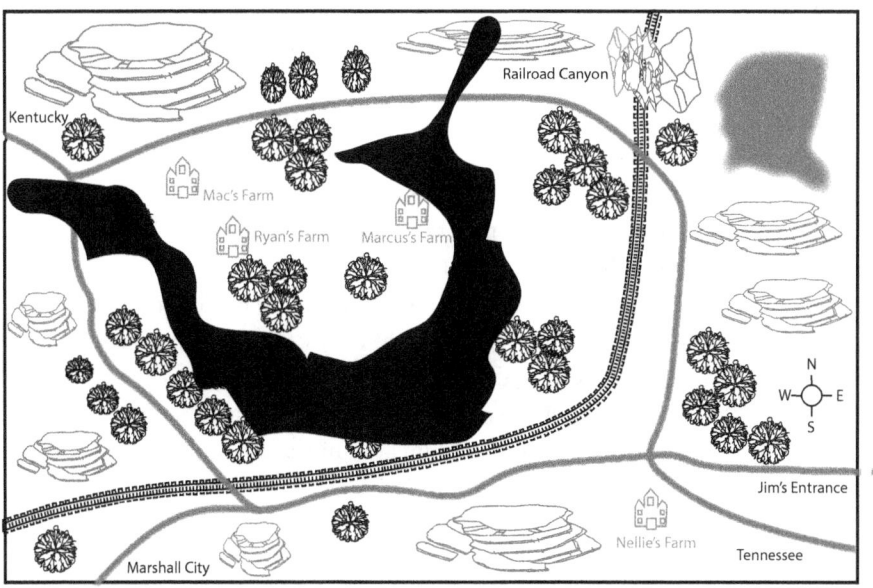

When the dust settled, Marcus and Mac found each other. They stumbled through the debris of buildings and mangled farm equipment in search of survivors. They dug into collapsed structures following the sounds of faint crying, coughing, or muffled gasps within the rubble. Soon other stunned survivors started to frantically lift heavy timbers off frightened livestock and injured people.

They ministered medical care to the wounded and carried the dead to separate locations. They setup a medical facility in Mac's living room and placed lifeless bodies, covered with tattered bed sheets or canvas tarps, in his root cellar. When nightfall arrived, Mac's team accounted for all their residents, alive or dead. Almost half of the community died in the earthquake; now the living focused on either burying loved ones or tending to the injured.

Incredibly, very few animals died. Before the earthquake struck, fearful livestock escaped the looming danger by running through barbed wire fences, kicking apart wooden stables, or breaking out of metal pens. Now, as shadows lengthened, the nervous livestock slowly returned to their farms in search of fodder and protection.

Newscasters reported that people living within five miles of the earthquake's epicenter felt the tremor, but the greatest impact occurred in the Appalachian Mountains between Virginia and Tennessee. Valley residents experienced the brunt of the quake. No one was excluded.

West of the valley, Shirley McGuire, Gloria, and most of the children fell into the chasm as the earth split through the mountain range. Only two valley children survived the mountain calamity: Destiny, Shirley's teenage daughter, and Brady, Gloria's two-year-old son. Minutes before the earthquake began, Destiny took Brady for a short walk near the river. When the ground shook violently, the teenager fell on top of Brady, pinning him defensively to the ground.

"Be still," she whispered into Brady's ears as the boy cried fitfully.

Throughout the tremor, Destiny not only kept Brady from slipping into the fissure; she protected him from falling branches and tumbling stones. When the earthquake subsided, Destiny sat up. She dusted dirt and leaves off the boy, inspected him for injuries, then squeezed him tightly to her chest, saying repeatedly, "You're alright, sweetheart. You're alright."

⌀◦◉◦⌀

Oddly, TJ and BoJed's cutthroat gang survived the earthquake without a scratch. They lost neither horses nor their ill-gotten gains. Hiding close to TJ's camp, Talia watched the renegades with fear and loathing. She remained alive because she clung to a tree during the upheaval, but she stayed hidden from the outlaws and continued to watch them with trepidation.

Before sunset on that dreadful day, TJ built a fire to prepare dinner. Enticed by the aroma of roasting meat, Destiny and Brady walked wearily into the camp, thinking they were reuniting with their families. The teenager realized her mistake when she saw silhouettes of tall men standing near to the firelight instead of her friends and family.

Panicking, Destiny picked Brady up and paced backwards keeping her eyes steady on the men. After taking a few steps, she turned and ran out of the camp as fast as she could, stumbling over rocks, slipping on icy grass. Brady shrieked with surprise by her sudden change of behavior. Ignoring the child's terrified wails, Destiny rushed through dense forest undergrowth. Wild, thorny brambles raked their tender skin, ripping their clothes ragged, but she didn't care about torn clothes or skin abrasions; she only wanted to get away from these wicked men.

Then Destiny stopped abruptly. In front of her and on both sides lay a two-hundred-foot drop into a deep, dark hole. Behind her stood two demented pursuers. She turned around swiftly with her back to the fault; she faced the men. Clutching Brady tightly to her chest and panting heavily, Destiny looked over the child's back to see the men approaching her slowly, steadily.

Motioning her to move away from the precipice, one skinny man said unconvincingly, "Come over here. We won't hurt you."

Looking into their brutal, dark eyes, Destiny knew he was lying.

"We have food. Wouldn't you like something to eat?" lured the other man with a lecherous smile and foul-smelling breath.

Destiny glanced over her shoulder, peering into the depths, hoping to find a ledge to move farther away from these evil men. But there was nowhere to go. *These men will kill Brady as soon as we return to camp. And me? They'll probably molest me and kill me before sunrise.*

"Come on, whatta ya say? Let's get Baby Bumpkins something to eat and we'll give you some new clothes to wear." Both men started to laugh when they thought of discarding her torn dress, but Destiny understood their thoughts.

There are no clothes or food for either of us, she concluded sadly.

She walked backwards toward the edge of the cliff, keeping her eyes fixed firmly on the men. Brady no longer cried but sucked his thumb, whimpering softly.

"Hey now, slow down, girlie; you'll slip and fall down that cliff," warned the first man, his voice trembling slightly.

Destiny glanced over her shoulder again, looked gently into Brady's fearful eyes, then returned her gaze to the men. Softly, she said, "Father, forgive me."

Holding Brady tightly, she turned around briskly and ran forward, off the bank, into the abyss. The men rushed to the canyon's edge, frantically trying to clutch her dress, but to no avail. Stunned, they shook their heads in disbelief as they watched the two bodies crash into pointed boulders lining the canyon floor.

"Why did she do that?" asked one of the men, scratching his chin.

His partner raised his shoulders in dismay. Both men turned to walk back to camp without a blushing teenage girl or a chubby toddler. Kicking the dirt, "Boss is not going to be happy with us," complained the skinny man.

His smelly partner sighed, "Boss is never happy but he probably won't beat us as long as he has that stupid kid to kick around." Even though the boss wouldn't kill them, neither man hurried back to their camp. Skinny rolled a cigarette, took a drag, and passed the cigarette to his putrid buddy.

When the two men finally returned to camp, they retold their story to the rest of the outfit. Their boss shouted, "Fools! Idiots! Can't you do anything right?!"

"I almost had her, Boss," sniveled the skinny man. "One or two more steps and I woulda grabbed her arm!"

Snatching the emaciated man by the collar and breathing on Skinny's face, BoJed (the men's nickname for Boss Jedidiah) snarled, "Not good enough. If she weren't too damaged after we was done with her, we coulda sold her! Blonde, pretty teenagers are worth a bundle!" The boss threw the thin man across the fire and then backhanded the smelly man in the face, knocking him to the ground.

"Let this be a lesson to all of you." BoJed glared at each man, pointing a finger at them emphatically, "Captives are more valuable to us than anything we can steal from these starving farmers." Glimpsing at TJ squatted by the fire, frying potatoes, the boss stormed over to the silent teen, "Are there any more women where you come from?"

TJ stood up and looked evenly into BoJed's menacing eyes. Capitalizing on his knowledge, TJ said, "Yeah, there are more women, but you'll need me to get in good favor with the valley folks."

The boss stepped back and looked at TJ with surprised interest. Smiling with a grudging new respect for the teen's boldness, "What do you suggest, Mr. Good Favor?" Several men jabbed each other in the ribs, waiting for the boss to hit the presumptuous young man.

"Let me ride ahead of you. Get the lay of the land. I'll report what I find, and we can make our plans from there," TJ responded coolly.

Talia pressed a hand over her mouth as she listened.

The boss sat down on a log to consider TJ's proposal. After a moment, BoJed reached into his pocket, withdrew a pinch of tobacco and a slip of rolling paper. He spread a thin line of tobacco on the paper, licked the paper, rolled the ends closed, and put the cigarette into his mouth. Leaning over the fire, he picked up a burning twig to light his cigarette. Leisurely stretching his legs in front of him as he smoked his cigarette, BoJed continued, "I don't trust you. What would prevent you from riding ahead to warn your kinfolk?"

"I left that valley because I hated it," TJ answered plainly. "But if you want, clean up one of your men so he can ride with me into the valley. If I betray you, he can kill me and ride back to you. No harm, no foul."

A smile twitched on one side of BoJed's mouth. Biting the cigarette in his teeth, BoJed snarled, "You pick the man you want to ride with; we'll wait to hear what you find."

TJ nodded his head. "When do you want us to leave?"

"Not now. We'll all ride together until we reach the edge of the forest, then you can go into the valley with one of my boys."

TJ met the man's eyes, smiling confidently. "If there are any women left in the valley, I'll serve 'em up to you on a platter."

Talia crawled backwards deeper into the forest. Shaking from cold and fear, her mind raced as she thought about her friends still living in the glen. *Somehow I have to beat TJ back to the valley to warn the others.* She slithered down the hill, mindful not to make any sounds. When she felt she moved far enough away from the camp, Talia stood up quietly and ran toward home.

17

JIM'S EXTENDED FAMILY FELT the earthquake but they were protected from its devastation. After the tremor subsided, Miah climbed a fire tower he found and looked across the mountain range. Lying before him were hundreds of miles of unspoiled forest, and in the far distance he viewed the valley.

He sighted the massive crack that split the once-pristine cove. Slicing through the western mountains, the fault cut a U-shaped gash in the meadow and proceeded over the northeastern mountain range. Scanning the vista, Miah could see that Nellie's farm remained intact and another cluster of farms persevered on the fissure's opposite side; but overall, the rest of the farms no longer existed. *God have mercy on those poor souls,* thought Miah.

Miah reported what he saw when he returned to the station. "The earthquake split the valley in two. Nellie's farm sits in one corner and the rest of the farms lie on the other side." Then he added darkly, "Juan's house is gone."

Sara sucked in her breath; a chill ran down her spine; everyone hoped that Juan and Rosa survived. Jim put his arm around Sara's shoulders, motioning for Miah and Beth to come close to them. As the foursome joined hands, Miah said a word of prayer. Afterward Jim mentioned, "Maybe we should go back to the valley to help our friends."

Deliberating for a moment, Sara answered reluctantly, "Someone needs to stay here. We see needy people all the time."

It was true. Despite Jim's efforts to keep a low profile, after the goat rescue story circulated throughout the mountains, people visited them regularly. Mountain people brought whatever they owned—berries, milk, eggs, whatever resources they had to barter—to pay for Jim's medical skills or Miah's mechanical knowhow.

Jim and Miah often gave the food to other families because they met starving people daily. Sara and Jim's household practiced a very relaxed system of commerce based on love and need, not greed and power. Unfortunately, Jim feared one day their compassion would also be their undoing—a band of renegades or looters destroying the station—so he and Miah regularly searched for more secure lodging, somewhere off the traveled roadway.

As Jim looked for better housing, Sara expanded their influence among the mountain people. Before they arrived at the gas station, she knew nothing about medicinal plants. But after finding a botanical reference book in the store and listening to the locals discuss home remedies, Sara quickly learned the names and healing properties of a wide variety of plants. Using this knowledge, she created a section in the store exclusively for herbs to make homemade lotions, teas, and tinctures.

The station became more than a store; it was a one-stop location for basic provisions, medical care, mechanical repair, and daily news. Sara had a variety of dried herbs on hand, so whenever someone stopped by, she always offered them a mug of tea. Every time Sara sat down to drink tea with company, she fondly remembered the old woman in the bookstore, and that memory led to a free lending library in another section of the store.

The station soon evolved into a general meeting place. Although the only outdoor signs marking the former gas station simply read "Groceries" and "Garage," the mountain people now called it "Doc's" or "Doc's Place." Jim tried to tell everybody that he wasn't a doctor, but their neighbors ignored his explanations. After a while, Jim stopped correcting people and simply accepted his new name.

"Hey, Doc, my dog got tangled up with a porcupine; can ya help him?"

"I think my son broke his arm; will you set it?"

And it wasn't just medical calls he received; "Doc, can you help me repair this old rifle?"

Jim always helped. He filled his backpack with hardware, antibiotics, sutures and needles, adhesive glue, bandages, and Sara's various homemade salves and distillates. Whenever called upon, Jim slung the backpack on his shoulders and hiked over mountains to help others. Sometimes he knew what to do and other times he didn't, but what he didn't pick up in the army he learned by actual experience, or just dumb luck.

But Jim wasn't the only one receiving attention; the four shared their talents liberally. Because many children lacked a formal education, Sara and Beth created a school in the back of the store to teach basic reading, writing, and arithmetic. Miah simply solved problems; he became the go-to guy to fix practically anything or assist with odd jobs. Occasionally neighbors just needed a strong back to do some heavy lifting and Miah always helped.

Thinking of their daily tasks, Jim reconsidered his original idea of returning to the lowlands. Yes, they could offer help to their valley friends, but they were also important to their mountain friends. That evening, Jim spoke with Miah, "As much as I'd like to return to the valley, I believe we're needed here even more."

Miah agreed, but added, "I've been thinking a lot about that . . . Doc's Place is special. And the work we do is important," hesitating to choose his words wisely, "but I still want to go to my grandpa's farm this spring; I really wanna find my family. Or at least see if Papaw is still alive."

Jim shook his head, agreeing. "I understand. Juan and Rosa should be here by spring." Seeing apprehension in Miah's face, Jim said, "I don't think they died in the earthquake, Miah. When they arrive, you and I can take a trip to your grandpa's farm. If for some reason I'm busy, I'll bet Juan will go with you; he's always game for a new adventure."

"Really?"

"Absolutely. We're a team, Miah. If your family is alive, we'll find 'em." Jim put his arm around the young man's shoulders, "I love you like you were my own son. Honestly, I can't imagine a better son than you."

Miah replied, "I love you too, Jim." Jim patted Miah's back; nothing else was said but they understood each other. Miah would continue to search for his family and Jim would help him. Jim would do whatever Miah needed, without question. Miah pondered this paradox; he was leaving one family to find another, leaving his adopted dad to find his real one.

⋘⊙⋙

Strangely, after mentioning Juan's name the night before, Jim saw Juan and Rosa ride to the station the next day. He didn't recognize them at first; they were over two miles away, but there was something familiar about the distant shapes. Jim picked up his rifle, holding the weapon easily in his grasp. As the riders talked together, Jim watched their horses shuffle up the road. The couple ambled along at a slow, unthreatening pace.

Suddenly, Jim heard a surprised woof from Happy. The big dog barreled past him, almost knocking Jim over. She ran toward the two riders in her clumsy gait. Panting excitedly, Happy barked so loud that everyone in the station heard her, *"Juan! Juan is here!"*

As soon as Mattie saw Happy race down the road barking, she joined the chase. Quicker than Happy, Mattie rushed past the Newfy to greet Juan and Rosa first. When she reached the riders, Mattie jumped up and down, yipping with delight. Laughing, the couple dismounted their horses and knelt down to pet the dogs. Happy snuffled her nose in Juan's hair, inhaling his scent, crying excitedly.

Juan wrapped his arms around his huge, bearlike dog, "Oh man, it is so good to see you again, Hap!" Happy's tail wagged furiously as she lavishly kissed his face and hands.

Rosa giggled as Mattie licked her face and hair. "Oh, you sweet little dog." Turning to Juan, "Look how big she's grown!"

Juan gazed at Mattie, "Yep, she's a full-grown dog now."

Hearing Miah whistle, Juan glanced up the road to see their welcoming committee. Farthest away, Miah shouted and waved his arms. In front of Miah, Sara and Beth ran so closely together that they looked like a blur of colors and curls. And Jim led the procession with his long legs jogging effortlessly toward them, yelling enthusiastically.

Rosa and Juan stood up just in time to be overtaken by a group of laughing, cheering people. The road was filled with a din of loud voices and barking dogs. Several mountain people joined the confusion, then stepped aside; they wanted to be a part of the excitement but suddenly became embarrassed by their boldness. Not wanting to exclude anyone, Jim introduced Rosa and Juan to their new neighbors. After their greetings, the assembly of people and animals moved slowly toward the store, a jumble of boisterous people and prancing, barking dogs.

Almost immediately, Juan noticed the wedding band on Jim's hand. Pointing to the ring, Juan asked, "Hey, what's this, guy? Did you get married without us?"

Putting his arm around Sara's waist, Jim answered, "Yep, couldn't wait on you. I had to move on this fine woman before she slipped away."

Juan hugged Sara again, "Congratulations, Sara! I'm sorry you have to look at Jim's ugly mug every day, but at least I know he's in good hands." Looking over at Miah, Juan said, "Hey, dude, what did you do?

Gain twenty pounds of muscle and grow two inches taller?" Miah smiled self-consciously as they bumped knuckles.

While the men reconnected with rowdy laughter and jokes, Rosa quietly moved over to Beth and Sara. Noticing Beth's sparkling eyes and radiant complexion, Rosa said, "Beth, you look lovely; the mountain air must suit you."

Beth met Rosa's eyes, "I'm in love," she whispered.

"That's the best beauty treatment in the world," Rosa commented as she glanced at Sara; "just look at Sara's face."

Sara smiled, admitting, "Second chances. I've been given a second chance at love and family."

"Family?" Rosa arched an eyebrow.

"Miah, Beth, and our students are my children now," she said, but added in a secretive tone, "but Jim and I wouldn't mind having our own baby someday."

Rosa held Sara and Beth's hands in each of her hands, "Well, we'll have to pray about that, won't we?" The women smiled and walked hand in hand into the store, talking quietly with each other.

That night at dinner, the conversation covered a wide range of subjects. Miah described the earthquake damage he saw from the fire tower; Sara boasted about Jim's success as a country doctor; Jim bragged about Sara's herbal expertise; and Beth talked about her experiences as a teacher. Juan related some of the trials and mishaps they encountered on their travels through the mountains. As the conversation flowed, Rosa listened quietly to their stories, smiling.

Noticing her stillness, Jim finally placed his hand on hers, "Rosa, what've you been up to?"

Rosa looked calmly at Juan, "I married a wonderful man and we're exploring a strange new world together." Then she looked at each person at the table, "I'm eating a delicious meal with wonderful friends and we'll sleep in a real bed tonight." Everybody laughed because they understood the harshness of travel and the joy of sleeping in a bed after a trip ended.

Pausing to emphasize her next comment, "And I waited for this very special moment to let you know that Juan and I are expecting a baby." Juan stared at his wife dumbly. He widened his large brown eyes, his mouth gaping open.

Juan didn't need to say anything. The room erupted with shouts and applause. Rosa lit up the room with her firecracker smile.

Jim turned to the newlywed bride, "Look at that, Rosa. You're the first person I ever saw take words out of Juan's mouth."

"Is it true?" Juan gasped. Rosa nodded, her cheeks flushed.

Juan stood up quickly, accidentally knocking over his chair. He gathered his young wife into his arms to kiss her. His lips gently caressed her closed eyes, her cheeks, her hands. "My beautiful, beautiful wife," he murmured. He pulled away, looking at her face, "Why didn't you say anything to me?"

"I only had suspicions; remember, my grandfather raised me, not my mother. Anyway, when I described my symptoms to Sara, she gave me a pregnancy test Beth found in the pharmacy cupboard." Rosa gave Juan a flirtatious smile, "I took the test . . . and passed with flying colors! Let me rephrase that: passed with a blue color."

Juan beamed, "A baby." Shaking his head in amazement, "I'm gonna be a father!"

Thinking about the responsibilities ahead, everyone at the dinner table watched Juan's whole countenance change. He stood taller, straighter. He looked at the young woman beside him with open admiration, "You will be such a great mother; our baby is so lucky to have you. I'm so lucky to have you!" He kissed her hands, adding softly, "I love you."

Rosa placed both hands on Juan's face, "I will always love you, mi amor. Now my big, strong man will have another mouth to feed."

"Besides Happy?" he teased.

"Besides Happy."

Juan embraced Rosa, picking her up in his arms so that her feet no longer touched the ground. He closed his eyes, "Thank you, Jesus." When he reopened his eyes, he looked at their friends sitting at the table, quietly watching, listening. Glancing at Rosa's plate, he asked, "Rosa, are you finished with dinner?"

"Yes."

Juan addressed his friends, "Please excuse us. I'm gonna take my lovely wife outside and we're goin' on a little moonlight stroll. We have a lot to talk about."

Jim graciously stood up, looked out a window, and said, "This is a beautiful evening for a walk. Take all the time you need; we'll leave the door unlocked. Come inside whenever you want." As a precaution, Jim added, "Just take your weapon with you; there are a lot of wild animals prowling at night."

Juan grabbed his rifle and the joyous couple left their friends. They walked among stately evergreens and moss-covered rock formations with Happy and Mattie. They talked about probable trials they foresaw in the future but reaffirmed their dedication to each other. They understood the dangers of bringing a baby into this fractured world, but they trusted Jesus and they trusted each other.

Despite their best efforts to avoid pregnancy, Rosa now carried a child—their child, their baby. Realizing the enormity of his new obligations, Juan assured Rosa, "I will always be with you. I'll love you and I'll protect you. I will *die* before anything happens to either you or our baby." Gazing tenderly into Rosa's eyes, "You're my treasure."

Plodding silently behind her master, Happy said to Mattie, *"Juan should not worry. I will not let anyone hurt my family."*

Mattie looked earnestly at her companion, *"I believe you, Happy. I'll protect my family JUST LIKE YOU."* Happy wagged her tail. Thus, having made vows to each other, the dogs padded faithfully behind their companions. Each dog instinctively committed to guard her family and home because, as every good dog knows, people are really just members of their dog pack anyway.

18

Try as she might, Talia could not keep up with men riding horses during the day, but she recovered her mileage in the evening. Exhausted after walking for hours, she usually stayed at least a half a mile away from the gang's campfire. Her only reprieve was that the men usually stopped traveling at dusk, set up camp, then spent the evening drinking and quarrelling.

Talia took advantage of the nighttime hours. Once she located TJ's campfire, she made a bed of fallen leaves or evergreen boughs and went to sleep. Sometimes she continued to walk. Usually she walked past the men's camp and made her bed late at night. She fell asleep later for two reasons: she wanted to elude the outlaw's tracker, and she longed to see her father again.

Although vulnerable, Talia refused to give up. Frigid night temperatures, along with the wind, cut mercilessly through her thin clothes, chilling her to the bone, but she persevered. Because wolves prowled in the dark, she sometimes rested in a tree. Tall trees offered Talia safety from wandering predators but the treetops also exposed her to bracing winds. To minimize this problem, she tied herself to tree trunks with tough kudzu vines, wrapped her arms around her waist, slouched into her coat, and tried to stay warm. Needless to say, she slept restlessly.

Besides fatigue, Talia constantly fought hunger. She gathered nuts and berries to eat when she found them, but most often she ate grass and sedges to fill her empty stomach. As she walked, Talia dreamed of eating bird eggs or small animals, but in the winter birds don't lay eggs and most small animals hibernate in snug dens. To compensate, Talia sucked on icicles or chewed frozen plants to fight her hunger.

Despite these harsh conditions, Talia thanked God for her life because she remembered those who started the journey with her. All the women and children died; the men left; and TJ joined a group of bandits. She escaped the horrors that many in her group suffered, so she pressed onward without grumbling. Although memories of those who died haunted her, Talia's deepest desire was to seek her father's forgiveness.

Is my dad still alive? What will he think of me now? She looked at her half-frozen, chapped hands and her skinny legs, and touched her nappy hair. She wondered, *Will Dad even love me anymore?* When uncertainty overwhelmed her, Talia opened her Bible to reread her father's inscription, "If you ever want to come home, follow this map. It shows you the names of the roads you'll need to take."

She pressed the Bible to her chest, weeping. She wept for the dead children, for herself, for her father: the guiltless, the guilty, the forgiving. Sometimes she read passages from the Bible and thought about Scripture as she walked. Before long, Talia developed a routine that strengthened her: as she hiked, she looked for food; but when she stopped to rest, she read the Bible. Once she resumed walking, she considered what she read and prayed for understanding.

As she walked and prayed, Talia also listened for danger. Within days of traveling alone, Talia recognized the sounds of hunters—those walking on two legs, or four—and she avoided contact with both enemies. Until her fifth day of travel.

Talia heard wild cheering from the outlaws. Hidden behind thick shrubs, she watched as they brought a freshly killed deer into their camp. The smell of roasting venison nearly drove Talia mad as her empty stomach growled incessantly. She stuffed weeds into her mouth to appease her raging hunger. As Talia feverishly gathered vegetation for her bed, she suddenly noticed a strange form in the forest vegetation, a sleeping fawn partially covered by leaves.

When the fawn looked docilely into the teenager's eyes, Talia's hunger vanished. She whispered gently, "I won't hurt you." Remembering the needs of foals and calves, she realized, *You poor little thing. They killed your mother, and you're going to need some milk soon.*

Thinking quickly, Talia yanked thin vines from the soil to weave a simple net. She wrapped the netting loosely around the fawn's body and bound the fragile creature to her chest. Motivated to save a life rather than watch another innocent perish, Talia moved soundlessly through the forest toward her father's home. Choking back tears, the young woman spoke softly, "Jesus, please help me get this little deer to Dad's house before she dies. Please!" Talia slipped into the darkness without any concern for her own welfare, because now the only life that mattered was nestled next to her heart in a primitive sling made of dried vines.

⋐◉⋑

After the earthquake, life changed radically in the valley. Nellie, Toynell, and Brant could sometimes see their neighbors but they would never be able to cross the gigantic fissure that separated their farms. Not only did the fault split the valley, but it continued out of the valley in both directions and over two mountain ranges. The crevasse swallowed many people during the earthquake and now the only survivors left lived either in Mac's cloistered area or on Nellie's farm.

Nellie grieved over lost friends but she still thanked God for sparing lives on both sides of the valley. Nellie could travel to Marshall City or venture up the mountain road Jim's group followed, but she couldn't visit Marcus, Ryan, Mac, or Pastor Greg. Feeling isolated, Nellie expressed her concern with Brant and Toynell.

"Do you want to leave our farm to look for Juan and Jim?" Nellie asked.

Brant rubbed his chin and looked at his wife, "Toynell and I talked about that but we're not ready to leave yet. This is our home."

Toynell nodded her head, concurring, "We have a beautiful farm with healthy animals. We sleep in warm, soft beds every night and there's always something to eat." Lifting her shoulders, "We're blessed."

"I just don't want you to stay here because you feel like you need to take care of a broken-down old woman." A tear ran down Nellie's cheek. "You see, I love you. And you shouldn't take any unnecessary risks for my sake."

Toynell held Nellie's hand, "What risks do you have that we don't already share?"

Nellie answered, "You're right." Counting her fingers, "Raiding gangs, government forces, crazy weather, oddball diseases—take your pick." She paused, "But I wonder . . . does living here make us more exposed?"

Brant smiled. "If current rumors are true, we're living in the last days. Where would we go to hide from disasters?"

Nellie spoke meekly, "Mac and Marcus's co-op might provide more security for us. The fault acts like a barrier to thieves. And our friends work productive farms inside the fault's perimeter."

"I'll tell you what, Nellie: when we feel led to move, I'll follow the fault line through the mountains. If I find an area where we can cross the crevasse, we'll move to Mac's place. If not, we'll take the same road that Juan and Jim traveled. In the meantime, we want to stay here with you."

Toynell added, "Besides, you're not a broken-down woman to us, Nellie; you're like our grandma. We'll be with you until the end, period. You're family. You're one of us. So if we move, we're taking you with us."

Tears welled in Nellie's eyes, "Thank you."

Brant and Toynell wrapped their arms around Nellie to hold her. Nellie simply rested in their arms. After a minute, she sniffed, dried her damp eyes with her apron, and looked at the two young people in front of her. With renewed vigor, Nellie straightened her shoulders, pushed a lock of gray hair off her forehead, and announced, "You know, for a woman that never had any children of her own, I have the kindest, most generous family in the world!"

❧

Across the valley, Marcus spied a strange apparition in the dusky twilight. He saw a tall, spindly person shuffling toward their small community. It looked like a woman. *Maybe a pregnant woman? Or a woman carrying a baby?* Although he couldn't distinguish any specific features, there was something familiar about this person's gait. *I must be dreaming*, he thought; *that woman walks just like Connie!*

Marcus dropped his shovel and ran toward Ryan's son. "Jason, let me have your horse for a few minutes. I see someone coming. I want to ride out there to check 'em out!"

Jason swiftly turned to look in the direction that Marcus pointed. "Sure, take her, Marcus. Do you want me to saddle up another horse to join you?"

"Yeah, but I don't think this person will give us any trouble." Marcus mounted Jason's horse, slid his rifle into the scabbard, swiftly turned the gelding, and dashed down the road toward the stranger.

As Marcus's horse kicked up dust on the road, Talia stopped to watch the rider bearing down on her. When she recognized her father's beat-up cowboy hat, she whispered, "Dad." Talia started to run toward Marcus. She waved, screaming his name, "Daddy, it's me! I'm home!"

Marcus pulled the horse to a sudden stop beside Talia. The horse's front legs plowed stiffly into the dirt. In one fluid motion, Marcus dismounted, letting his reins fall to the ground. The big man picked up his frail child, held her tightly to his chest, and spun her around in a circle. "Talia, you're home! Thank God, you're home!"

With his face wet with tears, beaming a broad smile, Marcus looked into Talia's eyes. "Welcome home, my beautiful baby girl."

Talia collapsed into her father's arms, weeping with joy. "Oh Dad, I never thought I'd see you again. I'm so sorry I left you."

"I watched the road every day. I hoped you'd come back to me." Marcus probed the furry body with his large, calloused fingers. "Hey, what's this little bundle you're carrying?"

"Oh, this is a fawn I found after her mother was killed. I named her Aimee . . . but Dad, she's famished."

"Well, let's get her some food!" Marcus answered heartily. Without effort, the strong man put his left foot into the saddle's stirrup, and swung his right leg over the gelding's back while holding Talia, and Aimee, securely in his arms.

By this time, people rushed down the road to help Marcus. When armed men rode up to Marcus and his daughter, they overheard her say, "Dad, some really bad guys are coming here."

Turning to the men, Marcus ordered, "Double up on guard duty." The men consented; they knew the drill.

"TJ's with them."

Marcus looked sharply at Talia, "Willingly, or as a captive?"

"Willingly."

Marcus paused. He clenched his teeth, adding, "Tell the guards not to trust anyone. Not even people they think they know." The men acknowledged his order with slight nods, but no one looked directly into Marcus's eyes.

Marcus turned his attention back to Talia. TJ's folly wasn't going to steal Marcus's delight of seeing his daughter again. After he noticed mothers cradling babies and roughhousing children join the clutch of people on the road, Marcus introduced Talia to everyone.

The crowd welcomed her arrival. Joyous, Talia laughed and waved. She never expected such a warm homecoming from anyone; certainly not from the father she abandoned, or a group of well-wishers she didn't even know.

She was home; she and Aimee were home at last. Half-starved and exhausted, Talia found her way home to discover her dad *still loved her*. Talia knew she deserved to live in the cold forest eating grass and sleeping in trees because she freely decided to leave the valley; no one pushed her away. *Stupid!*

But when she returned to her senses and came home, she realized her father would always love her, with no strings attached. *Amazing! I don't deserve this kind of love*, she thought. Afterward, she whispered a proclamation that only God heard, "I will never leave my dad, or his God, again. Ever!"

Although food supplies were scarce during the long winter, no one skimped on the meal to honor Talia's return. Mac roasted meat over an open fire pit as women baked rolls in the fire's coals. Jason hauled milk from the icehouse and Ryan returned from the root cellar carrying a wooden crate with carrots and potatoes. One woman even found enough ingredients to bake a presentable blueberry pie. As the cooking progressed, everyone helped carry assorted tables and chairs into Marcus's living room for the banquet.

While they waited, children played hide-and-seek outside in the darkness while parents talked about their families. Teenagers cringed or denied some of the exaggerated stories their parents told, but no one cared too much about the reliability of anyone's story. Parents were just having fun; everyone understood that the bigger the tale, the funnier the story.

Listeners sat on the front porch drinking hot spearmint tea, rocking in chairs or swinging back and forth on a glider. Once dinner was ready, the group shuffled into Marcus's house. Although hungry, they didn't want to lose that rare sense of peace they felt that evening; the playful banter of children, and the amusing stories about those children, blanketed the assembly with good humor.

As a fire snapped in the fireplace, the remnant sat down to eat together. After Pastor Greg blessed the food, Marcus stood up, lifted his glass of milk, proclaiming, "This is a day to rejoice! I'm standing in a warm, dry house, eating with all my friends, and celebrating the return of my lovely daughter. I love you, Tal." Afterward he looked at his guests and opened his arms, "I love all of you." Looking upward, he concluded, "Thank you, Jesus!" And the crowd shouted, "Amen!" amid their loud praises and clapping hands.

The men decided to keep the news of impending danger to themselves for the evening. With so few lighthearted moments in their grinding lives, they wanted to give the women and children time to simply enjoy themselves. People laughed loudly, told stories, sang songs, and prayed together. No one wanted to leave, but as children fell asleep in their parents' arms, families reluctantly left the fellowship to return to their bedrooms spread throughout the cluster of farms.

It was a night to remember, for everyone. For Talia, she remembered her father's love and forgiveness. For Marcus, he remembered the thrill of reuniting with his daughter and the pain of losing his son. For partygoers, they remembered the closeness of friends and the goodness of thanksgiving.

For Pastor Greg, he remembered scripture that described the wedding supper of the Lamb.[1] The pastor encouraged others to endure daily hardships because their eternal hope in heaven far exceeded any temporary pain on earth. Talia's dinner reminded all of them of Jesus's promise of their permanent home in heaven: a land without tears, abounding in love, and filled with joy.

⊷⊙⊙⊶

Early the next day, Marcus found his daughter tending to her fawn in the barn. "How's Aimee doing today?" he asked.

Smiling radiantly, Talia marveled, "Look at her! She eats like a pig. I can hardly hold the bottle steady because she sucks the milk out so fast."

Marcus bent down to examine the small animal. "You know, Tal, I think I'm going to let you take care of all the orphaned babies around here. They need to be fed on a schedule, just like your fawn. I also think you need more experience handling animals."

"Why do you say that?" she asked with false indignation.

"Well, for one thing," Marcus joked, "you need to learn how to identify the sex of an animal."

"Okay . . ." she said suspiciously, "What are you saying, Dad?"

Smiling he answered, "Aimee's a male. *He* needs a new name."

"Really?!" She glanced upward, "Hmm, well, let's see . . . that shouldn't be too hard." Placing a finger on her lips as she thought a moment, "I'll name him Amos. How's that?"

"Sounds good to me."

---

1. Rev 19:7–9.

"Amos is kind of an old-timey name, isn't it?" She looked at the fawn ravenously sucking on the bottle. "Ah, I don't care; Amos is gonna survive. Someday, he'll be big and strong; he'll walk around with his huge antlers and nobody'll push him around."

Watching his daughter, Marcus said, "Well, if anyone can raise a stag, it'll be you." He hugged Talia, "When you finish with Amos, I'll show you the other babies that also need attention."

As Marcus turned to leave, Talia added, "Uh, Dad, before you go, we . . . um, need to talk about a few things." Setting the empty bottle on the ground, Talia stroked Amos's fur as the fawn pushed the empty bottle with his nose. She chewed nervously on her bottom lip.

"What's up, Tal?"

"It's about mom and TJ."

"Okay," he urged, "go ahead."

She blurted, "Mom-was-shot-and-killed-by-a-bad-man-that-rode-into-our-camp-with-his-gang."

Marcus closed his eyes; he exhaled loudly. "Go on," he said reluctantly.

Rather than rushing, she could barely get the next words out of her mouth, "And . . . rather than travel with us . . . TJ joined the gang."

Marcus snapped his eyes open. "TJ joined the same gang that killed your mother?" With renewed seriousness, he asked, "Is there anything else?"

Now she practically mumbled, "Yes, I hid in the bushes to watch TJ in the bad guys' camp. After TJ heard how much the outlaws wanted young women and children for slaves, he agreed to bring them to our valley to help them find more people for trade."

Marcus gazed even deeper into Talia's brown eyes. He spoke slowly, emphatically, "You mean to tell me that my son, my only son, wants to be a slave trader?"

"Yes," she answered with a lump in her throat.

His countenance darkened; fury burned behind his eyes. Inwardly, he vowed, *No one—absolutely no one—under my protection will become a slave.* Marcus blasted out of the barn; his deadly silence amplified the volume of his rage.

19

THE NEXT FEW DAYS provided Juan many opportunities to integrate with others around Doc's Place. Personable and outgoing, Juan made friends wherever he went. Jim enjoyed Juan's company when he visited sick people or ailing animals because Juan carried extra supplies, and recounted endless stories. Juan told his stories to Jim, the mountain people, anybody willing to listen. Privately, Jim doubted the truth of Juan's embellished accounts, but he didn't care; Juan told humorous, outlandish tales that always helped pass the time and broke the ice with shy shut-ins.

Rosa also endeared herself to her new companions. Having lived most of her life on a farm, she understood animal care almost as well as Jim. Whenever Jim was away, Rosa automatically assumed all veterinary responsibilities at Doc's; many times they worked as a team when one set of hands wasn't enough to handle a large animal.

Additionally, Rosa's grandfather taught her how to do everything he did—ranching, hunting, cooking, and cleaning. The lovely Latina could make homemade tortillas, change a tractor's oil filter, or help birth a breached calf. Rosa also played as hard as she worked. Once the local children discovered how accurately she could throw a softball, they begged her pitch for all their games, which she did whenever she had free time.

One week after Juan's arrival, Jim and Juan came home at dusk, ecstatic. "We found it!" Jim exclaimed. "We found a permanent home. It's beautiful!"

"Oh, Rosa, you're not gonna believe this place," marveled Juan. "It's a huge log cabin. A billionaire must've built it, but it's empty now. A gigantic kitchen, a large stone fireplace, eight bedrooms upstairs, and that's just the house. Outside there are fenced paddocks, a massive stable, and a four-car garage."

Jim interrupted, "Not only that, it's on the rim of a mountain, next to an artesian well!"

Juan counted on his fingers, "Secluded, defensible, clean water."

"It's a dream come true, Sara," Jim looked at his wife. "Oh, one more thing . . . the mansion has a large room off to the side. Maybe they used it for entertaining—I don't know—but you could use it for your school, your store, your plants, whatever you want."

"I want you," Sara said simply. "I know you've never been comfortable living on this road." Jim shook his head, *Yeah.* "So I can't wait to see it," she added enthusiastically.

Jim said, "Until today, I wanted to find my army buddies' stronghold somewhere in these hills. But with this new place, we'll have a secure home near our new friends, and far off the beaten trail."

Unaccustomed to seeing Jim so excited, Juan suggested, "Let's take a hike tomorrow. We'll show you what we found."

Everyone agreed wholeheartedly. This was fantastic news: out-of-the-blue, smack-a-homerun-into-the-stands news! This was an answer to prayer.

❦

That night after dinner, Juan smiled at Rosa, "Let's take a little stroll."

Rosa grabbed her coat and mittens as Juan opened the front door. Before he shut the door, Happy squeezed behind Juan to join them on their walk. Watching his dog, he remarked, "I don't think Hap is ever gonna let me out of her sight again. She walks up steep trails with Jim and me every day." He patted Happy's head, "She even runs ahead of us to flush out birds and rabbits, just for fun. Silly dog!"

Rosa stroked Happy's coat. She squatted down, held Happy's big, floppy face, and looked into the dog's droopy eyes, "Happy, you are such a good dog. Always take care of Juan for me, okay?" Happy licked Rosa's face, wagging her tail.

Grimacing Juan said, "Man, Rosa, even I don't have the guts to look Hap straight in the face. She's a drool monster!"

"She's the loveliest creature I ever met," countered Rosa. Turning to her husband with an arched eyebrow, "Is there something you want to talk about in private?"

Juan faced his wife, holding both of her hands, "Honestly, how're you feeling?"

"I'm fine," she answered easily.

"Well, Jim wants to help Miah find his family, but I've watched Jim; he's really needed here. Miah said his grandfather's farm isn't too far away from the Tennessee River. Looking at a map, it'll only take a few weeks to make the trip—"

"And you want to take Jim's place," she finished.

"Yeah, but not until we've moved everyone to a safer location; and not if you need me here."

"Our baby isn't due for a long time and I'm feeling great. Actually, I would love to go with you, but I better stay here. If anything happened to me, or the baby, while you're gone, Sara and Jim would take wonderful care of us."

"So you think you'll be okay until I return?"

Touching his worried face, "Of course, mi amor. Help that fine young man find his family, and come back to me as soon as you can."

Juan pulled his young bride into his arms. As he embraced her, Juan whispered into her ear, "I will always love you. I'll come back to you as soon as Miah gets to his granddad's farm."

Pulling back slightly so she could see his eyes, Rosa asked coyly, "So what are you going to do with Happy?"

At the mention of her name, Hap stood at attention, opened her mouth, and stuck out her tongue. Juan replied, "Umm, I think I'll have to take her with me. We won't move too fast." Juan studied Happy's rugged, muscular build, "I think she'll be okay. She seems to like the fresh air and exercise."

As the couple murmured endearments to each other, Happy smiled. *"I will never leave you, Juan. I will protect you, and guard you, and love you."*

Juan smiled as he looked down at his dog. He could hear Happy grumbling softly as she wagged her tail. Then she started her big dog dance: she rocked back and forth on her front legs while her back legs shuffled in place. *What a funny dog*, he thought aimlessly. *If Hap could talk, I'll bet she'd say all kinds of nice things.*

∽◉◡

After Marcus left Talia in the barn, he promptly found Ryan and Mac to tell them about TJ's proposed plan to disrupt their lives. "I suspect his outfit will be here in a few days, maybe a week on the outside."

"Whatta you want to do?" asked Ryan.

Mac interrupted, "Actually, I already have an idea. I wanted to talk with everyone about constructing a fence on the exposed side of our properties. Since the fault protects most of our perimeter, we only have a couple of miles open to attack."

"What kind of fence are you talking about?" Ryan wondered.

"I don't know . . . maybe just a barbed wire fence to start, but if we keep gettin' attacked, we might want to build a walled fort out of trees."

All three men fell silent as they considered the immensity of this project. A practical man, Marcus suggested, "We need a fence to keep our livestock from wandering all over creation anyway; let's start with barbed wire, and if we need something more substantial, we'll build it."

By this time, Jason, Pastor Greg, and three other men joined the conversation. As they discussed the project, the men calculated supplies they needed to build a fence. The fence posts wouldn't present a big problem because they could cut down trees from the forest; the bigger issue was the availability of wire and staples.

"We might have enough wire for half the fence. But there's a lotta metal roofing that was torn and scattered all over creation after the earthquake," a listener said. "We've been stacking corrugated metal panels in piles for weeks now."

"You know, that's not a bad idea," Mac reflected. "The fence might look weird, but a solid metal fence would confine our animals and create a great barrier against attackers. Let's spend the rest of today gathering hardware, tools, and fencing. We'll meet again tomorrow after breakfast to see what supplies we have on hand. We'll figure out what kind of fence to build." The men agreed and dispersed quickly to begin consolidating supplies.

The next morning, men, women, and children assembled to discuss the fence. Besides barbed wire, hardware, and metal roofing, residents found stockpiles of solid oak pallets, dozens of fallen trees, huge barn timbers, and mountains of rocks and rubble throughout the compound. It was a hodgepodge of building supplies, but everything was sturdy.

One grizzled farmer examined the assorted materials and wiped his brow before he remarked, "Well, it sure ain't gonna be pretty but we can build one tough fence out of this stuff." Knowing that they needed to construct a fence quickly, residents agreed to begin the project immediately using the available salvage.

Erecting a fence from scavenged items gave residents a chance to be creative and resourceful. After establishing the boundary, people built the fence in steps. They filled low areas with rocks, dug holes for fence posts, laid out sheets of metal between the posts, and calculated the amount of barbed wire needed to complete the fence.

After days of moving rocks and digging post holes, builders began to visualize the fence. A gate was positioned in the middle of the fence. On either side of the front entrance gate, they would stretch a barbed wire fence. After using all the wire, the builders would attach long sheets of metal roofing to fence posts. The metal fence would extend to the edges of the fault line.

Anyone flying over the valley would view a compound—almost completely encircled by a precarious cliff—with a small section of fence protecting the land still attached to the meadow. The two-mile-long fence would have sheet metal, on both ends, next to the fault line. Where the metal barrier ended, barbed wire would be attached to fence posts. The barbed wired ended at a center gate made of thick timbers and wooden pallets. So, looking at the oddball fence from left to right, a person would see cliff–metal–wire–gate–wire–metal–cliff; a strange but effective design.

"There should be enough metal and wire to complete the fence from end to end," observed Marcus.

"Yeah, I think you're right," smiled Mac. "This is going to be one *ugly* fence. I can't even imagine what Juan would say if he saw what we're doin' now!"

"Aw, you know Juan. He'd insult our fence every time he saw it. But he'd be the first man up in the morning carrying rocks or the last man at night nailing metal to posts," concluded Ryan.

Looking toward the mountains, Mac said wistfully, "I hope Rosa and Juan are okay." Recounting the timing of their departure, he added, "They just missed the earthquake. Hopefully they didn't get caught in rockslides caused by the tremor." Sighing, "I think of them every day."

"We all do," Marcus said in his deep voice. "Juan and Rosa are more family than my own flesh and blood."

The men eyed each other apprehensively before they walked back to their workstations. No one knew what to say to Marcus. They were constructing this atrocious fence to keep TJ and others like him from hurting their families. No man, especially someone as compassionate as Marcus, should have to endure this reality; yet in these last days, daughters betrayed mothers, wives deserted husbands, sons challenged fathers, and fathers killed sons.[1]

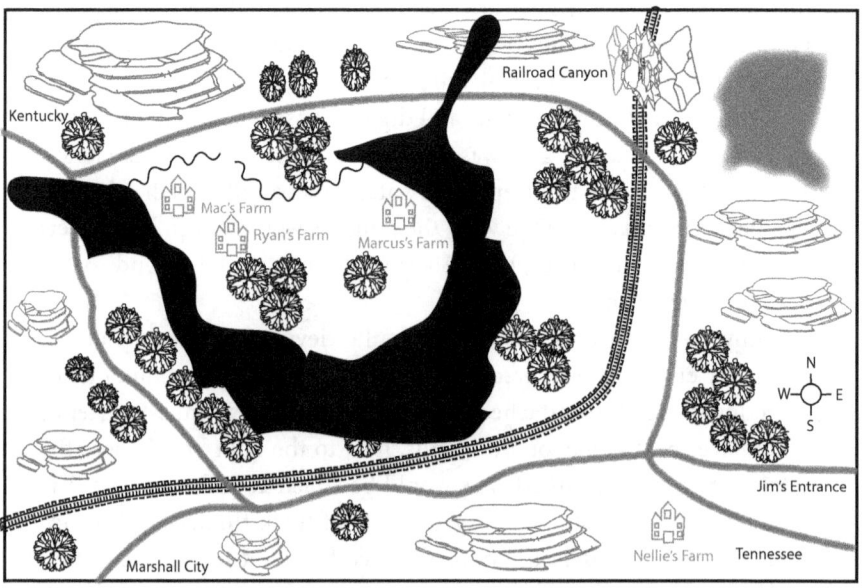

Fortunately for the fence builders, TJ's disreputable company didn't come to the valley as quickly as anticipated. The night Talia found Amos, the outlaw's drunken leader, BoJed, slipped down an outcropping of stones and broke his leg. Several men carried him back to their camp after they heard him screaming for help. They made a splint from a straight branch they found and tied it to his leg.

He did not have a compound fracture but he still couldn't ride a horse well, so without a wagon the party decided to wait in their camp until BoJed could sit in his saddle again. Each man found diversions to stay busy: some men gambled, a few went hunting, one man whittled little figurines, but all of them drank the liquor they stole from unsuspecting victims. With time on his hands, the gang's tracker found something interesting: evidence of another person in the woods, a person that paralleled their route through the mountains.

Concerned, the tracker followed the stranger's trail until he discovered a complex of houses, barns, and fields protected primarily by a jagged

1. Luke 12: 49–53.

fault. He watched people inside the barricade working feverishly on a fence that would prevent an easy approach by invaders. Turning his horse carefully to avoid detection, the tracker returned to camp to report his findings.

"You should see the fence this bunch of hillbillies are building!" the tracker recounted. "Both ends of the fence start at the cliff and they're building toward a gate in the middle." Looking directly at TJ, he continued skeptically, "It's almost like they knew we was comin'."

BoJed stood in the middle of the group, leaning on a crutch made from a stout branch. He hopped on his good leg to a tree, leaned against the tree for support, and viciously struck TJ in the face with his crutch. TJ dropped to the ground, unconscious. BoJed roared, "If this kid warned anybody, he'll wish he died in the earthquake instead of facing me!"

The gang laughed at TJ's expense. They hated the kid. Ever since TJ joined their party, BoJed treated him better than the rest. TJ heard their grumbling insults: "That kid's like BoJed's pet puppy!"; "What's so special about him?"; "He ain't nothin' but a worthless freeloader."

Now the murderers reveled in BoJed's anger with TJ. Maybe they could stoke BoJed's fury by throwing a little kerosene on his fiery temper—always a fun game to play. "Hey, BoJed, have you seen that kid anywhere, or is he out sending messages to his lowland pals?" or "Why does the kid always burn dinner?" or their never-ending gripe, "I think that kid is stealing my tobacco."

It didn't matter what his gang said now; BoJed seethed with rage as his own imagination created lies about TJ. Initially BoJed thought TJ was his ticket to the gala; he was going to use the kid to waltz into a camp of unsuspecting do-gooders. Originally he wanted to kill all the adults, maybe spare a few fine-looking women, and steal the children. Now his gang needed another plan of attack.

BoJed still might let the kid talk to his dad to see if they could get into the farming complex without violence. He wasn't sure what he wanted to do, but he would supervise the kid closely now. BoJed narrowed his eyes as he watched TJ stir from unconsciousness.

TJ fluttered his eyelids as he rubbed his cheek, "What did I do?"

"I don't know yet," snarled BoJed, "but you better watch yourself because your life don't mean nothin' to me."

TJ stood up shakily, dusting off his pants. He lifted his chin in the air and answered insolently, "I didn't do anything!"

BoJed looked at the brash kid in amazement, smiled slightly, and smashed TJ in the mouth with his crutch again.

Spring

20

WHILE TJ LEARNED NEW lessons from lawless men, Miah grew in obedience to God. Everyone trusted Miah explicitly. They explained their needs or problems to Miah and he helped them. The young man was resourceful and intelligent; he shared his natural talents freely, never expecting repayment.

As Jim's group packed to move into the log mansion, Miah sat down to examine an old pedal sewing machine for Rosa. He thought if he could fix the machine before the move, he'd pack it; otherwise, they wouldn't bring it with them. Concentrating deeply on a faulty mechanism, Miah didn't hear soft steps approach him from behind. He nearly jumped out of his skin when Beth cleared her throat.

Startled by her presence, he stammered, "Beth, I . . . I . . . didn't know you were there!" He looked up into her sky-blue eyes, admired her stunning blonde hair, and lost every thought in his head. He couldn't think of one thing to say to the young woman standing in front of him.

Sensing his confusion, Beth touched his hand lightly, "Miah, I'm afraid when you go to find your family, I may never see you again." Still trying to recover from his surprise, Miah looked at her, swallowed hard, but remained dumbstruck.

Smiling, she reached behind her neck with both hands to unclasp her necklace. "Here, take my necklace with you on your trip." She gave him a dainty chain with a small silver cross. "You can put it in your pocket or something, but it will help you remember me."

He closed his hardened hands around the necklace, slipping it into his left shirt pocket. "I'll keep your necklace next to my heart, but there is no way I'll forget you." Finding the courage to say the next few words, "I love you, Beth." He stood up, placed his hands on her rosy cheeks and kissed her lips gently. Afterward, he backed away slightly, "I'll come back to you. As God is my witness, I will return to you."

Beth closed her eyes as she thought about his words. When she reopened her eyes, she promised, "I'll wait for you. I don't care how long you're gone; I'll wait for you."

He continued excitedly, "When I get back, we'll get married; and I promise that I will *never* leave you again." Reconsidering the word 'never,' he stammered, "At least I won't leave on my own free will."

Beth smiled awkwardly, tears in her eyes, "I'm only sixteen. We might want to wait a while before we get married." Glancing at his determined face, she added, "But when you return, I'll be the first one to welcome you home . . . and the last one to say goodnight."

Miah held Beth tightly in his arms as he professed, "Once I find my family, I'll come back to you as soon as I can."

"Good." She paused, then added, "I can imagine a pretty fast trip." Miah smiled; her honesty was one of her many attributes.

Leaving the world behind, the couple sat on the dusty garage floor with their fingers intertwined and simply talked. The two young people discussed Miah's family, his upcoming trip, and Beth's new interests. Minutes stretched into hours, but for two young lovers there wasn't enough time to say everything in their hearts.

When she finally noticed the setting sun, Beth stood up. She promised to help Sara with dinner, so she needed to go. Before Beth left the garage, the couple reaffirmed their love, vowed to wait for each other, and sealed their plans with a lingering kiss.

⁓◉⁓

After helping everyone move into the mountain lodge, Miah and Juan prepared for their trip through the Smoky Mountains. They left on a crisp, early spring morning, probably in March. Everyone understood Miah's need to search for his family but no one cheered their departure. Wrapped in a woolen blanket to buffet the bracing wind, Rosa walked Juan to his saddled horse.

Rosa smiled faintly, "Be safe, my love . . . and hurry home."

Juan embraced his small, strong wife. "I'll be back as soon as I can." He touched her tummy, "You might not even gain a pound before I return."

Knowing Juan's tendency to exaggerate, she smiled and countered with brass, "I doubt that!"

Then Beth broke away from the crowd to approach Miah. In front of everyone, Beth stood boldly on her tiptoes before Miah and kissed him on the lips. "I love you. Take care of yourself," she said.

Although the wind rumpled his sandy hair, Miah calmly brushed the hair away from his face, and kissed her a second time, tenderly. As he held Beth, Miah whispered into her ear, "Start to make plans for our homecoming. I'll be back before you know it."

After some lengthy farewells, the two men mounted their horses and rode away. Happy followed closely behind them with her tail wagging, her tongue lolling out of her mouth. Mattie chased the trio up the road to talk with her big friend.

Confused, Mattie asked Happy, *"Where are you going? What should I do?"*

Hap licked the worried Aussie's nose, *"Do not worry about us, pup; we will be fine. When I come back, I will tell you all about the things I smelled. Maybe next time, you can come with me. Now, you need to go home to take care of our family."*

Mattie sat down dejectedly; she watched the explorers leave the secluded cabin to begin their journey through the mountains. Suddenly, she heard Jim's sharp whistle, her cue to come to him. Mattie turned, stopped, took one last look at her friends, then raced home as fast as she could.

When Mattie came back to the mansion, she saw Beth sitting behind a barn, crying. Crawling on her belly toward the distraught teen, Mattie politely put her nose between her paws, wagging her little tail. Beth looked down at the submissive dog and flung her arms around Mattie's neck.

"Oh, Mattie, I'm going to miss Miah so much!" she cried.

Mattie licked Beth's face and hands to cheer her. *"I'll take care of you. Nothing bad will happen."*

Beth buried her face in Mattie's thick, soft fur. "You're such a good dog." Studying Mattie closely, the pup's inquisitive eyes and eager expression, Beth brightened, "Thank you for coming to see me."

And starting that day, at that precise moment, Mattie became Beth's dog. Mattie went to the barn with Beth, walked with Beth to gather herbs, slipped quietly onto Beth's bed at night to sleep. The two became inseparable. Jim didn't mind Mattie's abrupt change in loyalty; he knew Beth needed a companion and he admired the Aussie's tenderness.

Sara also noticed Mattie's new allegiance but she said nothing to Beth. One night, Sara mentioned offhandedly to Jim, "I see Mattie follows Beth everywhere now."

"Isn't it great?" marveled Jim. "The poor girl was heartbroken after Miah left, but little Mattie stepped in to become her best friend."

Sara simply gazed at her perceptive husband. Amazed by his sensitivity, she wrapped her arms around him, "I love you, Dr. Wilkins."

Jim laughed at her teasing tone, gathered her into his arms, and said, "I love you too, Sara Wilkins." Working in unison, the couple blew out candles and threw more wood in the fireplace. After Jim locked the doors, he walked back to Sara, put his arm around her, and the pair retired for the night.

⁂

Juan and Jeremiah quickly adopted a traveling routine that worked well for them. They rose early, drank some coffee, ate hardtack, saddled their horses, and set out on their trip. Juan usually saved a chunk of meat from dinner for Happy, so while they chewed on hard biscuits Happy devoured meat and biscuits.

Although the men grudgingly ate hardtack, Happy loved the tough biscuits. Hardtack tasted like chew bones to her. Truth be told, the men also imagined that hardtack probably tasted like chew bones, but neither one complained about their food.

They walked the horses at a slow, steady pace so Happy had no trouble keeping up with them. Most of the time, the Newfy ran ahead of the horses to flush game out of the brush. Juan knew when Happy was hunting, so he kept his rifle handy. Whenever frightened birds or rabbits scattered in front of them, Juan usually killed enough food for dinner.

In the evenings, Miah and Juan would talk about hundreds of things. Women, love, faith, dogs, horses—it really didn't matter because they discussed everything. Sometimes they didn't say a word; they just listened to owls hooting or coyotes howling.

One night Miah said, "I have the strangest feeling that we're being watched, Juan."

"Yeah, I felt that way all day. I kept looking over my shoulder thinking that I would see something," he frowned, "never did though."

"Did you notice Happy?" asked Miah.

"Yeah," answered Juan. "She walked stiff-legged with her hackles raised and growled most of the afternoon." Happy lifted her head at the mention of her name, thumped her tail a few times, then resumed chewing on a bone.

As darkness fell and stars blanketed the sky, Miah sat by the warm fire, staring at the heavens. Feeling talkative, Miah began, "What do you think of these strange times, Juan?"

Juan did a double take because Miah rarely started conversations. Juan actually laughed as he patted Happy on the head, "I think we're living in the Bible's tribulation, so I count each year like a dog's birthday."

Miah stared at Juan with confusion, "What . . . ?"

"Yeah, you know how veterinarians say for every year we live, a dog ages seven years?"

"Uh huh."

Juan went on, "Well, to me, it feels like every year since the U.S. fell, I age seven years." The pair chuckled at Juan's ridiculous analogy. "Yep, by the time I'm thirty, I'll have gray hair and wrinkles. I probably won't be any wiser either!"

Just at that moment, Happy stood up and ran to the edge of the firelight. The hair on her back stood up straight; she growled with a ferociousness that surprised both men. *"Get away from my family,"* threatened Happy to the intruders.

"Why should we?" snarled the alpha male wolf. *"You're just an old dog and there are five of us."* The other wolves grumbled in agreement as they crept closer to the firelight, amber eyes glowing. Muscles taunt, senses alert, the pack advanced steadily toward Happy's family without fear of the Newfoundland.

Hearing the growls as the pack prepared to charge their camp, Miah and Juan turned around just in time to see the wolves' profiles. Juan shouldered his rifle in seconds. But just before he took a shot, Miah stood up, raised his arms in the air, and spoke commands in a loud, foreign language that Juan never heard before.

The wolves immediately stopped at the edge of the forest, suddenly quaking with terror. One wolf yelped at the sound of Miah's voice; the alpha male cowered as if Miah beat him with a club. Tails tucked between their legs, all the wolves ran back into the woods, tripping over each other to flee from the terrifying men.

Juan lowered his rifle from his shoulder to stare at the panicked wolves. He swiveled toward Miah but all he saw in the firelight was Miah's dark figure standing steadfast, his hands still raised above his head. Juan stared at Miah in amazement, his mouth gaping open. "Wha . . . ? What was that?!"

Miah turned rigidly to gaze directly at Juan, "I think Jesus demanded that the wolves leave us alone."

"I didn't hear Jesus," Juan disputed. His voice gradually increasing in intensity, "I just heard you, and you . . . sounded . . . scary, bro!"

Still violently shaking with fear, Miah nodded his head, "I felt an overpowering urge to shout in the Spirit, so that's what I did. God's Spirit told the wolves to leave."

Spreading his arms in front of him, Juan exclaimed, "Are you kidding me? We've been traveling together for days, talking about . . . I don't know, everything. Suddenly, when our lives are in danger, you pulled out the big guns, and blew up the whole shebang! Wolves ran away from the sound of your voice!" Trying to comprehend what he heard, what he saw, Juan declared, "Why didn't you tell me about this Spirit-shouting thing?"

"Not everybody wants to hear about gifts of the Spirit."

"Well, I'll tell you what, compadre: you now have my complete attention."

Still agitated, the men moved nervously around their campsite, holding their weapons securely, listening to every sound in the forest. They checked their horses and walked into the woods with torches to make sure that the wolves were gone. After their pulses settled down, they tried to relax but talked incessantly; both knew they were hours away from sleeping.

Aware of Juan's astonishment, Miah walked to his saddle, rummaging through his things to retrieve a Bible. Miah sat on a stump near the fire's glow, thumbed through the New Testament, and began to read Scripture out loud. He found passages in 1 Corinthians where the Apostle Paul describes spiritual gifts. As the Bible opened up another dimension of Christianity, the two men discussed their opinions and compared their ideas to the Word of God. They talked late into the night.

Before retiring, Juan said, "How do you want to handle guard duty tonight?"

Yawning, Miah said, "It doesn't matter to me. I don't think we'll see those wolves again, but there's probably something else lurking in the woods."

At that moment, images flooded Juan's imagination: bears, mountain lions, renegades. He even heard rumors of cannibals prowling the country. He just nodded to Miah, half afraid of the teenager. Juan replied cautiously, "Well, I'm wide awake; I'll take the first watch."

Miah smiled, "Okay. Wake me up when you're tired; I'll take the second watch." Acting as if he chased away wolves every night, Miah tossed more wood on the fire, then spread out his sleeping bag. Miah curled up in his bed and quickly fell asleep.

Juan watched Miah sleep. The Latino had a new appreciation for this young man and an awesome fear of God's power. *The kid spoke some words that scared away a pack of hungry wolves!* Juan pondered with wonder. Considering his earlier conversation about aging like a dog, he randomly thought, *Well, I'd say I aged three years tonight.*

Juan wrapped a blanket around his shoulders, leaned his back against a tree trunk, and listened carefully for snapping limbs or crunching leaves. He glanced over at Happy. He smiled as he heard to her muffled woofing and watched her feet wiggling. *Chasing rabbits*, he thought nonchalantly. In his quiet surroundings, Juan prayed for continued protection over all his loved ones. He thanked God for his divine intervention, humbly asking for a greater understanding of the spiritual gifts Paul described in the New Testament. But unlike Happy—presently entertained in her own dream world—Juan knew he wasn't too old to learn new tricks.

21

As the barrier fence neared completion, Mac looked at the horizon and spotted a dark figure walking toward their encampment. Thinking it might be TJ, Mac whistled and pointed out the figure to Marcus, who was patrolling the area on horseback. Marcus quickly rode out to the lone traveler. He discovered it was not TJ, but Brant.

Brant waved and grinned with his usual friendliness; Marcus beamed. Sliding off his horse, Marcus stepped over to the young man, giving him a powerful hug. "What are you doing in our neck of the woods, Brant?"

Removing his wide brim hat to wipe his brow, Brant replied, "Just touching base with you guys. I found a narrow passage over the fault a few miles away, so I jumped over the crack to see how you're doing." Looking at the barbed wire and corrugated metal fence, Brant pursed his lips discreetly, "It looks like you've been busy."

Putting his hand on Brant's shoulder, Marcus answered, "That's an understatement." Gathering his horse's reins, Marcus walked beside Brant to explain the reasoning behind their construction project. Marcus also answered Brant's personal questions about his family. "Talia lives with me again. I know she's going to want to hear everything about you and Toynell."

Brant nodded, "Talia's a good kid; it'll be great to see her again." Shaking his head in disbelief, "I'm sure sorry to hear about TJ, but if there's anything I can do to help you, just let me know."

"Will do," said Marcus, forcing the image of TJ out of his mind.

By this time, everyone came out on the road to greet Brant. Marcus introduced Brant to those who didn't know him yet. Men took off their leather work gloves to shake Brant's hand; women, wanting to look a bit more presentable, used aprons to wipe sweat off their brows; and young children eagerly watched the grown-ups from behind their mother's legs. As an escaped refugee, Brant was a newcomer to valley old-timers, but he was a familiar face to other escapees, and his former friends received him warmly.

After the excitement of his arrival ebbed, Brant sat down with a few people to talk. "Listen, we need to think . . . since we can see our farms across the canyon, we should find a way to communicate without spending a day walking. Any ideas?"

"Do you know Morse code?" asked Mac.

"No, but it's a simple code of dots and dashes, right?" responded Brant.

"Yep."

"I programmed computers with ones and zeros, so I can figure out codes made with dots and dashes. Just gimme a codebook to decipher your messages."

Jason's face suddenly lit up, "Hey, I have an old Boy Scout manual in our house. It has the entire Morse code alphabet! I'll go home and look for the book; I think it's somewhere in my closet." The teen got up and raced toward his house.

Under his breath, Ryan conceded, "This may take a while, fellas. Jason's closet is a nightmare."

"Ah, that's okay," replied Brant; "we have plenty a time." Thinking logistically, he added, "Once we have the codebook, maybe we could use flashlights to send messages. Does anyone have a spare flashlight and batteries? Because I sure don't."

"I think I can help you with that," remarked a grandmotherly listener. "Let me go home and rummage through my junk drawers." Looking at Ryan, she confessed, "If you think Jason's closet is a nightmare, you would lose your mind if you saw the drawers in my kitchen. But don't worry; I'll find what you need." With that assurance, she left the group to search for batteries and a flashlight hidden deep within the confines of her junk drawers.

Enjoying the camaraderie, Brant sighed, "I really wish, Toy, Nellie, and I could talk with you like this every day."

"Why don't you move over here with us, Brant. There's plenty of room to build another house on the property," suggested Marcus. Everyone listening agreed.

"I'll tell Toynell and Nellie that we're welcome here, but right now our fields are ready for tilling and the cows are having babies." Everyone understood Brant's rationale because in between working on the fence they also had planting and birthing concerns.

"Well, let's get some supplies for you to take back home," offered another woman. "What time are you going back?"

Before Brant could answer, Marcus interrupted, "Why don't you have dinner with us, sleep at my house tonight, and return to your farm tomorrow? By then, we should have ample food and supplies gathered for you. I'd like to walk back with you so you can show me where you crossed over the fault."

"Sounds good!" said Brant. "I told Toy that if I wasn't coming home tonight, I'd build a fire near the edge of the cliff and I'd wave to her."

"That's a great idea!" marveled Marcus. "Let's build a bonfire tonight, roast some food over the fire, and we'll all wave to Toynell and Nellie. We have a pile of branches and broken pallets left over from the fence that need to be burned anyway. We'll just make a party out of it."

So that's exactly what they did. Residents stacked all discarded wood from the fencing project—splintered timbers, unusable oak pallets, and branches from fallen trees—until the pile of wood look like a small mountain. Using brown pine needles for kindling, they started a blaze and fanned the flame into a raging bonfire. They charred meat over the flames and baked side dishes in Dutch ovens banked in the coals; cooking over an open fire was second nature to everyone now.

When a little boy saw two people standing on the other side of the crevasse, he yelled, "There's Toynell and Nellie!" The entire crowd within the compound stood along the fault's edge, staring intently. From their vantage point, they spied two tiny silhouettes over a mile away straight across the precipice. Everyone at the party waved their arms, clapped, and shouted. Nellie and Toynell jumped up and down, waved, and whistled back to their friends.

Communicating with others overjoyed Toynell and Nellie. They were no longer isolated! They could converse with others again, and they relished that connection.

As he watched the two women across the ravine, Pastor Greg suddenly had an idea. "Brant, when you return home, why don't you take my shofar with you?"

"What's that?" asked Brant.

"It's a ram's horn. Israelites blew a shofar when they wanted to call an assembly or warn people of danger. During daylight hours, we might not notice you sending Morse code with a flashlight, but we'd sure hear a shofar blasting across the gorge."

"So if I need to send you a message during the day, I'll blow the shofar first?"

"Yeah. Once you have our attention, you can send us a message with your flashlight."

"You wouldn't mind giving me your ram's horn?"

"Not at all," assured the pastor. "That's what the shofar was designed to do. I'll go home and get it for you."

As Greg turned to go home, someone in the crowd asked, "Hey, pastor, is your shofar in a cluttered closet or junk drawer?"

"No," smiled Greg, unfazed by the ribbing, "I know exactly where to find it." Turning aside, he left the group to retrieve his horn.

Marcus spoke loudly to get everyone's attention. "Arright," he said as he looked around the gathering, "tomorrow Brant will show me where he can jump over the ravine. Does anybody else wanna go?" Before anyone answered, Marcus held up his hand, "Wait a minute," he glanced at Brant, "what time do you want to leave?"

"I'd like to be on the road by 7:00," answered the young man.

Marcus continued, "Anybody that wants to walk with Brant and me should meet at my house before 7:00 tomorrow mornin'."

Brant added, "If others want to go all the way back to our farm, we should bring a sheet of plywood or a couple of wide planks to act as a bridge across the fault."

Several men and women volunteered to accompany Brant for the entire trip. They wanted to visit with Nellie and Toynell, maybe even explore the valley after the earthquake. Brant was excited to bring others with him; he knew both Toynell and Nellie would be thrilled to see their friends again. After the group discussed their morning plans, they settled around the bonfire to eat dinner, watch the stars, and talk.

⌒◉◉⌒

After a particularly challenging day of travel, Juan and Miah studied the same stars and galaxies as their friends in the valley. The sky seemed alive with falling stars. "Maybe it's because I grew up in the city, but I'll never get used to looking at the night sky," revealed Juan. "We're so small—"

"And God's so big. Right?"

"Yeah. Why would the Creator of heaven and earth die on a cross for someone like me?" Juan said quietly, stirring the fire with a stick. He threw another log onto the coals.

"Love," answered Miah simply. Staring at the fire, thinking out loud, "He gave his only Son to die for us. Can you imagine that kind of love?"

Juan answered honestly, "No." He couldn't do it; he couldn't sacrifice his baby for someone he didn't know. He couldn't sacrifice his baby for all the bad people he knew, or even the nice ones.[1]

"Neither can I," admitted Miah. "I know it's true but I can't get my head around that much love. I just accept it, but I sure can't explain it."

A few minutes passed without either man saying a word. Eventually, Juan broke the silence, "You know, you're an odd guy, Miah. You look like a regular teenager but you talk like an old man."

Miah chuckled, "Maybe it's your 'dog age' theory. I spent the last few years being overwhelmed or mystified by life, then Nellie gave me a Bible to read. When I read it, the puzzle pieces started to fall together. It changed me. All of a sudden, I understood the most peculiar things; I became an old man overnight." The young man threw Juan a lopsided grin. "I may look seventeen but I'm really forty-five."

Juan laughed, "Okay, you're aging like a big dog! Hap is fourteen years old but a vet told me she's like . . . one hundred in dog years." When she heard her name, Happy stood up, walked over to Juan, and nudged his hand. Juan patted her head, looking at her with admiration, "You're my pal, Hap." Happy wagged her tail, then she lay down again to pull cockleburs off her coat.

Miah sat down on a log as he stared into the fire. "I wonder how much dogs understand us."

"I don't know but Hap knows I love her, and Happy loves *everybody*." Juan petted her husky frame again, "I'm glad she came with us."

"Yeah, me too."

The men became quiet again, listening to the crackling fire, watching sparks drift upward. Thinking about their trip, Miah brought up tomorrow's journey, "Before it got dark, I noticed that we're just a few miles away from the Tennessee River. You can see the river from that mountaintop over there," he gestured.

Juan poured himself another cup of coffee, warming his hands on the steel mug. "How far is your granddad's farm from the river?"

---

1. John 3:16.

Shaking his head, Miah answered, "Not very far, maybe five or ten miles. My family used to travel this road when we went to Papaw's. I know where we are."

Juan looked down the road, "Good." Contemplating the river, Juan asked, "How are we going to cross the water?"

"Well, hopefully the bridge is still intact; otherwise, we might need to find a boat to get across."

"So we'll cross that bridge when we get there?" joked Juan.

Miah rolled his eyes, "Oh man, that's terrible!"

Raising his hands in mock surrender, "No arguments there." Tossing his sleeping bag near the fire, Juan said, "Let's get some sleep. I want to cross that river as soon as we can. First thing tomorrow, if possible."

Miah checked on their horses again; afterward, he sat on a stump with his rifle across his knees. "If we rent a small boat or canoe, we'll have to stable the horses on this side of the river for a few days." Giving Juan a sidelong look, "Do you have a lame cliché about stabling horses?" challenged Miah.

"No," Juan replied quickly, "but I'm still waiting to say, 'Let's head them off at the pass!'"

"Sheesh!"

22

THE NEXT MORNING, MIAH and Juan set off. When they reached the top of the hill, they looked at the Tennessee River but neither man spoke. Over half a mile wide, the burgeoning river moved swiftly with water from the spring runoff. Their eyes followed the road leading to the river; finally Juan exhaled.

"No bridge," Juan said heavily. "And that's a huge river."

"It is," Miah answered gravely. In all the years he visited his grand-dad, he never saw the water level so high or flowing so rapidly. Maybe something happened to the dam upriver.

Juan confessed, "You should know that I never learned how to swim. I hate open water." Taking a deep breath, he pointed straight ahead, "Look. PeaceKeepers are checkin' everyone's papers before they can get on a ferry."

Glancing downstream, Juan suggested, "Let's see if we can find a boat farther away from the sentries. Maybe we can negotiate a ride without government interference." Looking at Miah, he advised, "Lower your hat over your forehead and keep your leather gloves on. We don't need to stir up any trouble with the New Order troops."

Following Juan's directions, Miah adjusted the brim of his Stetson and slipped on his leather gloves. Both men hunched down in their saddles, looking at the ground, plodding listlessly down the road as a pair of dejected refugees with an old dog. Fortunately, there were still a lot of people fleeing cities, so Miah and Juan appeared as harmless and inconspicuous as hundreds of other homeless wanderers riding skinny donkeys and horses.

They rode along the shoreline for a mile downstream from the bridge until they found a ferry without troops standing guard. Wanting to discuss their fare, Juan dismounted to approach the vessel's captain.

Partially obscured by deadwood and beach shrubs, Miah stayed behind with the horses and Happy, watching closely.

Walking confidently over to the ferryman, Juan started to negotiate with bravado, "I have two passengers, two horses, and a dog that need to get across this river. How much do you want?"

Grinning, with a set of rotted teeth, the calculating man sneered, "Whatta ya got to trade?"

"I have two coins," began Juan, flashing a silver dollar, "I'll give you one when we start, and you'll get the other when we get safely across the river."

"No can do, mi amigo," the ferryman said curtly. Opening his arms expansively to flaunt his disreputable, rotting ferry to Juan, "I don't like to get my ferry dirty with Mexican deportees."

Juan stepped forward, inches from the man's face, stared at him with steely eyes, and said through clenched teeth, "I am a United States Army sergeant."

Not backing down, the ferryman countered rudely, "Technically, there is no United States anymore."

"There's no Mexico either but that didn't stop you from talkin' trash." With a calm but deadly edge, Juan said, "Take us across the river now or your last breath is moments away."

"Says who?" countered the man.

"Says me, and my loaded Glock." Juan jammed a pistol into the man's stomach, waiting for a response.

The ferryman hissed, "Where'd you get a gun?"

"It doesn't matter," growled Juan in a quiet voice. "Do we have a deal?"

"Yeah, we have a deal," the man decided grudgingly. He broke eye contact with Juan and walked across the ferry's greasy floorboards. He began to pull a thick rope attached to a post on the pier, letting the rope wind around his scuffed, worn boots.

Juan waved Miah over to the ferry. With Happy in the lead, Miah led their horses onto the rickety watercraft. Before they cast off, the ferryman asked greedily, "So where's those coins you talked about?"

Juan fished around in his pocket, never taking his eyes off the ferryman. He took out one coin, holding it in front of the thief's face. "Here's a dollar now; you'll get another when we reach the opposite shore," Juan repeated, still itching to kill the man.

As if he didn't want Juan's money, the man scoffed in disgust. In reality, he was impressed to see the rare silver dollar. One ounce of silver was worth at least one hundred digital coins, but a Morgan, an old Morgan, was worth twice that amount on the black market. He usually earned a chicken or homemade preserves for his trouble, but not today. Today, he was going to score big.

He wouldn't haggle with Juan because he had another plan. While Juan and Miah secured their horses onboard, the sleazy captain motioned to his partner. The extra man quickly jumped onboard, moments before the ferry departed. Three quarters of the way across the river, the ferryman stopped his boat. With a malevolent grin, the ferryman pulled out what looked like a Hi-Point .45, and pointed it at Juan and Miah. "Okay, cabrón, gimme the rest of your cash. All of it."

Anticipating a double cross, Juan quickly responded with supple, decisive movements. He ducked down, grabbed an extra oar, and knocked the captain off the boat. The captain fell into the cold rushing water, and floated swiftly downriver. Retrieving the .45, the ferryman's accomplice tried to shoot Juan but Juan kicked him in the stomach. As the man bent over, wheezing with pain, he reflexively discharged his weapon into the boat. The fight ended abruptly when Juan shot the accomplice in the head with his Glock.

Unfortunately, gunshots caught the attention of government soldiers on the shore behind them. Pointing to the stranded ferry, a commander ordered his soldiers to fire upon the boat. With wood splintering all around them, Miah crawled frantically to the ferry's steering assembly, restarted its engine, and pushed the accelerator to full speed.

Despite Miah's rapid response, a constant barrage of bullets quickly splintered the already flimsy ferry. The horses died rapidly from gunshot wounds. Miah lay on the floor of the ferry's remaining bulwarks to guide the boat with a hand tiller. Unfazed by slivers of wood piercing his hands and legs, the young man kept his eyes on the shore in front of him. Juan threw himself on top of Happy to protect her from the incessant pummeling of bullets but the assault was unrelenting. Fortunately, the dead horse's bodies blocked the bullets from hitting Juan; otherwise, he never would've survived.

When the pulverized ferry started to sink, Miah screamed as loud as he could, "Juan, grab a life jacket or hold onto a plank of wood! The boat's not gonna make it to shore!"

But it was too late to grip anything. Juan sank into the icy current, gasping for breath, flailing his arms frantically. Bullets followed him into the depths, but the shells swiftly lost accuracy and velocity in the water.

At this point, bullets didn't matter anymore; Juan was drowning. To save himself, Juan kicked his feet and flailed his arms, but all he did was fill his mouth with more water. He managed to reach the surface once for a few seconds, looked around wildly, but he couldn't find anything to grab. In his panicked state, Juan heard a woman's voice say, "Be still, Juan; I will save you." Juan felt a tug on his shirt collar, then passed out.

Juan vaguely remembered Miah pulling him out of the river. With extraordinary strength, Miah threw Juan over his shoulders and ran into the forest. Harassed with government troops on their heels, Miah rushed through the forest, still carrying Juan, until he ran into a granite wall. Panting, Miah screamed, "Lord, save us!"

Suddenly, Miah noticed a split in the granite wall. He pushed Juan into the shadowy crack and wedged himself between Juan and the encroaching troops. Realizing that the crack widened, Miah kept shoving his friend deeper into the fissure. Before long, Miah realized the crack led to a cave. With one last thrust, practically a bone-breaker, Miah pushed Juan through the entrance, and then wedged himself into the dark enclosure.

Miah sat motionless as he listened to the soldiers track their trail. Once troopers reached the forbidding granite landscape, all traces of Miah's steps vanished on the rocky surface. The guards prowled the area extensively but they never found the cave entrance, or the fugitives.

Finally, a lieutenant declared, "They're not here. Sergeant, take your men to the other side of this mountain to continue your search. They're probably a mile ahead of us by now! Get moving!" The men broke away from the steep rock walls, dividing into two separate groups; they hunted for tracks on the ground or broken branches that would lead them to their quarry but, to their disappointment, the trail turned cold.

Miah relaxed his posture and looked at Juan. Amazingly, Juan was still alive. With his teeth chattering, Juan shivered from the cold but he was breathing. Just as he started to relax, Miah heard a noise outside the cave entrance. Grabbing a large stone, Miah pulled his arm back to throw the rock when he recognized a big, shaggy face looking into the cave.

"Happy," Miah whispered. Taking her time, Happy squeezed into the cave. She wagged her tail rapidly when she saw Miah. After Happy snuffled the ground briefly, she stepped over to Juan to sniff his hands and face.

"We need to warm up our friend, Hap," Miah said as he removed most of Juan's wet clothing. Instinctively, Happy dried Juan with her tongue while Miah furiously rubbed the quivering man with his hands. Miah was also freezing but it was too dangerous to start a fire; he didn't want to attract the guards' attention, or asphyxiate them in the cave.

Body warmth, Miah thought. Miah removed his saturated clothes. He grimaced several times as his clothing snagged on wood chips embedded in his face, hands, and legs, but his discomfort was minor compared to Juan's low body temperature. Once Miah draped the garments over rocks to dry, he encouraged Happy to lie on top of him and Juan.

Although displeased with this awkward arrangement, Happy eventually relaxed enough to fall asleep. As the shaggy dog snored, Miah smiled to himself when he considered their situation: he and Juan were nestled under a 130-pound dog that woofed and wiggled while she dreamed. Despite the discomfort of sleeping under a hefty wet dog, he reflected with admiration, *Thank God for Happy; she saved our lives today.*

The next morning, Juan opened one eye, thinking, *Am I in heaven?* It was too dark to see much but Juan changed his mind, *No, this can't be heaven because it smells like a wet, moldy rug.* He tried to focus his eyes, thinking, *Who's sitting on my chest?* "Hello?" he groaned feebly.

"Hey, Juan, welcome back to the world of the living!" Miah's voice rang cheerfully inside the tight quarters.

Trying to shift under the weight, "Man, you covered me with the heaviest, smelliest blanket in the world. Did you kill a buffalo or something?"

"No, buddy, that's your guardian angel, Happy. Come here, Hap," Miah patted a hand on his thigh; the big girl stood up stiffly, shook her head, throwing slobber everywhere, and turned around to look at Juan. Before Juan could say anything, Happy gave him a sloppy kiss on the lips.

Juan sat up quickly, wiping his mouth with both hands. "Ugh, Happy, God love ya, I'm not Rosa." Looking around their restricted quarters, Juan presumed, "I'm guessing there's a good story behind this place."

Happy just stood next to Juan, wagging her tail. *"I am so glad you are alive, Juan!"* Hearing Hap's groans, Juan petted his panting dog, barely able to see Miah through the shadows.

"What happened?" groaned Juan. "The last thing I remember was looking up . . . and seeing the surface of water way over my head."

"You bobbed to the top a couple of times; Happy grabbed you by the collar with her teeth and swam to shore with you," answered Miah. He added solemnly, "She saved your life, Juan."

Amazed, Juan studied Happy. He glanced at Miah, gauging whether or not he should say anything more, but ultimately decided to elaborate his experience. "You wanna hear somethin' weird? I *swear* I heard a woman tell me that she was gonna save me." Happy wagged her tail, smiling with her long tongue hanging out of her mouth.

Miah scratched his head. "There wasn't anybody close to you; maybe you just dreamed you heard a voice."

"Yeah, that must be it. It's hard to say what your mind does when you're gulping water instead of air." Glancing around the small cave, Juan noticed his clothes spread out on some rocks. Realizing that he was just wearing underwear, Juan reached over to grab his clothes. He got dressed in a prone position because the cave was too low to stand up straight.

"So how did we get into this little cave?" Juan asked.

Miah described their escape from government troops in detail. After he finished, Miah added, "We don't have very much, Juan. We lost almost everything in the river: the horses, our money, even our food."

Juan stood up unsteadily, crouching slightly to avoid bumping his head on the cave's ceiling, and leaned against a rock wall. "Yeah, but we didn't lose our lives, my friend." Smiling down at his dog, "And we didn't lose Hap either." Shaking his head in bewilderment, "I can't believe this old dog rescued me from drowning; she must have the biggest, strongest heart in the world."

"That she does," agreed Miah. "We couldn't have asked for a better scout." Concerned, Miah asked, "What do you feel like doing today?"

"Honestly? I feel like getting as far away from the river as possible."

"We can do that," smiled Miah. "We're less than ten miles away from Papaw's house. We can walk the rest of the way, if you're up to it."

Waving his hand forward, Juan prompted, "I'm game. Let's get out of this cave. I need to catch a breath of fresh air anyway." Leaning over to whisper in Happy's ear, "First chance I get, I'm gonna get you the fattest, juiciest bone you ever saw." Knowing how much starving people valued bones, he continued, "If anyone asks why I'd give such a big bone to a dog, I'll just say, 'Because Happy's more than a dog; she's my hero!'" Although Juan believed Happy couldn't understand a word he said, he knew she was glad to see him alive.

In response to Juan's attention, Happy danced in place. Resuming her role as expedition guide, she squeezed through the narrow cave opening first. Miah and Juan followed Happy and the three intrepid travelers began the last leg of their journey.

23

WHILE JUAN AND MIAH walked in the Smoky Mountains, a small contingent of valley residents visited Nellie's house. In the morning, they walked with Brant to Nellie's farm; later, they spent the afternoon visiting with Toynell and Nellie. A few men ventured into the surrounding fields to gather scrap metal, usable lumber, and hardware thrown helter-skelter by the trembling earth.

The biggest find occurred in the late afternoon. The men located several groups of stray horses and cattle that survived the earthquake. The stockmen slowly herded the animals back to Nellie's farm, leading the livestock into fenced paddocks. They gave Brant some of the animals to add to his own herds. The men pledged to return in a week to take the remaining stock back to their community on the other side of the fault.

The following morning when they left, a rancher explained, "Before we return for the horses and cattle, we'll build a little bridge to lay over the gorge."

Nellie gave the man a questioning look. "How big is this gorge?"

"It's less than two feet from both sides of the crack, so we don't need a *long* bridge; we just need a wide bridge with solid wood sidewalls. If animals looked down and saw how deep the hole was, they'd freak out. We'll lead them across single file. They can walk casually on a solid wood bridge without knowing what's beneath them."

"Actually, that's a relief to me too," replied Nellie. "I don't think I'd want to even jump two feet over a deep crack."

Reminiscing, the man scratched his chin, "Yeah, the jump is a little unnerving but you won't have to worry about that. When we come back to your house next week, the bridge'll be done. When you visit us, you can walk down the middle of the planks without looking over the sidewalls."

"It's a deal," Nellie exhaled with relief. "I hate heights."

എൕൟൟ

Although drained from their travels, Juan, Miah, and Happy felt revital-
ized when they found Papaw's farm. A half a mile from their destination,
Miah pointed to the entrance of his granddad's property. "There it is!"
remarked the young man triumphantly. "And look, there's a lot of activity
going on down there."

Miah saw dozens of people moving about the barnyard: men carrying logs on their shoulders, a small boy clutching a duck, two women
talking while they ground flour. It looked like a storybook drawing of life
during the eighteenth century.

"Wait a minute," cautioned Juan as he pulled Miah into some cover
bushes. "Do you know any of these people? Are they friends or strangers?" Miah squatted beside Juan; he understood Juan's apprehension.

Miah studied the activity closely. After a moment, he exclaimed
excitedly, "Friends! Family! I think I just saw my baby sister!" Without a
moment's delay, Miah stood up from their hiding place and started to run
the last stretch of road to his grandpa's farm.

Juan and Happy walked faster but they didn't hurry; Miah needed
some time alone with his family. In truth, Juan didn't want to overex-
tend Happy's strength. Regardless of her upbeat personality, Juan noticed
lately that Happy sometimes stumbled with weariness, even on short
travel days, yet she seemed even more unsteady after her strenuous swim
across the Tennessee River. Her age concerned Juan but now that Happy
detected a favorable change in the men's attitudes, she trotted beside Juan
with renewed vigor.

Juan patted her head, "We're here, big girl, but remember to mind
your manners. I'll make sure you're treated like a queen!"

As Juan talked casually with Happy, Miah ran into his granddad's
yard, waving his arms, shouting and whistling to announce his arrival.
Papaw ran outside carrying a shotgun but when he spied his tall, handsome grandson, he shouted, "Jeremiah! As I live and breathe. I never
thought I'd see ya again!" The two embraced each other warmly. Miah
lifted his grandfather off the ground in a loving squeeze while his granddad whooped a hair-raising yell.

Running as fast as her chubby legs would carry her, Miah's three-
year-old sister, Nora, wailed, "Mia, Mia!" She reached up longingly to
her brother. Jeremiah released his grandfather to pick up his little sister.

Tossing her in the air and catching her, the little girl squealed with ecstatic delight. "Mia ees 'ome," she garbled in her near English language.

"That's right, little bug, I'm home!" Holding his sister straight out in front of him, "Look at how much you've grown, Nora! Where did you get that black curly hair and those rosy cheeks? Last time I saw you, you were a chunky little baby with fuzzy hair!" Miah hugged his sister tightly again while Nora giggled in his arms.

"I reckon it's been awhile since you'ns seen each other," said Grandpa scratching his long white beard.

"It's been over a year," replied Miah. "How did Nora even recognize me?"

"I'm more surprised that *you* recognized *her*," his grandpa said. "As far as Norabelle knowing you, that's easy." Tossing his wrinkled hand in the air, "Pshaw, I been showin' her pictures of you ever' night. She knows all about 'cha."

With a cockeyed smile, Miah responded, "That means I'll have to straighten her out later, doesn't it, Papaw?"

His granddad laughed, "I tol' her some of the wildest tales you can imagine." Tapping the tip of Nora's nose softly with his index finger, "But that's what grandpas do when little girls don't go rat to sleep."

"Yeah, you probably shook her up so much she never wanted to sleep!" said Miah knowingly.

The old man's eyes crinkled with mischief, "Well now, you can put her to sleep tonight with all yer boring old stories about fixin' machines or choppin' down trees." Stretching his back, "I arready feel a yawn coming on me now."

Miah arched his eyebrows in fake surprise as he looked at his grandfather. At that moment, he saw Juan and Happy enter the front gate. Rushing over to his companions, Miah said, "Papaw, I want you to meet my good friends: Juan Peña and his dog, Happy."

"Pleased to meet'cha," said Grandpa. The men smiled at each other, but didn't shake hands. Juan understood that shaking hands was kind of a valley thing. Papaw stroked Happy's shaggy coat; she looked a bit disheveled with cockleburs and twigs tangled in her fur, but Papaw didn't care. "That's a mighty fine dawg ya got thar."

"Yeah, she is," smiled Juan proudly. Happy sat next to Juan, enjoying all the attention.

"Does yer dawg like other dawgs?" Papaw asked.

"She likes everybody, people or dogs; it doesn't matter to Hap," answered Juan.

Papaw nudged Juan with his elbow, "Have I gotta surprise for ya'll. Folla' me." Walking with an arthritic limp, the old man led Miah, who was still holding his sister, Juan, and Happy into a dilapidated barn. "Now if ya listen real close, ya'll hear 'em," lured Papaw.

Juan and Miah strained their ears but heard nothing. Happy, on the other hand, looked up with renewed interest, bounding over to a secluded corner of the barn. There in a nest of straw lay two Border Collie pups moaning in their sleep.

Unable to contain her joy, Happy just looked at the adolescent puppies, her droopy eyes watering. *"Oh my,"* panted Happy, *"baby dogs!"* As her tail furiously fanned the air, the big dog immediately started to lick the puppies' bodies.

Astounded, Papaw remarked, "Golly Bill, a couple licks with that big ole tongue and them pups is clean!"

Shaking his head, Juan remarked, "That's the best present you could ever give Hap. She'll ignore dinner, a belly rub, even a bed by your toasty fire if it meant she'd have to leave these pups."

Lying gently next to the bed of straw, Happy continued to clean the puppies with her warm, soft kisses. When the puppies woke up, they instinctively nuzzled their noses into Happy's furry coat. One puppy walked around in tiny circles on Happy's tail, made a bed in the Newfy's fur, then curled into a ball, tucking its nose under its two front paws.

"I'm gonna have trouble pulling Happy away from these pups when we leave again," predicted Juan. He looked around the barn, "Where's their mother?"

"Don't know," the old man said. "They wandered in here a few days ago, skinny and dirty, so I been feeding 'em, keeping 'em in the barn. Do you want 'em?"

Covering a smile with his hand, Juan said, "I don't know if we can travel with two small dogs, but—"

"Happy won't leave without these puppies," finished Miah. Both men knew that if they wanted Happy to travel with them, they needed to make room for two puppies in their party.

"I guess I'll need a handyman to build some kind of dog carrier for the trip back," hinted Juan.

Gazing at his sister, Miah replied, "Ah, we'll figure out something. This little bug won't sit in a saddle all day anyway." He looked at the puppies, "And I don't think the pups will be any trouble. They're almost half grown anyway." Gazing at his granddad, "Papaw, where's Dad and Mom?"

His grandfather sighed deeply, "Yer mama passed away four or five months ago—the plague. And you arready walked past your dad twice . . . he never even seen ya."

⁂

Miah set Nora down so he could run out to the main entrance again. He looked around the yard. He scanned everyone's faces until he finally spotted a weathered, emaciated man sitting on the ground—his dad, or at least, a faded image of his dad. With deep concentration, the man stacked course gravel into separate, precise mounds, mumbling to himself, drooling slightly.

Miah edged closer as he studied his father's furrowed brow and intense expression. Miah spoke softly, "Hi, Dad . . . remember me?"

Miah's dad looked at his son with dull, uncomprehending eyes and said, "Do you know how many rocks it takes to build a city?"

Stunned, Miah silently shook his head, *No*.

"At least a million," his dad responded assuredly without looking at Miah. "I already figured the number of rocks it would take to build a city but I can't make a model of the design to fit my calculations." As Miah's dad stared at his make-believe city, he pursed his lips in anger, and with one swift movement knocked down the gravel mounds. Tightening his hands into fists, his father screamed in frustration, "How can I build a fortress to protect my family if I can't even design a model city?!"

With a wild expression, his father stood up, shaking with fury, cursing loudly. Taller and stronger than his father, Miah tightly embraced the crazed man. Miah intentionally pinned his dad's arms so he wouldn't hurt anyone, but his father continued to shriek and cry. Arching his back, his father stiffened every muscle in his body, convulsing uncontrollably. Coming to Miah's aid, Juan and Papaw also locked their arms around the insane man as he ranted and cursed God.

Fearful onlookers stopped everything to watch the men, expecting to see more irrational behavior. Miah closed his eyes, praying silently. When he reopened his eyes, Miah commanded, "In the name of Jesus Christ of Nazareth, Insanity, I cast you out!" As his father screamed even louder, Miah repeated his command.[1] The screaming ceased. Suddenly, his father's eyes rolled back in his head and he collapsed like a rag doll in Miah's arms. Working together, Miah, Juan, and Papaw stretched the man's twitching, thrashing body on the ground.

Miah sat on his knees, held his dad's hand, closed his eyes again, and prayed. Miah prayed quietly for a few minutes, then said aloud, "In the name of Jesus Christ of Nazareth, Depression, I cast you out!" One of his father's legs stopped kicking the ground but the deranged man continued to claw the dirt, growling, grinding his teeth. Undeterred, Miah continued to pray for discernment and proclaimed Jesus's authority over specific demons; this painful process lasted over an hour. Each time a demon left his father, a different part of his body stopped shuttering, and finally the obscene language ceased.

When Miah no longer perceived the presence of demons, he glanced up at Juan and Papaw. Miah licked his dry lips; he watched his father's face. His dad's eyelids quivered; finally, the man opened his eyes and he saw his son for the first time in over a year.

"Jeremiah," his dad exclaimed, "are you real?"

Overwhelmed with fatigue, Miah breathed a sigh of relief and whispered thanks to God. Gazing compassionately at his father, Miah replied in a shaky voice, "Yes, I'm real. My friends and I just arrived today."

Juan and Papaw crouched near Miah's father. Both men looked at each other with wide-eyed amazement but neither said a word. Miah, Juan, and Papaw helped Miah's dad, Bill, stand. Although disheveled, Bill looked at them with his brown, inquisitive, *rational* eyes.

Bill looked over both of his shoulders at the crowd gathered around them. "What happened?"

"Dad, you were demonized." Startled, Bill stared at his son doubtfully.

Unperturbed, Miah went on, "We cast several demons out of you; you're better, but you're not outta the woods yet. You need to be discipled to keep those unclean spirits from coming back to you." His dad studied Miah suspiciously, "If you don't do anything to guard yourself, Dad, those demons will return. Only next time, they'll bring their friends with them, which will be even worse for you."

Bill looked confused. Miah said, "Listen, Dad, it's a lot to take in all at once." As he considered the crowd watching him, Miah spoke in a softer voice, "Together, we'll study Bible passages dealing with demons;

---

1. Luke 8:26–39.

you'll understand what happened to you." His dad turned away, unconvinced. Miah grabbed his dad's arm, "Dad, this is important. Don't throw away the truth because people say that demons are just fantasies. They're real, and they're destructive."

Bill nodded his head slightly. Dazed, Bill recalled, "The last thing I remember was burying your mother." Suddenly his face became ashen as another memory struck him, "Nora! Where's Nora?"

Lifting the little girl to her father, Papaw responded, "She's rat here, Bill. I been takin' real good care a her."

Bill thrust his hands out eagerly as Papaw put Nora into her father's arms. "My sweet baby girl," Bill buried his face in Nora's curls. Nora pulled back to look at this stranger's face, perplexed, but she didn't cry. "Thank you, Dad," Bill said gratefully.

Weary from their travel and the day's remarkable events, Miah and Juan withdrew into the crowd without fanfare. Juan looked sideways at the teen. "You'll never cease to amaze me, Miah . . . I decided to give you a new nickname."

"Yeah, what would that be?"

"Viejo perro. It means 'old dog.'"

Miah laughed with Juan. "Well, I hope this 'old dog' can still learn new tricks because it seems like our life changes—every . . . single . . . day."

"Listen, buddy, I'm running in circles trying to keep up with your tricks. Let's go back to the barn to check on Happy and her pups. After what I saw today, I could use a cold nose on my face to slap me back into reality."

24

THAT NIGHT FOR DINNER, Papaw roasted a wild boar over an open fire. As with any group meal, everyone prepared food they found in nature or raised in a garden: roasted nuts, sautéed mushrooms, cooked water cress, fried okra, boiled peanuts, and baked sweet potatoes. While they ate, Miah and Juan learned that Papaw turned his farm into a loosely knit community of refugees. Despite the isolated location of his farm, Papaw welcomed people who wandered onto his property accidently and granted sanctuary to those who requested to stay. Those who stayed for a few weeks slept in reconverted storage sheds or barns but every unmarked person ate at Papaw's table; it didn't matter if they stayed for one meal or one year.

The wanderers helped Miah's granddad complete whatever work was needed: raise livestock, sow and gather crops, forage for food, or dig wells. A lazy person didn't stay very long because if they were healthy and didn't work, they didn't eat. A simple life with simple rules.

As they ate dinner, Miah overheard discussions about world events from several men sitting at a nearby table. Not having ready access to outside news, he listened intently to the men. Miah jabbed Juan, motioning for him to also listen to the conversation.

An outgoing man, Juan walked over to the men's table to introduce himself, "My name's Juan and this is Jeremiah. We couldn't help but overhear some of your conversation; can we listen to your news?" The men cheerfully moved their chairs closer together so Juan and Miah could squeeze next to them at the table. Juan mentioned, "Miah and I have been in the dark for some time now. We know the United States was overthrown but we don't have reliable communication where we live. We don't know how, or why, our nation fell. We don't even know much about the world government."

Two olive-skinned men leading the discussion smiled weakly, shaking their heads. The larger man spoke first, "You're not alone. Just about everywhere we go, we pass along intel and hear local gossip. It's kinda like building a massive jigsaw puzzle."

His partner added, "We'll tell you everything we know that's not hearsay; it's reliable information."

The large man went on, "We have intelligence backgrounds, but we bugged out when the supreme leader signed a proclamation to kill Jews." His friend nodded sadly. "It started with a general climate of hate and distrust in the U.S. Kinda like building a bonfire, Americans threw old, dried complaints into the fire. Oppressive taxes, entitled people, uneducated graduates—"

His friend continued, "—gridlocked traffic, city decay, weather calamities: each rotted log added to the pressure people felt daily."

The men explained that the worlds' monetary leaders tossed into this volatile environment the most incendiary matches they had in their arsenal: intentionally destroying the U.S. dollar and dismantling the flow of trade. The blazing economic inferno that ensued changed the world, for the worse, forever. Without the dollar, a person could no longer buy food, water, electricity, medicine, or transportation. Without the flow of trade, people couldn't find staple goods even if they had a viable currency.

Fueled by social media and one-sided international news outlets, people blamed the free market, conservatives, and capitalism for this global catastrophe. No one looked through the smoke screen to see the hideous schemes elites concocted in their closed, poisoned meetings. Some people suspected that financiers capitalized on a global viral epidemic to distract victims from recognizing the oncoming economic disaster.

Ultimately, the long-term plans of these power mongers reached fruition and the economic collapse precipitated domestic and international reactions. In the United States, hostilities arose between the haves and have nots, nationalism crumbled, information and communication sources faltered, and the debt-ridden society panicked. Rioters destroyed cities, looters ransacked homes, administrators closed schools, merchants locked doors, and anarchists overran the U.S. capitol. International markets fell, inflation soared, and governments toppled. Starvation, fear, and violence became the rule of the day, rather than the exception.

In the midst of their despair, people throughout the world cried for help. "Who can stop this violence? Who can give us water? Who can give us food? Who can provide medicine and power?"

After the endless questions, a unified voice of millions proclaimed, "We long for the days of security and plenty!"

Heeding the world's resounding cry, a mystifying figure walked onto the global stage, suave, educated, cultured, and diplomatic. Already a well-known presence in international politics, his benign countenance, dazzling smile, and silver tongue all served to mask his true intentions from billions of needy people. In reality, this "savior" hated people; but he loved power, prestige, and conquest. To this man, humanity consisted of destitute, disgusting, disposable creatures placed under his authority as means to an end.

With the United States fatally wounded, he stepped in to create a strong government to fill the vacuum of leadership felt worldwide. Controlling the flow of information, he created an impeccable media mechanism to regulate and disseminate information supporting his cabals. Before long, the world adopted a common currency. Universally, people claimed loyalty, love, and adoration for their new savior as he rescued them from certain death.

Or did he? His citizens were nothing more than objects of his scorn. Initially, he was not labeled as the Antichrist or the beast; only Bible readers knew his true name. Christians immediately disappeared when they heard that the Antichrist came into power; they hid, or if caught, became martyrs. They were shown no mercy from the beast's henchmen, and became known as insurgents, rebels, anarchists, the dregs of society. Even children were murdered at the behest of the New World Order's sovereign ruler. Now, apparently, the supreme leader targeted Jews for annihilation, along with gypsies, nomads, and anyone else not bearing his distinctive mark.

The larger man concluded, "It's bizarre; those who got the mark think they're safe from harm. They have utilities, receive healthcare, even accept a socialistic stipend of spending money."

His friend added, "They think they're saved, but they're just slaves. Foolish slaves that ask for more government handouts, binding them even closer to a leader who detests them."

❦

Juan and Miah sat still. Neither one could imagine this level of depravity. They knew the U.S. was gone, but now they realized the whole world, as they once knew it, was gone. Sheltered in the valley, they were unaware of the universal damage, until today. Now, they not only understood the destruction; they knew what caused this devastation: greed, power, and lust.

"You don't have to look any further than the bankers and politicians that pursued a globalist agenda," revealed the big man. "They controlled the purse strings to set up a one world government through a single currency, killing millions of people in the process."

"Bean counters," mumbled Juan.

"What?" asked Miah.

"Bean counters! Corporate bigwigs, banksters," growled Juan.

The big man added, "The Gnomes of Zurich."

Frustrated, Juan said, "I spent my life protecting the U.S. from enemy forces, and who overthrows our government? Sniveling, cowardly elitists! Business leaders! Lawmakers!" In disgust, Juan stood up abruptly, knocking over his chair. He stopped, picked up the chair, and took a deep breath to regain his composure; afterward, Juan thanked the men for their information and left the table, appalled.

25

MIAH WATCHED JUAN WALK briskly away from the crowd. He knew Juan needed time to think, to pray. Miah looked back at the men staring at him. Not knowing what else to say, Miah stood up, thanked the men, and walked quietly to his grandfather's table.

Papaw noticed Miah's deferential manner as he seated himself; he nodded to his grandson but continued talking to his friends with exaggerated gestures. Later, when his friends moved to another table, Papaw nudged his grandson with his elbow, "So, Miah, what're your plans now that ya found yer family?"

Miah withdrew from his reverie, "I'm going to take Nora and Dad to my new home in the mountains, Grandpa." Pausing for a moment, "I love a beautiful girl; her name is Beth, Elizabeth. When I get back, I wanna marry her."

Papaw's toothless grin brightened his aged face. This was delightful news for the old man.

"Grandpa, would you like to come with us?"

Extending his arm toward the crowd, "Nah, this here's my home, with my people." Then Papaw asked, "Who's goin' with ya?"

"Dad, Nora, Happy, Juan, and the two puppies, so far. If you know anyone else who'd like to travel with us, we'll be glad to talk with them."

"Ya know a couple of those fellers you was talkin' to? They'd make great hands. They're young, full of beans. Smart fellers. I think they're itchin' to move on anyway. I'll talk with 'em, see if they're interested. When are ya leaving?"

"As soon as possible. Juan's wife is expecting their first child so Juan wants to hurry back home." Blushing slightly, "And I'm anxious to see Beth again."

"Let me get the word out tonight. We'll see if anyone else wants to join ya."

"Thanks, Papaw; and thank you for taking such good care of Nora and Dad. I needed to find them before I could think about starting my own family."

Papaw hugged his grandson, "You're growin' up to be a fine man, Miah. I'm proud a ya."

Embarrassed, Miah stared down at his feet, "I only did what you taught me."

"Well, son, ya listened and obeyed. There are a lot of people living today that did neither and they're in a world a hurt right now."

Sucking on his bottom lip, Miah's grandfather considered his next words carefully, "Now, ya know that I love Bill; course he's my kin," shrugging his shoulders, "but 'cha gotta understand that he's a wildcard. He's unreliable. I don't wanna say he's bad, but he ain't wired right. 'Member that, ya hear?"

Miah shook his head slowly, debating if he should even take his father on the trip. He would talk with Juan this evening. Together, they would decide whether or not to take Bill with them.

Putting this thought aside, Miah asked, "Papaw, if you don't mind, Juan and I would like to sleep in the barn tonight with Hap and the puppies. We have heavy coats and gloves so we won't get cold. And after sleeping under the stars while we traveled, it will feel great just to lie down inside a barn on straw."

"Be my guest, Jeremiah. They's plenty a horse blankets in the tack room if you need more coverin'." Hesitating as he thought about the deliverance, Papaw shook his head in wonder, "Rest up; ya had a crazy day. I'll see ya in the mornin'."

Papaw turned away, limping over to the fire where a group of old men smoked pipes, whittled wood, and told lies. He settled easily into the conversation and soon began to spin his own tall tales to the amusement of his cronies. "Did I ever tell ya 'bout the time my dad accidentally punched a bear in the nose? Yeah, he was sleeping in a tent, sawing the logs . . ."

Shaking his head, amused by his granddad, Miah began to search for Juan. He found the Latino, back to his boisterous self, telling a group of people about their adventures. With his arms spread wide, Juan said, "— then Miah started to talk like an alien or something. The wolves tucked their tails between their legs, tripped over each other trying to get away from us, and disappeared into the woods!" Mesmerized, the listeners gawked at Juan, then turned to stare at Miah in awe. "Talk about making a perfect entrance . . . here's the man of the hour: Jeremiah Rubinstein!"

If only the ground would open up and swallow me, agonized the modest young man.

Putting his arm around Miah's shoulders, Juan gracefully led Miah away from the gathering, "Well folks, we need some sleep. I'll be glad to talk with you more tomorrow. I should get this pathetic old dog to bed."

The two friends left amid the listeners' excited whispers and polite applause. "You're killing me, Juan," moaned Miah.

"Ah, buck up, guy. Your faith is an inspiration to scared and homeless people. Besides, they weren't clapping for you; they were praising Jesus! Let's get back to the barn, make some cozy straw beds next to Happy and her puppies, and sleep like the dead."

The following morning, Juan and Miah were awakened by the high-pitched yips and pin-sharp teeth of curious puppies. Rolling over to pet Happy, Juan shoved his big dog good-naturedly, "C'mon, sleepyhead, it's time for breakfast!" Ruffling her fur, "I don't know about you, but this looks like a perfect day to wade in that ice-cold river at the bottom of the mountain."

Juan poked Happy again but the big dog lay still, her tongue hung limply out of her mouth. Juan sat up abruptly, *This isn't right.* He immediately rubbed her body all over, shaking her to wake up. Hoping against his greatest fear, Juan said playfully, "Come on, Hap, wake up! Come on, girl . . . come on, buddy . . ." but Happy's body remained motionless.

A battletested soldier, Juan squeezed his eyes shut momentarily, but gradually reopened them, slowly. Touching Happy softly, Juan whispered, "Oh, Hap," he sighed heavily, "you were such a good friend." Tears welled in Juan's eyes as he laid his head upon her chest, hoping to hear a faint heartbeat or a wisp of breathing, but Happy was gone. Leaning against Happy, Juan stroked her coat tenderly, his shoulders quivered as his tears fell quietly on her fur.

Upon hearing desperation in Juan's voice, Miah sat up, alarmed. He watched Juan's actions, listened to his words; nevertheless, Miah's thinking was blurred, his mind still foggy from dreaming. Then the realization hit him: *Happy died last night in her sleep.*

Reflexively, Jeremiah put his hand over his mouth. Out of respect for his friend or maybe his own social awkwardness, Miah averted his gaze away from Juan and Happy. *What should I say? What can I do?* he thought anxiously. Ideas jostled around in Miah's head but words eluded him. Feeling helpless to do anything, Miah just sat quietly, clasping his hands together tightly, waiting for Juan to say or do something.

In time, Juan stifled his tears. He sat up, took his blanket, and gently covered Happy's body, neatly tucking the corners under her huge frame. He muttered softly, "There are a lot of hungry people walking around here but nobody's gonna touch you." Catching his breath and sniffing his nose, Juan cleared his throat, "Miah, would you help me bury Happy today?"

"Absolutely," Miah said, relieved to help. "She was the bravest, kindest, friendliest dog I ever met." Wiping his nose with a rag he kept in his pocket, "It would be an honor."

26

AFTER NELLIE'S VISITORS—THE STOCKMEN and their families—walked across the chasm to begin the final leg of their journey home, the tracker in TJ's gang watched their progress with intense interest. The tracker slipped quietly back to BoJed's camp to report the news. Unable to control his excitement, he jabbered about a group of men and women walking unescorted toward the barricaded community.

"Slow down! What're you saying?" snapped BoJed, now healed well enough to ride his horse.

Taking a deep breath, the tracker repeated in a controlled voice, "I'm saying . . . that this is a *perfect* time to nab several young women and children away from the local yokels. They're not protected by a cavalry from the fort."

Smiling at his good fortune, BoJed decided spontaneously, "Let's do it!"

The bandits jumped onto their horses and rode quickly down the mountain. Just before reaching the unsuspecting walkers, the outlaws split into two units: one group to stop in front of the line to prevent their progress, and the other group at the rear to prevent any runaways. While the travelers still remained out of view from the walled compound, the gang rode in front and behind the surprised walkers, immediately stopping them.

BoJed's horse reared up on its hind legs in front of the lead man, swiped the air with its front legs, and dropped to the ground menacingly, pawing the dust. Restraining the horse's reins in his left hand, BoJed pointed his pistol directly at the lead man's head. "Don't move or make a sound, or you'll be the first to die," he snarled.

The front man looked to his left and his right but realized they were surrounded by a vicious, ugly band of men. Stammering, the man said, "We don't have anything of value, mister. We're just a bunch of farmers."

"Nah, you're wrong there, buddy. You got several beautiful women and teenage girls that we'll just commandeer from you," BoJed smiled coldly at the man, leering at the women.

"I . . . I . . . can't let you do that!" the exasperated man said. "You're talking about my wife and daughters."

Eyeballing his victims hatefully, BoJed shot the lead man in the chest. Women and children screamed in terror. The dying man's two daughters collapsed to the ground, crying, while his wife ran to her husband, fell to her knees, and cradled his head in her lap. She stroked her husband's hair, speaking softly to him as he stared at her face, struggling to breathe.

BoJed yelled over his shoulder to his men, "Get the women away from that guy. He'll be dead in a minute and I don't want to smell dried blood on their clothes tonight." Grinning scornfully, "I might lose my appetite."

Laughing, several men slipped off their horses to grab the women. The two girls screeched in horror, clinging to each other. After the men brutally yanked the wife away from her husband, the woman stood up unsteadily, bravely facing her abusers.

Waving at the two other herdsmen within the group, "Hey, BoJed, do you want any of these men?"

"Naw, haven't you heard?" BoJed sneered. "We're at war with un-marked people. Just take the men *and* those no-account children into the woods. Kill them, but do it quietly." Noticing his crew's surprised expressions, "We don't want to rile other valley do-gooders. And we don't need a posse hunting us down for five spindly women and girls."

"But, boss, what about the kids?" asked a bandit, still unsure of BoJed's order.

"We can't slow down to babysit kids right now. Kill them too, but use your knives."

Unbothered by the bloodletting of BoJed's orders, TJ and the other outlaws separated the men and children from the women. Using their rifles as clubs, they beat the two stockmen unconscious; after that, they dragged wailing children and the two men's bodies into the woods. The women and girls shrieked wildly, clutching for their loved ones, but their tears only inflamed the killers' fury.

To quiet the growing noise, the outlaws hit mothers and daughters with their rifle butts and knocked them to the ground; one woman passed out, another spit out two bloody teeth. Cowed, the conscious women held each other, weeping softly. For a moment the women heard muffled crying and pleading from the forest, then nothing. Absolute silence.

Terrified, the women looked at the ground but said nothing. They listened to the sound of crunching leaves as the murderers returned from the forest. Cleaning knife blades on their jeans or handkerchiefs, TJ and his cohorts returned without the stockmen or their young children.

BoJed ordered, "Grab the women. Throw them over your laps so we can get outta here!"

Each man pulled a female by her hair or arm, hoisting the prisoners onto their horses. The killers forced the women to stretch across their laps like bags of grain, and braced the women with their free hands. The gang disappeared into the forest with their captives whimpering in terror, leaving little evidence of their kidnapping on the road.

☙◌֎◌ல

Outside the outlaws' purview, Brant was already experimenting with Morse code. Using a flashlight, he sent preliminary messages across the wide chasm and waited for answers. After hearing the shofar echo across the valley, Jason was the first person to notice the periodic flashes of light, so he started to decode Brant's messages.

"Brant wants to know if our families arrived back home," relayed Jason.

"Not yet," answered Mac. "Ask Brant when they left and how long it should take for them to get home."

The initial coding process was very slow. Jason wrote a message on paper, coded each letter from his Boy Scout manual, then sent a stream of short and long flashes of light to signify dots and dashes. After he finished, they waited for Brant's slow response.

"They left at 9:00 this morning," Jason replied warily. "Brant's message says, 'Slow walk three to four hours.'"

By this time, Ryan and Pastor Greg joined the group. "It's gotta be close to 6:00 now," Ryan said uneasily. "Something happened to them."

Without delay, Mac directed, "Grab rope, rifles, and ammo. Jason, round up some horses and saddle 'em up. Greg, find a few more people to join us. We need to locate our friends before it gets too dark. I'm afraid they either fell down the cliff or someone attacked them."

Within fifteen minutes, Jason returned holding the reins of seven horses. Greg returned with Marcus, Alicia, Monica, and Ryan.

"Dad, let me go with you," begged Jason.

Ryan considered the assembled posse: on one side, Jason and Greg, two people who never experienced bloodshed, and on his other side, experienced soldiers who understood the cost of battle. Looking at Mac, he asked, "Whatta you say, Mac?"

Mac responded decisively, "If we need to pull people out of the gorge, we could use the extra muscle." But as he considered the possibility of a fight, Mac added, "Greg, you and Jason can ride with us, but if we have to attack with force, stay behind us. When guns start firing, I need soldiers that can fight instinctively, without hesitation. You don't have that training yet." Jason and Greg agreed. "Okay, let's go find our families." With those parting words, the crew mounted their horses and sprinted out of the compound.

⋐ ⊚ ⋑

Since the renegades saw no one following them, they relaxed, deciding to set up camp before dark. Within the circle of men, mothers and daughters huddled together and kept a close watch on their captors. One of the teenaged girls, Carly Parsons, recognized TJ; she whispered to the others, "Let me talk to TJ. He might help us escape when it gets darker."

The captives closed their eyes and prayed for deliverance. Mothers who knew TJ feared the worst but said nothing to their trusting daughters. Having recently escaped from a reeducation center, several mothers prayed with conviction for another heavenly miracle.

While the criminals ate and drank, TJ brought a small portion of food for the women to share. Taking advantage of the moment, Carly waved TJ close to her side. "I'm so glad to see you, TJ. You can save us from these men!" she murmured.

TJ scoffed, "Why would I want to save you? There's a lot of money in trafficking slaves. I plan to make plenty of money with you."

Horrified, the young woman persisted, "TJ, how could you? You, Talia, and I played together when we were kids. What's wrong to you?"

"Nothing's wrong with me, and after tonight you're not going to be so perfect either."

"TJ, you're not serious," the frightened girl answered. "Help us!"

"Yeah, I'll help you. I'll help *myself* to you." Pleased with his cruelty, TJ laughed and strutted back to the fire to join his cutthroat friends. As she watched TJ's retreat, Carly's mouth gaped in terror.

⌒◎⌒

With the aid of Ryan's tracking skills, Mac's company quickly narrowed the distance between the two parties. When Ryan noticed firelight in the woods, Mac's unit silently dismounted to devise a plan. Monica, a slim Asian woman, spoke, "Since these drifters steal women, why don't you let Alicia and I blunder into their camp looking for, oh, I don't know," she lifted her shoulder slightly, "a cup of coffee, something simple—"

With a knowing grin, Alicia interrupted, "A simple request from two simple-minded women."

"Right," conspired Monica. "While we distract them, you can move in."

Pastor Greg's eyes widened, his face blanched as he looked achingly at Monica. "Are you sure you want to risk your lives?" he asked numbly. Although he hadn't confessed his feelings to Monica, everyone noticed Greg's attraction to the young woman.

Looking at the love-stricken man, Alicia answered, "Don't worry, Pastor; Monica's a soldier. She knows how to handle herself." Turning to their leader, "I like Monica's idea, Mac."

"So do I," said Mac. Looking at the men, "Marcus, Ryan, head over to the opposite side of the camp. Pastor, Jason, stay here with the horses. I'll come up the middle." Mac turned to the women, "Make some noise as you ride into the camp; they'll think you're just a pair of clueless females. We'll follow your lead."

"Thanks, Mac," said Monica. "We won't let you, or those poor women, down." Alicia and Monica prodded their horses forward at a leisurely pace as the men swiftly ran to their positions.

Talking to Monica as they approached the firelight, Alicia addressed the men first, "Hiya, fellas! We saw your campfire, and thought we'd stop by to see if you have any hot coffee."

Standing up and trying to smile charmingly, BoJed said, "Ladies are *always* welcome in our camp." The other men tried to suppress their lascivious laughter.

Coolly, Monica swiftly scanned the outlaws' positions. In her peripheral vision, she confirmed that Mac, Marcus, and Ryan were in position, ready to strike. Monica tossed a sidelong glance at Alicia, smiled winningly at the men, and said, "Coffee would be great!" Turning their backs to the men, the women slid off their horses. With their chests pressed against the horses' bellies, they discretely pulled pistols out of their shoulder holsters, and quickly dropped flat on the ground. Lying prostrate, they aimed their weapons and began to quickly shoot the outlaws.

As soon as the shooting started, Marcus, Mac, and Ryan entered the fray. The entire campsite erupted with gunfire. BoJed fell into the fire with two bullets in his forehead. The tracker was hit in the gut with Marcus's shotgun. A fleeing outlaw shot Mac in the chest but Ryan ended his escape with several shots in the back. Alicia put two rounds in a drunk's chest before he could even grab his weapon and Monica killed the remaining kidnapper with a tight grouping in his heart.

In the confusion of battle, Carly ran to the fire. She grabbed a hot, sharp twig used as a skewer to protect herself and the other women. When TJ ran over to the women to find a hostage, he grabbed Carly's mother.

"Let's go," demanded the agitated young man. "You're my hostage now!"

Realizing that she might lose both parents in one day, Carly screamed like a wild animal, "Noooo!" She ran forward in blind anger, tackling TJ with the full force of her body.

TJ hastily recovered, jumping to his feet. Feeling both embarrassed and enraged, TJ announced, "Then you'll be my hostage, Carly!"

"I don't think so," Carly said through gritted teeth. When TJ furiously seized Carly's left wrist, she swung her right hand forward, thrusting the skewer into his left eye.

TJ screamed with tortured pain, frantically trying to pull the skewer from his eye. Without wavering, Carly slammed her palm against the butt of the skewer as hard as she could, jamming the branch deep into TJ's skull. TJ dropped to the ground without uttering another word.

Staring down at the dead teenager, Carly hissed contemptuously, "You already killed my father today; I won't let you kill my mother!"

She stared at TJ a moment longer, breathing heavily. Still prepared to fight anyone that threaten her or the other women, Carly picked up a heavy stone to use as a weapon. Turning swiftly toward the fire, she heard men screaming, smelled the acrid odor of discharged weapons, but saw little of the resulting action because of their seclusion in a copse of trees.

Carly looked down and noticed her shaking, bloody hands, one hand still tightly gripping the jagged rock. When she glanced up, she saw pity and sorrow in her mother's eyes. Carly's mother, Mrs. Parsons, wrapped her arms around Carly to shield her daughter from flying bullets. While both women huddled near the ground, Mrs. Parsons kept repeating, "Be still, Carly . . . be still."

When the shooting ended, Carly's mother didn't raise her head; she simply held her child. In the silence that followed, Carly's mother cautioned, "Stay down, Carly."

Glancing toward the campfire, Mrs. Parsons said, "Let me see what's happening. If I call your name, run as fast as you can into the forest, and don't stop running. Don't let those animals get a hold of you!" Without another word, Carly's mother crept toward the campfire to investigate.

She saw a heinous landscape of blood and bodies. Still on her knees, she pushed through the dense forest undergrowth to see Marcus and Ryan run swiftly to a fallen man. Mrs. Parsons wondered who was on the ground, until she recognized the fallen man's clothing—*Mac!*

She ran next to Ryan to watch as Marcus sat on the ground, holding Mac in his arms, assessing his friend's injury. Mac wheezed gasping breaths as Marcus inspected his chest wound. Pointing across the fire, Marcus barked, "Get Mac that flask of whiskey! Hurry!"

Ryan ran over to a discarded flask, picked it up, and unscrewed the lid as he rushed back to Marcus. Ryan dropped to his knees, then carefully lifted Mac's limp head. "Here, buddy, let's have a drink." He dribbled some alcohol on the dying man's lips to ease his pain.

Mac looked into Marcus and Ryan's faces. He tried to speak but his lips wouldn't form words. Mac reached his hand toward Ryan. Ryan grabbed his friend's hand, squeezing it. Mac licked his dry lips. After he assumed a fixed stare toward heaven, his ragged breathing stopped.

For a moment, all was quiet. Supporting Mac's neck and shoulders with his left arm, Marcus closed his friend's eyes with his right hand. Marcus rested his hand on Mac's forehead, dropped his chin, closed his own eyes, and mumbled a prayer.

After Marcus finished praying, one of the kidnapped teens shyly approached the troupe huddled around Mac. Sensing her presence, Alicia turned to the girl. She reached out to touch the teenager's hand, "Are you okay?"

"Um . . . I'm alright, but Mr. Washington's son, TJ . . . is dead," she answered haltingly.

Still on his knees, Marcus looked up at the girl with his bloodshot brown eyes. He stood up stiffly; feeling strangely very old, he followed the girl to TJ's body. When he approached his son, he saw the end of a hot poker sticking out of TJ's eye; Marcus turned his head away.

Nearby, Carly stood up on unsteady legs, walked over to Marcus, admitting, "It was me, Mr. Washington. I killed TJ."

Her words expressed neither joy nor pride; they merely stated facts—the cold, bare facts. Marcus looked at Carly with overwhelming pity; she was just a scared kid. A ripped, soiled dress barely covered her frail body, her hair fell in a mass of tangles, and her black eye and bruised cheeks bore the evidence of multiple beatings.

Marcus smiled gently at the teen and slowly reached for her hand. When she walked tentatively toward him, he protectively wrapped his strong arms around her. Carly cried in his arms. She cried for so many things: the loss of lives, the loss of security, the loss of innocence. Marcus spoke softly, "I'm so sorry you had to kill, TJ, Carly. Not because he didn't deserve to die, but because you didn't deserve to kill him."

Marcus patiently held the young woman as Carly wept. He prayed, "God, forgive us all for our sins. I pray in the name of Jesus that Carly will dwell in the shadow of your wings. I pray for the healing of her mind, her spirit, and her body; she suffered so much today. I pray for all these women; please give them your peace and comfort. In Jesus' name I pray, amen."

By now, almost everyone from Mac's company ministered to the women. Even Jason and Pastor Greg rushed into the camp as soon as the gunfire ended. The fighters talked calmly to the shocked captives. They helped women onto the backs of waiting horses, covering their quivering shoulders with blankets scattered on the ground.

While the others focused on the living, Ryan cared for his fallen friend. Ryan lifted Mac onto his horse and tied his body to the saddle. After Ryan hitched the last knot, he recited a silent prayer. Thinking of the trials they already endured, Ryan pleaded aloud, "Lord, please come back soon; we need you here."

As they regrouped to return to the fenced community, the troop gathered their belongings and collected some the gang's property. They saddled the outlaw's five horses, placed extra rifles in scabbards, and packed food in saddlebags. Each rescuer tied a captive woman's horse to their mount so the women could ride without concentrating on a trail. After tying Mac's horse to his own, Ryan pulled himself into his saddle.

As the group started down the road, Carly's mother pleaded for her husband's body. Thinking of the missing children and stockmen left in the forest, she asked, "Could several of us ride together or walk? I want to bring my husband's body home tonight before wild animals find him."

Marcus nodded his head, "You're right, Ms. Parsons. Tell us where you think we'll find them. We'll bring them home now." He looked steadily at Alicia. Knowing the woman's resourcefulness, her strength under pressure, "Alicia, can you oversee this detail?"

"Absolutely," she stated. "Pastor Greg and Jason can help me. We'll get everyone home." Relieved to help, the two extra men nodded their heads in agreement.

"What about TJ's body, Marcus?" asked Mrs. Parsons cautiously.

"I'll return for TJ after we get you home safely," sighed Marcus. "TJ doesn't warrant the same respect or attention that you folks need right now."

In the glow of sunrise, Marcus rode his horse to the front position to lead the procession home. The assembly of weary travelers willingly followed Marcus. Their unspoken allegiance to his directions began Marcus's new role as leader of remnants still living in the valley. Marcus never planned to lead a small contingent of refugees, but now he knew with certainty that he would die before he'd let anyone hurt these unfortunate, beleaguered souls again.

27

HUNDREDS OF MILES AWAY from the valley, Miah and Juan prepared Happy's burial. Unwilling to let anyone know Happy died, Juan and Miah dug her grave far from prying eyes, in a beautiful forested spot near a cliff edge, overlooking a river. To keep her grave secret from hungry scavengers, the pair decided to carry Happy's body out of the camp in a trunk. Before they carried the trunk to the gravesite, Miah adjusted the blanket on Hap's body. Inadvertently, the blanket slipped off her frame and Miah stared at her with disbelief. "Juan, come here; you gotta see this. Look at Happy's face."

Juan walked sideways to the trunk; he glanced down apprehensively. Doing a double take, Juan asked, "Is she smiling?"

"It sure looks like it," admitted Miah. Although dead, Happy's mouth was pulled up in both corners, and her cheeks were rounded. Happy's dancing face.

"Could be the muscles in her face tightened," concluded Juan, "but I'd like to think that she had sweet dreams before she died." Contrary to a moment earlier, now Juan couldn't take his eyes off her.

Studying the dog, Miah replied, "I don't know much, but I recognize that expression; I saw it a hundred times. It looks like she's smiling."

For the first time in hours, Juan chuckled, "Leave it to Happy to die with a smile on her face." He gently shut the trunk. He looked at his young friend, "Can I ask you a question?"

"Sure. What is it?"

"When I was a boy, a priest told me that once an animal dies, we'll never see them again. He said that animals don't have souls, so they can't get into heaven." Juan paused, "Do you think that's true?"

"Heaven's still a mystery to me, but I think we'll see animals in heaven. In Revelation 5:13, John writes, 'Then I heard every creature in heaven and on earth and under the earth and on the sea, and all that is in them, saying, To him who sits on the throne and unto the Lamb be praise and honor and glory and power for ever and ever!'"

"What? Every creature on earth and in the sea? Does that mean whales will be in heaven, whales will talk?"

"Sure sounds like it," said Miah. "If you want to read another cool animal story, study Numbers chapter 22. You'll find out about Baalam's *talking* donkey."

"Are you kidding?!"

"No. This guy, Balaam, was hired to place a curse on the Israelites. While Balaam rode his donkey to pledge the curse, an angel stood in the way to block Balaam's path. His donkey could see the angel but Balaam couldn't. The donkey kept trying to avoid the angel so she wouldn't follow Balaam's commands. Furious with her disobedience, Balaam beat her three different times. The angel finally opened the donkey's mouth; the donkey asked Balaam, 'Why are you beating me? Aren't I your donkey?' Now here's the kicker: rather than stopping and saying, 'Whoa, you're a talking donkey!' Balaam told his donkey that if he had a sword, he'd kill her!"

"What happened?"

"The angel opened Balaam's eyes, so Balaam finally saw the angel too. The angel told Balaam that if his donkey hadn't turned aside three times, he would've already killed Balaam but spared his donkey. You gotta read the story; it's amazing!"

Juan rubbed his forehead, "Talking donkeys, singing sea creatures . . . are you sure you read that in the Bible?"

"The Bible's full of surprises; those are just two examples. Ezekiel and Isaiah describe some fantastic heavenly creatures. All I know is, the Lord will return riding a white horse. I'll just be happy to see horses in heaven." Taking a breath, he added, "So to answer your question, yeah, I think we'll see Happy again; only the next time we see her, she'll probably talk with us."

Juan's eyes misted. He turned his head away to wipe his nose. Mumbling, "I look forward to that day, viejo perro."

As Juan and Miah carried Happy to a picturesque location above the river, they reminisced. Their stories were a tribute to Happy's life. Although Miah wanted to give Juan his complete support, he found that Juan gave him just as much encouragement to overcome his own grief. They were a team; no, they were brothers. After the burial, they sang praises to God for his creation. Afterward, they sat peacefully on the cliff, overwhelmed with the Lord's blessings; their funeral service for this kind dog was a good ending to a good life.

❦

Similar to the legendary mists of these notable mountains, Juan and Miah's praises drifted over the Smokies and settled in lowlands, blanketing areas for miles with God's blessings. So despite the horrors of the preceding night, valley residents maintained attitudes of hope to carry on with their lives. They trusted God and they trusted each other.

As a pastor, Greg started to prepare the burial of four men and three children. Although several women already knew of their loved ones' deaths, Mac's wife, Patricia, was unaware of her husband's passing. Monica and Pastor Greg decided to speak with Patricia together in case she wanted more details about the raid. Steeling his nerves, the youthful pastor took a deep breath and knocked on the McFadden's door at daybreak.

He heard the soft padding of footsteps moving across the floor. As Patricia opened the door, she smiled brightly when she saw her minister. "Pastor Greg, Monica, come inside. It's chilly on the porch." After the pair stepped over the threshold, Patricia closed the door gently. "Please sit here at the table. I'll start a kettle of water for tea to help us warm up."

Fumbling with his hands, the pastor sucked in his cheeks, took another deep breath. "Mrs. McFadden, we have some bad news . . ."

With her back to her guests, hands clutching a tea kettle, Patricia froze in place. She took a deep breath, then turned around to study the couple. Patricia sat down at the table, nervously clasping her hands, "It's about Mac, isn't it?" Scanning their faces closely, "Is he dead?"

"Yes," the pastor answered. "I am so sorry." Knowing that Monica fought several battles with Mac, Patricia looked at the young woman, "Tell me what happened."

Monica held Patricia's hands as she explained events from the night before. Patricia dropped her head as she listened. After Monica finished, Pat lifted her face to look at both of her guests, "Thank you." She paused, "Coming here must've been very hard for you."

Patricia continued, "Before we go any further, I'd like to tell you something about Mac and me. Living in these last days, we both understand the dangers we face daily. That being said, we agreed that if one of us outlived the other, the survivor would celebrate their beloved's arrival in heaven. A celebration is better than drowning in sorrow."

Exhaling, choosing her words carefully, "Even though my sons and I will miss Mac terribly, we're going to sing our praises to the Lord." She continued, "I believe Mac is living in a really great place now. I wish the boys and I were with him today, but we'll wait."

Squeezing both the pastor's and Monica's hands, "We'll wait with hope; we'll wait with joy; and we'll wait with songs on our lips because God is so good. We'll shout that truth so loud that our voices will shake this valley!"

Realizing her loud voice might wake the children, she snapped her mouth closed, and began to weep quietly. As Monica wrapped her arms around Patricia, she spoke soothing words to the mourning woman. Sitting silently, Pastor Greg allowed the women time to console each other.

After her initial sorrow passed, Patricia squeezed the bridge of her nose, sniffed, and wiped her eyes. She looked bravely into the pastor's face, emphasizing her conviction, "My promise to Mac stands, Pastor. Please give us a memorial service filled with joy and remembrance. My dear husband is home with the Lord now. As for me? I'm looking forward to the day when we'll see each other again in heaven."

Mustering her strength, "So blast your shofar, Pastor. Invite everyone to sing songs of victory. We'll triumph over the enemy by the blood of the Lamb and the word of our testimonies."[1]

Following Patricia's precedent, all the residents buried their family members with grace. Standing under the covered pavilion used as a church, Pastor Greg began the funeral with a prayer, "Dear Lord, from the clay of the earth, you designed us in your image . . ." Thus began the community's exultant farewell to their loved ones. After the pastor delivered his sermon, the congregation sang songs of joy, of hope, of salvation.

After the funeral, Patricia expressed one regret, "I only wish Juan were here to tell some of his outrageous stories about Mac." Rethinking that sentiment, a smile twitched on her lips, "On second thought, Juan's stories are better told outside by a campfire rather than in church."

Marcus grinned; he offered Pat his elbow. She laced her arm through his. Marcus gently escorted Pat and her sons into the tightly knit congregation of believers. They, and the other grieving families, basked in the love and support they desperately needed to find comfort, and to heal.

---

1. Rev 12:11.

တသော

The last thing Mac remembered was seeing his friends' faces. Ryan's features reflected worry and sorrow as he cradled Mac's head in his lap; Marcus's expression shone with compassion and mercy as he consoled his dying friend. Exhausted, Mac closed his eyes, and the world faded away in a vapor.

When he reopened his eyes, he saw a bright light. *Ah, the bright light I've always heard about; the light that scientists say is the result of a dying brain.* Mac continued to walk toward the light. *Except I don't feel dead; I feel very alive!*

Mac felt the soft texture of a warm, plush surface on his toes. Glancing down at his feet, he noticed that he no longer wore army boots. His bare feet walked on a springy surface of aromatic herbs.

Looking at his legs, he realized he no longer wore ragged, bloody clothes, but his body was draped in a white tunic. The loose-fitting cloth brushed smoothly across his skin—his unmarred, perfect skin. The tunic felt vaguely like velvet but it seemed weightless; more accurately, it felt like a soft breeze touching his skin rather than the rough scraping of crude, earthly fabrics.

Besides the soothing sensations on his skin and the delicate fragrances floating through the air, he now heard lilting melodies. The breeze blowing his sheath also sighed with a faint tune. *This is remarkable! The smells, the sounds, the feelings; it's a sensory overload.*

As he approached the light, he saw dark outlines of people mingling together. *Who are these people? Dead relatives, maybe?* he thought automatically. Mac walked toward the main figure standing in front of the gathered silhouettes. The figure's face shone brightly; his smile radiated gentleness, and his voice made Mac's heart leap with joy.

"Welcome home, my son," said Jesus. "I have been looking forward to holding you since the day you were born." With those words, Jesus wrapped his loving arms around Mac, and Mac, a huge, strapping Scotsman, fell into the Lord's arms like a child. Jesus had no trouble supporting Mac's heavy build or calming his weary soul.

With a trembling voice, Mac proclaimed, "My God. My Lord. My Savior." He paused, looking intently into the Lord's eyes, "I love you."

"I love you. I have always loved you. Come, I have so much to show you." Walking toward the assembled crowd, Jesus explained, "Before I introduce you to people you may not remember, I would like you to see someone that begged to be a part of this gathering."

Stepping out from behind Jesus stood a magnificent black dog. Her thick, long hair flowed elegantly as she walked; she stood tall, regal. When she smiled, her whole face emanated warmth. Without moving her lips—*Is he reading my mind?*—Mac heard the dog say cheerfully, "Hello, Mac!"

Mac's face lit up like a beacon. He ran to the majestic Newfoundland, dropped to his knees, and threw his arms around her neck. Filled with wonder, Mac gushed, "Happy! You're alive . . . in heaven . . . and you talk!"

Happy wagged her tail, prancing her special footwork. "Oh Mac, I always talked with my people; only now you understand me!"

Mac buried his face in her luxurious coat. Her fur smelled wonderful, citrusy, like juicy oranges and lemons; he inhaled the fresh aroma deeply. While he knelt next to Happy, Mac felt a gentle touch on his shoulder. Shifting his gaze back to Jesus, the Lord said smiling, "Let us go meet some of your family, Mac."

As Mac stood up, he realized that he would no longer experience fear, or doubt, or longing. No longer would he cry in torment or feel the pain of sickness. No longer would he speculate about the actions of people, Scripture passages that confused him, or the splendor of heaven. And no longer would he try to imagine Jesus's face, because Jesus stood directly in front of him. Radiant, handsome, alive! *All of my questions will finally be answered*, Mac thought.

Jesus looked tenderly into Mac's eyes, "Of course all of your questions will be answered, my son. You are home!" Jesus led Mac into a large assembly of people, who greeted him with elation. Mac basked in the laughter, hugs, and kisses of his heavenly family, never to experience unhappiness again.

⊱꧁꧂⊰

A few days later, Marcus followed Jesus's example with the Holy Spirit's guidance. As Marcus escorted Patricia into a gathering of believers on earth, the saints enveloped Pat with the same love and comfort that Mac felt as he entered heaven. A glimpse of one family's experience with God's perfect blending of mercy and righteousness, grace and forgiveness, heaven and earth.

Discussion Questions

1. Do you think animals communicate with each other? Why or why not.

2. Compare and contrast the living conditions of people living in the city and country during a natural or societal disaster.

3. Why do you think it's difficult for some veterans to reconnect with civilian life?

4. What do you think of Mac's decision to have everything on his farm destroyed if his family died of the plague?

5. Is there a character that you could identify with? Or a character that offended you?

6. Do miracles still happen today?

7. Was there an event in the story that surprised you? Why?

8. What do you think of the spiritual gifts referred to in this book?

9. Using the footnotes within this book, were there any miracles recreated in this story that you looked up in a Bible?

10. What is the battle in this story?

www.ingramcontent.com/pod-product-compliance
Lightning Source LLC
Chambersburg PA
CBHW050356030726
47503CB00006B/1883